MW00473204

THE EUROPE THAT WAS

THE EUROPE THAT WAS

Geoffrey Household

ST. MARTIN'S PRESS
New York

Library of Congress Cataloging in Publication Data

Household, Geoffrey, 1900-
    The Europe that was.

    I. Title.
PZ3.H8159Eu   [PR6015.07885]   823'.9'12   78-20671
ISBN 0-312-27058-5

Copyright © 1979 by Geoffrey Household

All rights reserved.

For information, write:
St. Martin's Press, Inc.
175 Fifth Ave., New York, N.Y. 10010

Printed in Great Britain

First published in the United States of America in 1979

CONTENTS

EASTERN APPROACHES

KINDLY STRANGER

It is an odd thought—at this date unworldly rather than disturbing—
that I am responsible for all the disasters of the last forty years, for
1914–18, for the Russian Revolution, for Hitler. No Martian arriving
from outer space could have changed the quietly running world into
so devastatingly wrong and fast a gear. And, as in a cautionary tale for
children, it all came about through disobedience.

My father had a dear friend named von Lech who was an undersecretary in the Austro-Hungarian Ministry of Education. They had
really little in common except the self-confident liberalism of their
time and a passionate interest in the art of teaching. Both of them
believed that when all Europeans—the rest of the world could follow
later—attended secondary school Utopia would have arrived. That
did not seem so comical a creed in 1914 as it does now. It was a bond of
idealism strong enough for them to visit each other, and even for their
wives to be polite to each other.

Von Lech was a hard-working administrator who kept two servants, but no car or carriage. That was just the position of my father.
Both of them could live comfortably and precisely in that state to
which emperor and king had called them, but holidays were always a
minor problem and illness a major one.

Thus it was natural that when von Lech discovered a very cheap
and hospitable hotel at Ilidze, an unknown summer resort in Aus-
trian Bosnia, he should write to my father about it. He knew that my
father was convalescing after a long illness and had been ordered by
his doctor to go abroad for a rest. Frau von Lech also wrote to my
mother in formal, diplomatic French. I think it was the use of French
rather than German or English which overcame her mistrust. Ilidze
was made to sound fashionable, which it wasn't, and romantic, which
it was.

Neither of my parents knew anything whatever about Bosnia. My
father, however, always accepted authority. Von Lech, it was plain,
counted Bosnia a normal province of the Austro-Hungarian Empire.
Provinces of the Empire were civilized and disciplined. It would therefore be an unwarranted misuse of the imagination to consider a visit to
Ilidze at all adventurous. They decided to start in the middle of June.
They would not hear of my travelling out by myself at the end of

term—rightly, for at thirteen I was absurdly helpless—so I was let out of school six weeks early, and accompanied them by train to Trieste and by boat down the Adriatic.

Ilidze was intensely excited by the coming visit of the Archduke Francis Ferdinand and his pretty wife Sophie, Duchess of Hohenberg. I cannot remember if she was really pretty. Even to a sophisticated eye all feminine royalty is dazzling. But I can see the Archduke now. I was immensely impressed by him. Not only was he going to become emperor, but he reminded me of a taller, fiercer and unsmiling edition of my headmaster.

The pair of them stayed at Ilidze for three nights while the Archduke attended the manoeuvres. On 28 June they were to make a state visit to the neighbouring town of Sarajevo; and the von Lechs, who highly approved of the solid glimmerings of liberalism in the Archduke, loyally determined to go over and cheer. Of course, we went with them.

We watched from a first-floor balcony on the Appel Quay. The house was some fifty yards from the cross-roads formed by Franz Joseph Street and the Latin Bridge, and belonged to some hotel acquaintance of the von Lechs—an old lady in black who entertained us with little cakes, and wine in coloured glasses. I think she must have been of rather lower social status, perhaps a native Bosnian, but I remember little about her except the coloured glasses.

The Appel Quay was a long, straight road, bordered on one side by houses and on the other by the river. It was Sunday, and so there was a thick hedge of public on each side of the route. In the distance, to the right of our balcony, the procession was coming up the quay towards us when we heard a sharp explosion. The cars stopped. Hedges wavered inwards and were held back.

The women of our party screamed that it was a bomb. My mother watched Frau von Lech to see whether it would be proper to faint. Frau von Lech, however, decided that my mother would show the famous English phlegm, and determined to imitate her. The old lady prayed, and fascinated me by the complicated gestures with which she crossed herself.

The men exerted their common-sense influence. Von Lech, who was still unused to cars, suggested that the noise had been due to a burst tyre or petrol tank. My father said that the public should not be allowed to purchase fireworks. The bomb as a political weapon was inconceivable to such believers in Progress; they easily assumed that—except in Russia—it was inconceivable to everyone else.

I myself, with the superiority of a sound preparatory school, accepted their unimaginative confidence that the incident was trivial. The melancholy procession—now of three cars instead of four—restarted and passed hurriedly below our decorated balcony. The cheering was so thin that you could distinguish individual voices. I was disappointed. It seemed hardly worth the short journey from Ilidze for so small and dull an affair. My only comparable experience had been a visit of Edward VII to Gloucester. There had been lots of yeomanry in gorgeous uniforms. The genial, top-hatted figure in the open landau had created, by the mere force of his expansive masculinity, an air of festival.

But now that the Archduke had passed, we could see the missing fourth car drawn into the side of the road. A crowd, at a respectful distance, was round it. Another and more active crowd, led by police, was running up the dry bed of the river. We saw an indistinguishable limp puppet caught and arrested.

Von Lech, allowing a decent interval for the stopped clock of civilization to start again, leaned over the balcony and made enquiries. Yes, it had been a bomb; a colonel in the last car had been wounded; some Bosnian students were, it was believed, responsible. Von Lech and my father took this awkward hurdle in their stride. Secondary education, they admitted, was bound to have its teething troubles.

I was silent with a new disappointment. One read of bombs in the newspapers. Anarchists with bombs occasionally blew themselves up (but no one else) in the *Boys Own Paper*. And now a bomb had been thrown practically in front of my eyes, and I hadn't even seen it.

The party returned inside for refreshments. The women were exclamatory. My father and von Lech discussed bombs with philosophic detachment. Nobody paid any attention to me. I made myself a nuisance, and was told that I could go into the garden and look at the goldfish until the Archduke's procession returned along the quay, but that on no account was I to leave the house.

In cold blood I should never have dared to engage myself in the streets of so very foreign a town; but curiousity about the bomb overcame all else. I was as eager to get the horrid details for my school friends as any reporter for his editor. I quietly opened and closed the front door, and slunk along the Appel Quay, keeping close under the houses in case anyone should come out on the balcony and spot me. I crossed Franz Josef Street and then, with enough people between me and the balcony, went over to the river side of the quay.

There was nothing much to see at the car. The right back-wheel and its mudguard looked as if they had been involved in a nasty smash—a sight far more familiar now than then. Imagination produced a few drops of blood on the road—or perhaps they were really there.

I wandered along the embankment with some vague idea of detecting traces of the would-be assassin in the river-bed. There were none, and I found myself a quarter of a mile from home with no satisfactory reason for being where I was. I became embarrassedly conscious of

11

my outlandish appearance. In honour of the Archduke I had been compelled to put on my Eton suit—then worn by all small boys on Sundays and formal occasions. I don't know whether Sarajevo had ever seen such an outfit before. No one assumed that I had escaped from a circus, so it cannot have been as startling as I supposed.

While I fiddled around, no doubt taking refuge in day dreams, the two hedges of police and public opposite our balcony had grown up again. The Archduke was due to return. Worse still, there was a third hedge stretching across the Appel Quay where the procession was to turn right into Franz Josef Street. I was completely cut off from home.

I disliked crossing the empty, wide road with everyone's eyes upon me. However, I had to get back to the balcony before my absence was discovered. I pushed self-consciously through the line of people into the open, and was at once turned back by a policeman. His reaction, I think, must have been one of sheer surprise. He was understandably nervous.

Turned back almost simultaneously was another spectator, a sharp-featured young man little taller than my over-grown self. He also was trying to cross the road and had left it too late. We exchanged glances. I remember his brilliant blue eyes in a yellowish face. He beckoned to me, and said in German (which I understood, though nothing would induce me to mumble it unless compelled): 'Come with me! I will take you across.'

Then he asked the policeman if he couldn't see that I was a little well-born foreigner and harmless. His tone almost implied that he was my manservant or tutor. With an arm round my shoulders, taking away by his middle-class poverty the shame of my resplendent Eton suit, he led me across the road.

We entered the crowd lining the corner of the Appel Quay and Franz Josef Street, and mingled with it. I began to bolt for home, but the procession was on us. The police car came first, then the car containing the Archduke Francis Ferdinand and his wife. I remember Count Harrach standing on the running board on the left-hand side of the car, shielding the Archduke with his body. It did not occur to me that such was his motive. It just seemed a gallant and genuinely Ruritanian way to ride.

The cars turned into Franz Josef Street. My kindly little friend leaned forward and fired twice. I was some distance from him and did not at first realize what he was doing. In 1914 we had not yet been educated by war and movies. Nothing spectacular happened, except that the Archduke leaned back and Sophie put her head on his knees. Then the wave of the crowd curved over Gabriel Princip. Above the bent heads and shoulders I could see Count Harrach put a handkerchief to the Archduke's mouth. It turned suddenly red as in a conjuring trick.

When I reached our door, the von Lechs and my parents came pouring out of it; they did not notice that I had joined them from the quay, not from inside the house. I never told them. I never said a word of my adventure at school. Guilt was already present, though it was many years before I admitted to myself that Gabriel Princip, seizing his opportunity, had used me to bluff his way through police and crowd to Franz Josef Street. Without me, he would have had to fire from some point on the Appel Quay past or through the protecting body of Count Harrach—a shot so long and hopeless that he would have drawn from his pocket only, perhaps, a cigarette.

GIVE US THIS DAY

Mirko Brancovitch was an old man, a calm link with the past; it seemed incredible that he could have been a bandit. He was not garrulous on the subject. There had been nothing gay in his trade, nothing dashing or even markedly virile. It was simply a way of life into which he had drifted. His reminiscences were not of stolen purses, but of poverty. He felt instinctively that thus he revealed the really essential difference between then and now. Other sufferings which had existed at the beginning of the century were still present in recognizable form, but extremes of hunger had vanished from all Europe, East and West.

The poverty of his mountains on the border of Bosnia and Montenegro had been unimaginable, he said. His fellow peasants were mostly freeholders and proud of it, though they had little benefit from their miserable patches of stony soil but freedom to starve. They were Serbs, unwilling subjects of the Austro-Hungarian Empire.

Military service was the greatest disaster. The soldier ate, but no provision was made for wife and children. The State took no account of such inglorious hindrances to patriotism. If he sent them all his pay, every single penny of it, his family would be alive when he returned. But pay could not dig the land and keep it dug, far less hire a labourer.

Exaggerated? When the young men in the café insisted that it was, insisted, before they left on their bicycles or even motor cycles, that such hardship was impossible, the ex-bandit used to lay it down that the test of how much a man fears his fate is what he will do to avoid it. He would quote Pavlo Popovnic as an example.

Pavlo had a young wife and two sons aged four and five—gallant little fellows but not yet able to lift their father's clumsy tools, let alone use them. By working fourteen hours a day on his four acres of mountain—only two of which could really be counted as cultivable—he fed his family, though neither he nor his brave Despina could ever be sure of it from year to year. Flood or the failure of a single crop could tip the balance against them. Remove Pavlo's strong arms and the place would not feed a couple of goats.

When Pavlo was called up for three years with the colours, he had to go. So far he had managed to avoid the alien service, but in the excitements of 1913 the empire was granting no exemptions, especially

14

to Slavs along the southern frontiers. There was nothing he could do about it. The military were up to such acts of desperation as cutting off the trigger finger. Authorities and their tame doctors looked very closely into any accidents at all which happened after a man had received his call-up papers. Even a genuine accident at so convenient a time could land him with ten years in gaol instead of three in the Army.

As soon as Danilo, the local policeman, had delivered Pavlo's orders and left, Despina abandoned herself to shrieks and tears. Then, like all generous women, she drew strength from her own exhaustion and started to make sensible plans. The goats, the sow and the seed potatoes could be eaten. There was an uncle who, at the worst, would give them shelter. Oh yes, she assured Pavlo, they would get through the three years somehow.

Pavlo agreed. He would have agreed to anything. He hated to see his dark-haired darling cry. But he knew very well that even if she and the children survived his years of absence the land and its stock could not. After his return, starvation was certain.

They were like morning and night together—Pavlo a golden Slav, Despina with the raven braids and thin-cream skin of the Mediterranean. We do not see such fine animals today, Mirko Brancovitch asserted. They won much more love than they ever knew, for they were shy of being loved except by each other.

The next morning Pavlo went down the mountain to see the bone-setter. It was spring, but the winter stores were finished and there were still some weeks to go before his work could produce anything solid to eat. A bunch of radishes was all the present he could bring her.

She was the only doctor peasants could afford, and they would have had to travel fifty miles to find a better, in spite of her odd pharmacopoeia of herbs and charms. She even had a medical beard of seven coarse black bristles. Pavlo was a little afraid of her, but he knew her to be well disposed towards Despina whose two sons she had delivered.

'If I break my leg, Mother,' he asked, 'how long before I can begin to work?'

'Four weeks,' she said. 'Perhaps five.'

That was all right. He would be up in time to get in the harvest. And while he was confined to bed he wouldn't need to eat very much. The children could have his share.

'You would set it crooked for me?'

'You will limp a little all your life,' she promised him.

Pavlo could not ask better than that; but it was not so easy to break a leg and harder still to do it so convincingly that the doctor in uniform and the lawyer in his black coat would write it down on their papers as an accident.

It was then that the bandit, Brancovitch, himself entered the story. All four went out to find him—Pavlo, Despina and the two children. They were quite confident. He did not rob peasants. He was as poor as they. When he had accumulated a little store of coins he bought powder and shot with them, just as the men who lived in cottages bought seed. He lived a lot worse than they and ate, perhaps, a bit better, for he had more meat—when he could swallow it down. It was not always very fresh meat. He used to hang it in a forked branch like a wild-cat.

The family found him sitting in the sun at the entrance to his winter cave, preparing a pine-marten skin. He made more out of selling shabby furs than banditry. There were few travellers really worth the trouble of holding them up.

While the children played in the scrub of the hillside, Pavlo explained the disaster of the call-up and made an eloquent speech such as his father might have delivered to a Turkish bey, begging for patronage. The formality was correct but unnecessary. Towards the neighbours Brancovitch was as benevolent as Robin Hood, within the limits of his charity. They were quickly reached. His largesse might perhaps run to a couple of sparrows on a wooden spit if a friend were ill.

'I want you to shoot me through the leg,' said Pavlo.

Mirko Brancovitch understood the urgency of it. But his weapon was not equal to his skill. He had only an old muzzle-loader. Normally he charged it with bird shot. On any game as big as Pavlo Popovnic he would have to use ball.

He pointed out that what Pavlo and Despina required was difficult. A leg was very small. He might give a flesh wound which wouldn't keep anybody out of the Army or, worse still, he might smash the knee-cap. Of course, at point-blank range he could make sure, and if he used a light charge of powder he could guarantee a clean break. But what about the powder burns and the wadding? The military examiners could be trusted to find that palpable evidence, for it would be just what they were looking for.

'Besides,' he had said, 'why in the devil's name should I shoot at you?'

Pavlo looked blank. He himself knew very well the sort of crime which Brancovitch would or would not commit, but he assumed that to the outside world a bandit was unaccountable; if caught, he would be executed in any case, so he was free to take a pot shot at anyone he pleased to amuse himself. It did not occur to Pavlo Popovnic that bandits had to have motives like anybody else.

Despina thought up a dozen reasons for shooting at her husband, but all of them were improbable and involved quite unforeseeable consequences. Brancovitch sadly refused to have anything to do with the plan. He accepted a bottle of Despina's plum brandy and gave in return a little bag of wild seeds for the hens. It was very welcome. At home there were few scraps fit for chickens, and of course no grain.

On their way back Pavlo was silent. His obstinate male mind was more impressed by the technical than the personal difficulties of firing a ball into a leg. He was an experienced shot himself. The death of the family cow had compelled him to sell his gun to buy a heifer.

He left his family to their thin soup and returned to the bone-setter, though it was now after dark and no time to disturb her. He begged her to tell him if there were not a way to hide powder burns and to make a bullet wound appear as if it had been inflicted from a distance.

Her memories went as far back into the past as Brancovitch's today. She knew a trick handed down from the time when the Turkish Janissaries raided the valleys to recruit Christian boys and drove the Serbs up into crags where liberty could be preserved at the price of hunger.

'You will buy two thick loaves,' she instructed him, 'of good wheat bread, not our peasant bread. Tie a loaf on each side of the leg and fire through them.'

Her prescription was obviously sound. Pavlo trusted it as if she had given him an infallible charm. He begged her not to reveal the secret to any of the other families who had husbands or sons called up for the Army. He did not fear that they would give him away. Mutual loyalty among the Serbs was absolute. No, he was alarmed lest they might all play the same trick and consequently all go to prison.

'They are as brave as I,' he said with a conceit which was national rather than personal.

'But their wives have not the courage of your Despina,' she answered.

It always took time—very naturally—to find Mirko Brancovitch. When at last they were able to tell him about the bread, he saw the point and was professionally enthusiastic. He suggested that the loaves should be at least a day old, since new bread might slow up the ball like a sandbag. And, to avoid shattering the bone, he was going to load with only a quarter charge of powder.

He was far more willing to oblige Pavlo and Despina than before. He explained that he had given his lonely thoughts to their problem. It was in his interest, too, that Pavlo's leg should be broken so long as it was plain that he had been shooting not at him, but at the police. And it was about time he did, or Danilo might be transferred to some other district.

Danilo was responsible for enforcing such law as he could over fifty square miles of rock. He and Brancovitch were of the same clan and most reluctant to interfere with each other; but for the sake of higher authority an occasional exchange of shots was essential.

17

'If you are willing to swear that I fired at Danilo from ambush and he fired back,' Brancovitch said, 'there will be no questions afterwards.'

Yes, he could ensure Danilo's co-operation and silence. No trouble at all there. The greatest difficulty still lay ahead. You, forty years later, the former bandit would explain, could never suspect it. The greatest difficulty was to get the bread.

Time was beginning to run short. In three days' time Pavlo had to report to the depot. The nearest baker was half a day's journey away, and even he did not bake town bread unless it were specially ordered. Neither Despina nor her neighbours had an oven which would bake loaves of the texture and thickness required.

Experiments with a little white wheat flour and inadequate fuel were hopeless. They dared not use any substitute. So one of the last precious days and nights of Pavlo and Despina had to be sacrificed while he walked to the town, gave his order to the baker, slept in the open and returned the next day with the loaves.

It seemed extraordinary that bread should cost so much when at home it cost nothing—nothing, that is, but Pavlo's indispensable labour and the children's scrabblings among the rocks to find dry, burnable roots. But all of them agreed that such loaves were a perfection of food, satisfying eye, scent and touch. The sons stroked the crust with little wondering hands.

The following morning Danilo turned up at the Popovnics' cottage with his rifle slung on his back. His presence there would be easy to explain to his officer. He was paying a visit to answer Pavlo's ignorant questions, to see what he was up to and to ensure that he was making no preparations for escape. The bone-setter was already boiling her remedies at the stove, with the splints and bandages under her skirt. It was unlikely that the Law would ever find out from her at what time she had come to attend to the patient. She accounted to no one for her mysterious movements and answered threats with crazy cackles of abuse and curses.

The children were left at the cottage. Pavlo, Danilo and the two women scrambled uphill to a just cultivable clearing, the size of a small room, at the top of the land. When they were there, Brancovitch detached himself from a cluster of rocks and patted Pavlo reassuringly on the back. Pavlo was pale and nervous. He was like mid-century man being prepared for an operation. It was going to save the future of his family, but it was not pleasant.

'Don't hurt him, Mirko!' Despina cried.

A ridiculous remark. But no doubt surgeons hear it today. And Brancovitch knew as well as they what she meant—that he wasn't to hurt Pavlo more than he must.

Now that the moment of their plotting had become reality,

Despina's anxiety was silent and terrible. It had no relation to our modern fears: of a dangerous compound fracture or of septic poisoning. Her medical knowledge was not up to that. In her experience—which in a country of blood feud was considerable—men always recovered from a broken limb though it was never as useful as before. That was why she and Pavlo had chosen a leg rather than an arm. The legs were only for carrying the arms to work.

No, her anxiety was not for the possible consequences, but a sharing of Pavlo's pain and distress. Yet she never doubted that it was his duty. She felt no horror at all for such an atrocity. It was the only alternative to disaster, and she would have unhesitatingly mutilated herself if it had been she whom the government wanted to take away.

Brancovitch insisted that the girl accepted the preparations naturally. She almost sanctified them by her love and simplicity, and the need of her children for food. Under those circumstances nothing in the act was criminal, nothing unclean.

Pavlo tied the loaves lightly on each side of his shin and stood with that leg advanced. The bandit knelt at a distance of two yards from him, his old muzzle-loader pointing slightly downwards. The trajectory of the ball would correspond to that of a shot aimed at the unsuspecting Danilo from higher up the hillside.

He fired. Pavlo sat down, biting his knuckles, free for ever of military service. Before the smoke of the powder had cleared, Despina had recovered the loaves and sliced out the circles of black and pink.

'For the children,' she sobbed, as she threw her arms and her long hair about her husband.

DIONYSUS AND THE PARD

His thumb was very obviously missing. You can know a man for weeks—if you are interested in his face—without spotting the absence of a finger, but you must miss the thumb of his right hand, especially when he is raising a glass at reasonably frequent intervals. A hand without a thumb is strangely animal; one looks for the missing talon on the under side of the wrist.

If you saw the back view of Dionysus Angelopoulos in any eastern Mediterranean port, you would at once put him down as an archaeologist or something cast up upon the beach by the Hellenic Travellers' Club. Judging by the tall, spare figure, slightly stooping, dressed in shaggy and loose-fitting Harris tweed, you expected a mild, pleasing and peering countenance with perhaps a moustache or a little Chelseaish beard; but when he turned round he showed an olive face with thin jowls hanging, like those of an underfed bloodhound, on either side of a blue chin, and melancholy brown eyes of the type that men call empty and women liquid when they are hiding nothing but boredom.

It was for the sake of professional prestige that Mr Angelopoulos modelled himself upon what he considered an Englishman ought to look like. He was the Near-Eastern agent for a famous English firm whose name is familiar to few women but to all civilized men. He was responsible for shining palaces above and below ground from Alexandria to Ankara. Wherever there were Greek priests and Turkish coffee one was faced sooner or later by his trade-mark (a little below that of his Staffordshire principals):

THE ALPH

Dionysus Angelopoulos

Sanitary Engineer

He was a man of poetic imagination and had read his 'Kubla Khan'. He was also a historian.

'Between myself and the fall of the Roman Empire,' he said when presenting me with his card, 'there was nothing but indiscipline.'

We had met on board a tiny Greek passenger ship bound from the Piraeus to Beirut: The cramped quarters and the Odyssean good cheer had swiftly ripened friendship. That is to say, he accepted me as a listener and, when he permitted me to speak, took note of any colloquialisms I might use and added them forthwith to his astonishing vocabulary.

'It is obvious,' said Mr Angelopoulos, 'that the ancients tighted themselves with more enthusiasm than we. Frenzy, no? Wine and poetry were the business of Dionysus, no? For Plato it was natural to see godliness in a tighted man. Today we see no godliness. We have changed. It is the fault of the religious. Dear me, what bastards!'

Considering he had just consumed two bottles of admirable claret made by the Jesuits on the slopes of Lebanon, he was unjust to Christianity. But Angelopoulos was a Wesleyan-Methodist. It was a really original point of Anglicism like the Harris tweeds. He had adapted his sect as well as his appearance to the respectable selling of sanitary earthenware.

'Godliness!' shouted Angelopoulos, raising the bottle with his right hand and placing an imaginary crown upon his head with his left. 'Do I tell you how my thumb goes to pot?'

'Not yet. I was going to ask you.'

'All right. You are my friend. At this table with you I am sitting a living example of Hubris and Nemesis. I am proud I lose my thumb. Do you know La Brebis Egarée?'

'I've heard of her.'

There were few travellers on the Syrian shore who had not heard of the Lost Sheep—a pale, rolling Frenchwoman whose habit it was, when she felt specially obscene, to declare in the unctuous voice of a priest:

'Monsieur, je suis une brebis égarée!'

Since, anyway, she looked like a gross white ewe, the nickname stuck. She was not the type to run mythical cargoes to Buenos Aires. She merely knew everybody. Whether you fell in love with a Kurdish princess in Smyrna or a German Jewess in Jerusalem, she could tell you what your chances were and whom you should approach.

'I tell you, old chappie,' said Angelopoulos, 'I thought she was no more of this world. I did not know till that evening where she now abided—hung out, I should say, no?

'The agent Socrates found for her a house in Athens, in the new suburb below Lycabettos. It is the last house in a little street that ends slap up against the cliff. The goings-on cannot be overlooked unless one should hang by his toes from the rocks. Only once was she taken at a loss. A Daphnis and Chloë were in the laurel bushes making love—how do you say that?'

I told him. He thanked me and, pulling from his pocket an expensive note-book bound in limp leather, made a formal entry in Greek and English.

'They were so happy they went right through the laurels and slid down the rocks into her back garden. A very proper place to find themselves, no?

'The Losted Sheep has a little restaurant upon the roof where the agent Socrates invited me to lunch. He does not pay there, I think. A meal ticket, no? He is a very useful chap. I will give you his card.'

Mr Angelopoulos searched through a portfolio full of badly printed cards, each of which set forth not only the name and address of its owner but his profession and any title to distinction he might have. He handed me:

SOCRATES PANCRATIADES

Agent d'Affaires

Hypothèques, Locations, Immeubles

Vins en gros

Publiciste

whereupon I understood that if I bought wines, a building lot or a political libel from Socrates Pancratiades I should be quoted a reasonable price and Mr Angelopoulos would get one of the infinitesimal commissions by which the Near East lives and is made glad.

'We were two upon the roof,' went on Mr Angelopoulos, 'the agent Socrates and I. The view was okay—the Acropolis, the Theseum, and to the south, Hymettus. Rather! God's Truth! We were content. And the Losted Sheep did us proud. The eats were top-notch. And we were served by two little Armenians—big-busted angulars you find seeing them dead upon the walls of an Egyptian tomb. Tartlets or Turtle Doves! O estimable dead!

'Attend to me, old chappie. It was Athens in the spring and the Losted Sheep's brandy was special reserve from the Achaea vineyard. You have seen the Achaea? Well, it is on the hills behind Patras. And there is the Gulf of Corinth at your feet with blue mountains beyond and the triremes skidding into the water at Naupactus. Splosh! No? And Aphrodite casts a veil about the swift ship. At that distance you cannot see oars and foam, but mist you see.'

'Triremes?' I asked, being a full bottle behind Mr Angelopoulos.

'In the eye of the spirit, old chappie. I will give you a card. Then maybe they will let you buy the special reserve and you shall see triremes, remembering where the grapes grow.

'The agent Socrates was soon tighted. I myself was tighted—but like an English gentleman. Or no. For an English gentleman always wants something. Barbarians! But I love you, my dear.'

'Hellas,' I said, realizing that this startling declaration was merely an apology, 'is the mother of all nations.'

'Incontestably all right!' agreed Mr Angelopoulos. 'I was content.

So, you see, I was not like an English gentleman. I wanted nothing. I was a god looking down upon Athens from the Losted Sheep's roof.

'She asked me if I would drink more brandy. I did not want more brandy. Then she asked me if I would make a visit to Fifi. I did not want to see Fifi. But the agent Socrates was asleep and the Armenians were asleep, and the Losted Sheep chattered. She did not understand that it was Athens and sunset and I, Dionysus, have a poet's entrails. I did not want Fifi, but if Fifi were young and would stay naked and quiet upon my knees, she would be better than the talk of the Losted Sheep, no?

'So I said: 'If your Fifi is beautiful, I will make her a visit. But if she is not beautiful, I will smell your fat, Brebis, while my priests eat you.' I was a god, you see.

'The Losted Sheep promised me that Fifi was more beautiful than any tail-piece I ever saw. So I went with her down from the roof and through the rendezvous house into the garden. In the side of Lycabettos was a cave with iron bars across the mouth.

'There is Fifi,' she said.

'I look. I see damn-all. A hole in the yellow rock and the shadows of the bushes where the Daphnis and Chloë entertained themselves. I do not know what to think. The Losted Sheep was a naughty one. She was maybe keeping a little savage behind the bars or a dame off her head with the bats. And then Fifi stretched herself and came to see who we were. She was a big leopard. Very beautiful, I bet you! The Losted Sheep had chattered, but she had watched me. She knew I did not want human things to worship me.

'Herself she would not approach Fifi. The bars were wide, and Fifi could get her paws through and most of her head. But I, Dionysus, had no fear. I spoke to Fifi. I sat on the sill of the cage and tickled her behind the ears. She liked that. She rubbed herself on the bars and purred. Then she was gone. I could only see her eyes in the darkness at the back of the cave.

'I called to her and she came at me through the air. So long and slender as if a love should fly down from heaven into my embraces. The Losted Sheep shrieked like a losted soul. But I was not afraid. I never thought to be afraid. I was a jolly god. Fifi knew that I would not hurt her. I knew that she would not hurt me. It was mutual confidence as in the sanitary or other business.

'She landed with all four feet together. I pulled her whiskers. She tapped my face with her paw to tell me she would play. So soft. So strong. I have felt nothing like it in my life. I shall never feel anything like it. They were created cats, you will remember, that man might give himself the pleasure of imagining that he caresses the tiger. To caress the tiger herself, that is for a god.

'I stroked her stomach. She purred. I stabbed into the fur my nails, up and down her backbone.'—Mr Angelopoulos held out his thumbless claw, crooking and contracting the fingers.—'She was in ecstasy. There was a communion between me and Fifi. All she felt, I felt. It tickled me delicately from the point of my fingers to my kidneys. I knew when she had had enough, when her pleasure could not more be endured. It was the same for me. If she had touched me again with her paw, I should have bitten her.

'And so we parted. I wept. I knew I should never feel such godly pleasure again. And there was the Losted Sheep shrieking and moaning. I put out my hands to her to stroke her as I had stroked Fifi. She ran. And so I woke the agent Socrates and we went away.'

Mr Angelopoulos was silent, brooding over the splendour of his past divinity.

'But your thumb?' I asked.

'My thumb—yes, my dear, I had forgotten. Hubris and Nemesis, of which is sitting with you the sad example. A week later I was in Constantinople. I had businesses near the port and I was coming home at night from Galata to Pera. There are streets with steps, no? Little stairs with stinks. There was a street with cats on all the steps. I stopped to talk to them—I, Dionysus, the catman who is chums with leopards. But I forgot that I was sober. I was a man and no more a god. I was a danger to all beasts. There was a pail of ordures and a grey kitten eating fish-heads from it. I stroked him and he bit me in the thumb. How should he know I did not want the fish-heads? If I had been tighted and a god, he would have known I needed no fish-heads.

'And so you see, old chappie, my thumb was tinctured red and then blue, and then it was green and white like marble. Thus I hospitalized myself, and they cut it off. Nemesis, old chappie, or the godly tit for tat as we say in English.'

LOW WATER

Gino's was an island. Its inhabitants had a single culture; it was surrounded by a sea as acquiescent as they. In summer the happy Mediterranean disturbed Gino's not at all; in winter harsh little waves, last remnants of storm beyond the narrow bay, spat fiercely at the weed-draped jetty and gurgled away in dark impotence beneath the flooring. The piles which supported Gino's were rotten; the planks which joined the café to the mainland stayed in place by sheer inertia. Every year the many slopes of the tiled roof, the angles of the wooden walls, became crazier by another inch. When anything fell off, Gino, eventually, put it back again. Neither screw nor nail would grip in the soft timber. A hole under the eaves which had mildly annoyed his clients for two seasons he stopped with a broken frying pan, leaning a balk of driftwood against the wall to hold the patch in place.

The culture of Gino's island was listless and Levantine. His nationality was Turkish; his father had been Maltese as much as anything, and his mother half Greek and half Italian. The ancestry of his girls resembled his own in so far as they were of mixed blood and obscure descent. The island industry was the provision of routine entertainment for summer visitors. Somebody had to undertake the job. It called neither for shame nor self-congratulation; it merely fulfilled a social need like unloading coal or selling hashish or cleaning sewers or becoming a policeman, and demanded—at any rate from Gino—no undignified activity of the body.

Gino was very long and very thin. His interior was full of national and foreign parasites, for he had been poor and a traveller. To him his island was home at long last, and upon it was no more need for energy or emotion. His only token of feeling was an undulation of the spine, which might have expressed satisfaction, at the same hour every morning when he rose from breakfast, took rod and line and started to fish from the stage outside the kitchen door. He fished from eleven to six, sometimes sitting, sometimes standing, hunched over the Mediterranean which sparkled and laughed at the foot of his steps and spread out beneath his island into a still lake of deep greens and browns sown with traps and nets of his own devising.

He caught fish. He caught fish continuously. They came, it was said in the town, all the way across the Mediterranean for him to

25

catch; and indeed Gino's island was about as far east as they could swim. It seemed to be a fish terminus and round point; after a quick nip from Gino's garbage or the soft ooze beneath his island there was nothing for it but to turn back to Greece and Gibraltar and the rich North African banks.

Gino himself looked like an old grey mullet set up by a bad taxidermist who had put back the skin over insufficient stuffing. His head was hairless and his dull eyes were too large. His fishlike mind knew none of the enthusiasms of humanity except the cooking of his catch. For this he was famous. Whether he fried to biscuit hardness in deep oil or adventured in the casseroles and herbs and wine of French cuisine or served his fish boiled and cold and decorated, they were products of high human art. His other cooking was vile. Indeed all of Gino that was not fish was distasteful.

He employed six performers. Each year they were sent to him by an agency in Alexandria. One of the batch had to be able to dance efficiently; two must be endurable however sordid their acts; the remaining three had just to get on and off the stage without incident and were usually over forty. He paid wages and commission to the upper three and commission only to the lower three, and put them all up in rooms like sunlit bathing hutches on the floor above the café. Gentlemen were strictly forbidden both by Gino and the police to visit this second floor; but the holiday season was short and the police were very poorly paid. As for Gino, he had signed a Notice To Customers and thereafter was indifferent to what went on upstairs unless the noise was too great. Then, in a barely audible voice, he pointed out that the house was very old and might fall down. If anyone were injured, he said, there would be a scandal.

That year there were scandals enough. They were the fault of Tatiana. She was an Egyptian with a Russian mother; and in her character a faint and purely traditional Russianness had remained proof against the lethargy of Egypt. Tatiana was the star performer and neither better nor worse than dancers whom the Alexandria agency had sent to Gino in other years. Her morals, which mattered to nobody, were above the usual standard. Her behaviour, for so conventional an island, was indiscreet. She gave parties to her favourites. She considered the whole upper storey as her own and dashed in and out of bedrooms at awkward moments. Her colleagues, who themselves observed the decent melancholy proper to Gino's, accepted Tatiana's instability as a new fashion from worldly Egypt and a useful topic of conversation.

The other two paid performers were Miriam and Elena the Greek. Miriam, being half Sudanese, was too black for popularity; Gino's clients preferred to cherish the illusion that they were being entertained by pure Europeans. Elena the Greek was born at Marseilles of port parentage into which, somewhere, had entered a strain of Chinese blood; she was called the Greek because that was the language she spoke most fluently. The three girls who worked for commission alone had the names and nationalities that the agency had given them. They were old, pink animals who answered to these names. How or in what memory each addressed herself could not be known. They lived in a dead present untroubled by remembered suffering. They had no clear thought left to them and little revealing speech.

Gino's season was short and it was not much of a season. The little town was Turkish; the islands which closed the western horizon were Italian; the inhabitants of both were largely Greek. It belonged nowhere and had nothing to offer the moneyed tourist. Yet the two hotels and the red and white villas set irregularly among dusty country lanes suited the pockets of small businessmen with the faiths and customs of Europe and were reasonably full of their families attracted by the hard and waveless beach. The fathers and elder sons, dignified and respectable by day, considered it proper to relax at night. Gino's represented for them the smart cabarets of French *plages* and Florida beaches familiarised by the cinema.

Upstairs and downstairs Tatiana disordered the island. She was always surrounded by two or three young admirers who were fascinated into outrageous behaviour though not into any lavish spending. She had a dashing habit of throwing her cocktails overboard 'to feed the fishes'. This might have been good for trade if she and her parties had not thrown the glasses and crockery as well. To Gino Tatiana was a liability, a shock, a devastation. She kept the older, slow consuming, steadily paying clients away. The noise and scandal raised the weekly subvention paid to the police. The glasses, if they could not be netted, were replaceable only at fantastic prices.

Gino increased the bills by erratic and exaggerated items which led to endless arguments with the clients and, after all, had to be reduced. He left his basic charges unaltered. They were reasonable—little more than those of the hotels although there were a band and three waiters and the performers to be paid, and a cook who attended to Gino's stove when Gino himself was reluctantly gazing at the dance floor. He felt that he ought to gaze—so far, that is, as *ought* had any meaning for him—but he said no word, he took no action. He had no interest in women, individually or collectively. They were like the bottles of Egyptian whisky. There was a demand for the stuff and he supplied it.

His fitful attempts to keep up with rising costs and wages were always a year behind. He had made his calculations when he bought and fitted out the island, and felt that the one effort should be sufficient for his life; it had to be done but thereafter there should be no necessity for thought. Beneath the floor the bountiful sea worked for him in darkness. Above was modest catering for eternal desires of men. Neither one nor the other could fail.

The season was disastrous. At the beginning of September there was nothing in the bank and the night's takings were paid out every morning. The wages of Tatiana, Miriam and Elena fell into arrears. As yet they did not complain. It was not the first time in their experience that the boss had been in difficulties.

On the next payless Saturday morning there was a row. Wages and commission were now three weeks overdue and obviously lost for ever. Even the three working crones, holding around their shapeless bodies wraps of pink and pale blue chiffon, stared at Gino with sad eyes in which was understanding of their fate. Tatiana, trim and terrifying in a beach suit, screamed at him in good Egyptian Greek. He was impassive. He bent his shoulders humbly over the till, as if it were the sea, and opened it and showed that there was nothing in it. Tatiana raged around the unswept room, buzzing like an angry insect of undoubted grace and comparative cleanliness between four greasy, wine-splashed walls, foul ashtrays, spilt food, tables stinking of sweat and debris. She hurled a bottle into the sea and was led upstairs weeping by Miriam and Elena. The other three returned to bed and their day-dreams of the impossible. Gino went out to fish.

The sun shone. The paintless wooden balconies of the upper storey gave back the light of the day and the stored light of a hundred years, sparkling with the fawn and white of timber on the southern edge of a forest. Tatiana, Miriam and Elena lay in the shade of the eaves, cursing Gino. When they were silent they could hear the plop of his tackle re-entering the water, or the reverberation of a sea bream smacking its arched body against the planks of the back-door jetty.

Night brought the end. There was no band. There were no waiters. There was no assistant cook. All had gone to the hotels to make what they could in the last week before the season finished. A few habitual customers drifted in across the creaking bridge of planks. They listened to abuse of Gino and agreed. They helped themselves and the girls to drinks and paid what they liked or nothing at all. Gino did not appear.

In an hour the café had emptied. There was no gaiety, no romance; the island and its inhabitants appeared exactly what they were. The girls, like the clients, had looked to the night and music, even at Gino's, to create an endurable illusion. Now there were only themselves and the sea and the slap of moths and beetles, before unnoticed, against the glaring lights. They sat still, scattered about the room at the tables where they had been left, without energy or desire to move together.

Gino came in from the kitchen bearing a huge casserole of fish. The scent, rich and appetising, overwhelmed the staleness of the room. He

28

put the dish on a table with six flat cakes of bread, beckoned to the girls and went out.

They moved to the food slowly, and as if ashamed by their failure to retain a single customer. Then with a brisk exclamation Tatiana threw away the filthy table cloth. The others, catching her mood of self-respect, swiftly washed knives and forks, glass and plates left untouched since the previous night. They chose clean chairs and sat down at the bare table, three a side, as in some institution for homeless females deserted by all but themselves. They began to laugh and chatter. Gino's fish was in no way institutional. It warmed and delighted.

They went to bed early, breathing for an extra four hours, instead of smoke, the cool air currents of the bay, and awakened to a vague feeling of holiday rather than disaster. Miriam made coffee and they breakfasted on the balcony. Then, as the heat of sand and dusty tracks consumed the morning, they saw their position in all its hopelessness.

It was Gino's responsibility to return them to Alexandria, and it was certain that he could not do it. They all spoke loudly of their contracts and of the Law that would, if necessary, compel him to sell his island to pay their fares. They gesticulated at a just and imaginary judge, but in their hearts they knew that they were terrified by the Law, upon whose edge they lived, and had no intention of calling to their aid the unknowable, uncontrollable gods of policemen.

They were too far east for chivalry. Tatiana and Miriam ran over the characters and probable bank balances of their devoted followers in the hope of finding one who might be gallant. Any, they decided, would provide food and especially bed for the few more days that he would remain at the seaside; not one would commit the generous folly of advancing the fare to Alexandria or even—in view of their known economic distress—of allowing it to be earned. There were no capitalists among the fathers and sons who took their holiday by that horned beach. Money counted, even when Tatiana was feeding the fishes and creating an illusion of imperial excess.

Either Miriam or Tatiana might perhaps make enough for herself to go, but not enough to release a companion as well. Though they had not hitherto been conscious of much liking for each other and though the three wage earners despised the three commissionaires, as Tatiana christened them, the solidarity of their profession—they called it the theatrical profession—prevented them from leaving behind any of their number to end, with certainty, in some horrible village brothel.

Tatiana could raise—probably—from an old friend in Alexandria the money for her fare. Miriam had a contract half promised for the winter and thought, not very hopefully, that the agency might lend her what she needed. Elena the Greek, who could dance just well enough for a joint such as Gino's but looked, without make-up on a blazing morning, like a slender Chinese grandmother, had no hope at all. The three commissionaires listened with dazed attention to the discussion among their betters. They would not have been surprised if Tatiana had produced thousands of piastres from a hat or if she had told them to go and prostitute themselves upon the beach. Whatever she decided they would perform.

Tatiana and Miriam decided nothing. They dived, exasperated, from the balcony into the caressing sea, two worn but serviceable arrows of black and white startling Gino and wrecking his fishing for that morning.

The day passed in intolerable nervousness. Tatiana, Miriam and Elena the Greek were not accustomed to be idle, to be without some vague and nearly objectless occupation. They rose usually at midday, fiddled with their breakfasts and complexions for a couple of hours. practised a few dance steps, showed themselves in whatever public place was temporarily in fashion, then passed the evening with some admirer until it was time to go to work. Now, however, with Gino's island ruined and the season nearly over, there was nothing to be gained by visiting the town, nor had they the heart for it. They remained in their rooms or on the balcony, quarrelling, screaming, in tears, demoralized.

At sunset Gino shut the wooden doors on the gangway to his island and put up a notice of CLOSED. Then he took his boat and lamp and fish spear and disappeared into the darkness of the bay. He said nothing whatever to the girls, accepting their forced occupation of his island without resentment, without pity, without helpfulness.

The soft splash of Gino's oars recalled them to sanity. They stared after him into the calm blackness of the sea. They could hear him; they could see the twin phosphorescent puddles of the oars receding into the distance, but the boat itself was invisible. Their fear of this isolation was extreme. All quarrels forgotten, they drew together on the balcony. The lights of the little town glittered half a mile away. The villas were nearer, but their lit windows were so scattered over the coastal plain that they only increased the sense of loneliness. In the girls' minds, and indeed in fact, they were castaways; it mattered nothing that their island was joined to all Asia by only a dozen planks.

They crept downstairs and turned up the lights in the kitchen. All day they had not had the energy to eat. There were bread and vegetables and a few eggs. Fish there was none, for Gino never kept it overnight. Miriam again turned cook. They ate in silence, exhausted and hopeless.

The effort of cooking and feeding did them good. Their washing-up extended itself spontaneously from the plates to Gino's revolting kitchen. They were six women who had seldom had goods of their own to

30

scrub and polish. Not one of them would have done a stroke of work for Gino, but this was for themselves. The silence, the closed door, the sea around and under impressed on them that it was for themselves.

By morning the unconscious, communal spirit of discipline was dead. No one made breakfast. They drifted down to the café and drifted back into the bedrooms to continue the interminable discussions. At least they were all calmer. One of the commisionaires had a touch of sunburn; it made her pudgy face look firm and elastic.

At ten Tatiana took command and persuaded Miriam to the kitchen. It was clean as they had left it. On the table were two flat baskets, a yard in diameter, piled with fish, among them a dozen fat, expensive soles. Tatiana, pacified by this industry, observed that Gino had eaten nothing. Outside on the jetty his indifferent back was towards them, hunched over the rod. Patronizingly she offered him a cup of coffee and the last of the bread. He accepted without pleasure or surprise and thanked her. His words were formal Levantine courtesies meaning nothing: phrases by which two human beings could converse for minutes without the need of any thought at all. She asked him what to do with the fish. Gino shrugged his shoulders. If people came to eat, they ate it; if they didn't, nobody ate it. He landed a red mullet and paid no further attention to Tatiana.

For all their working lives Tatiana and Miriam had depended on manager or proprietor. His was the responsibility, theirs the obedience. Even Tatiana's Russian liveliness was purely professional. Her plan for living was to make the clients spend in return for her wages and commission. Her future was a succession of engagements at third-class cabarets; her firm faith, founded on nothing, was that they would become first-class cabarets before she was too old.

The boss of the moment might be inefficient or exacting, lecherous or contemptuous, broke or miserly or generous; but the boss he was. He did not merely live as they between four walls from nine in the evening to three in the morning. He was in the mysterious outer world of contracts, arrangements, recommendations. Looking at Gino's back, it was evident to Tatiana and Miriam that they were for the first time without a boss and that Gino was in their own world of helpless resignation. He might as well have been the ghost of a fisherman sitting outside his own back door.

Even this understanding of Gino did not move them to any constructive plan. Indeed their angry chatter reached new depths of futility. All former schemes, however wild, had depended on Gino being forced to do something. They had at last realized that nothing would force him to do anything.

It was the fish that made the plan. There it lay, in quantity, luxurious. Alongside the baskets was the empty bread bin. Without need of imagination, the economic problem solved itself. Two of the commissionaires put on aprons of sacking and Gino's shoes—for their own had the high heels of their vocation—and shuffled off to the town with the fish baskets upon their heads. They returned at midday, weary, humiliated, miserable, but with bread and groceries and money over. Fresh sole was fifty piastres a kilo on the market. The girls were all ignorant of local commerce, and amazed.

Day after day passed while they ate and slept well, and fussed frantically to get themselves away. Gino wandered through and among them on his own plane, occasionally cooking, always unseeing and, after a while, unnoticed. Those who could write with ease wrote letters to the Alexandria agency, to cabaret proprietors in Athens and Istanbul, to old admirers, to anyone they had ever known with money to lend or employment to offer. The only result of all that fevered, impractical planning, that see-saw of hope, those hysterical visits to the post office to insist that letters had been lost, was that Elena the Greek was lent a pound by her sister. They tried to plan how it should be spent, but the island imposed its own solution. The pound immediately went on soap and a washtub.

The town returned to its winter peace. Gino and his girls had provided a week of scandal, conjecture and conversation, and a week was all they were worth. Nobody bothered them. They bothered nobody. On the island they were brown, healthy and rested, but neither knew nor felt the improvement. They were dull with fear of poverty, illness and starvation. When they thought, they had no hope; but they had little time to think. The island was their taskmaster.

Organisation grew though they intended none. Tatiana, by reason of her education, was general manager. Miriam was assistant cook. Elena the Greek, who had a passion for neatness perhaps inherited from that unknown Chinese ancestor, expended it upon the crusted dirt of Gino's hidden corners. Two of the commissionaires were becoming known in a more friendly fish market. The third was washerwoman. To all the girls their life seemed inactive and frustrated, for they were unaware of their achievement. Their only comfort was the superb fish supper that Gino often made for them. He seemed to enjoy their appreciation. He said nothing, but his body undulated graciously as he set the dish upon the table.

At the end of October the first storm roared down the Mediterranean and over the town. With Gino's island it merely played, for wind and sea were diverted by the sheltering promontory to the north. The wind was neither cold nor convincing; it whistled merrily round the ill-fitting eaves and slammed the bedroom doors. The sea, excitedly sucking and splashing, managed to wet three steps of Gino's jetty that had been dry all the summer. Gino lit the iron stove in the café, packing it with cut driftwood. Where the plates were thin with age and the blacking worn away the stove glowed red and comforting.

Wind, sea and fire emphasized the passing of time. Tatiana revolted. She shouted that they could not stay, that winter was coming, that this could not go on. She crashed a plate upon the floor and earned a reproachful look from Elena. They all listened while she cried and cursed; they had no answer to her repeated question of what they were to do. They looked at her, disconcerted by her vehemence as if she were destroying some feminine, delicately poised, illusive truth. In the silence the washerwoman spoke. 'Here we eat,' she said.

The comment was unanswerable. It referred to the present, that present in which the commissionaires had learned through timeless suffering to exist; yet in its profundity was hidden an illimitable future. If they wished, on Gino's island they might eat for ever. The warmth of the stove blended serenely with the warmth of the food within them. The storm was for others, not for them. Their dreams changed in that moment: those vague intentions which supported the lonely, personal life of each battered individual. They were back in the field of women—of eagerness and the possibility of love, of industry and of abounding health. They even had a willing servant who asked only to remain, unresisting upon his island. Impulsively Tatiana began the new world by a single act of creation. She rose from the table to give Gino orders for the morrow.

ROMANIA

SABRES ON THE SAND

The rules of the game of honour were really, you know, common sense. Like all conventions, they were ridiculous but prevented anarchy. I accepted them with a casual amusement which should have enabled me to handle them easily. Yet I am still bothered by the memory of an act which would have been condemned as unforgivably dishonourable by all my contemporaries. That it was for the sake of my sister made no difference—made it worse, if anything.

I must take you back to musical comedy of the year 1923. But it was not on any stage; it was the life of every week. Or, not exaggerating at all, the life of once a month. My sister and I were then Romanians. Before 1918 we had been Hungarians. As a Count of the Empire, I never really felt that I was either. So Magda and I took to our new nationality with decent resignation. We were flat broke, but one could have a lot of formal fun in Bucharest on next to nothing a year.

We had been asked to the royal ball at the Military Club. It was a scented night of late spring, but nerves were too edgy for enchantment. Chandeliers, which had only just been adapted from gas to electricity, gave too hard a light. The officers were made aware that cheap cloth of pale blue and gold was no more effective in a ball-room than it had been in battle. The women, wearing the short and unceremonious frocks of 1923 for the first formal occasion, felt disarmed—as if, Magda said, they were waltzing in their slips.

Only the few foreigners, dressed in the black-and-white of secure convention, were enjoying themselves without a care. They were mostly diplomats, but there were a few socially acceptable representatives of industry and finance—among, them, Rob Tymson. He was five years older than I, but I felt responsible for him. When I saw that he was contentedly knocking back champagne at the bar and exchanging pleasant reminiscences of sudden death in the St Quentin sector of the western front with a French banker called Delorme, I went off and danced.

My first premonition of something wrong was half an hour later. Magda and Rob were fox-trotting together, and everybody was trying hard not to stare at them. I thought that perhaps he had proposed at last and then committed the crime of kissing her in public. But it was not that. When I had managed to draw them unobtrusively out of the

37

crowd and on to a quiet balcony, Magda said: 'Rob is going to fight a duel.'

Well, it was just possible. If in the mood, Rob could play his part in our local comedy as flamboyantly as the British colonel in attendance upon Prince Florizel. But he was a typical Englishman, tall, fair, full of responsibility and common sense. He had come out to Bucharest for three weeks to sign a government contract on behalf of his family steel business. As soon as he realized that three weeks meant at least six months, he determined to stay on and enjoy himself.

'I am *not* going to fight a duel,' said Rob, very red in the face. 'It is barbarous to risk murdering a man just because he lost his temper.'

'You can choose pistols,' Magda advised him quite correctly. 'You were in the war. You must know enough about it to be able to miss him.'

'Will you try to understand, Magda, that Englishmen do not fight duels?'

'Oh, but you must, Rob! You can't help it,' she insisted. 'Ask Stephen to explain. He'll tell you how silly it all is.'

He stared at us as if we were two slim, eager, fallen angels from the pit. There we were, Count Stephen and Countess Magda, with no parents, no land, no money, nothing to hold on to but our conventions of honour, male and female, and intelligent enough to find them comic. The Romanian duel was normally a farce without any danger at all. My sister knew it as well as I did. That was why she was perfectly willing for Rob to do the proper thing although she was in love with him.

I sent Magda off to dance. She doesn't come into my story at all, the darling. She was a motive, nothing else. A most lovely motive for dishonourable conduct.

With some difficulty I got out of Rob what had happened. Delorme and he had been talking French and discussing the Romanian Army. Rob couldn't accept those gorgeous cockatoos upon the dance floor as real soldiers. A soldier to him was a bit of shapeless, suffering humanity, inexplicably cheerful and plastered with mud. What with champagne and disapproval, his voice was too loud.

'The cloak-room is stacked with their silly swords,' he said to Delorme. 'And they couldn't draw them if they wanted to, because the hilt is cast in one piece with the scabbard.'

His shoulder was roughly hauled round. He met the enraged eyes of a Romanian captain, who smartly slapped him across the cheek with the open hand. Rob was a competent welterweight and his reaction was nearly immediate. Nearly. Sheer surprise used up a fraction of time. So did reluctance—for he was not the type to start a rough-house in a ball-room.

Before his right hook could get fairly started he was gripped from

38

behind. Other bystanders were holding—but more conventionally—his opponent. Between the two groups a minor diplomat and a Romanian general were advising patience. I'm experienced in such scenes myself. One acts with the quiet decision of the knowledgeable man who throws the dog out just before it is sick.

'Damn it!' Rob exclaimed indignantly. 'I seemed to be caught up in a sort of ceremony without anybody asking me.'

Well, of course, he had been. Blue and gold officers closed in casually to hide the unfortunate affair from the dance floor. Between Rob's friends and the defiant captain's friends the general and the minor diplomat observed the frontier. Anybody who had not seen the slap would have suspected nothing. Delorme received the captain's card. He told Rob to go away and dance, and to look calmly composed.

When Rob at last got Magda to himself—partners were still booked on programmes with little white pencils—he found to his horror that she knew all about the incident. Everybody agreed, she told him, that it had been beautifully managed. They were bursting with curiosity to know what he would do, and trying hard not to show it.

'I shouldn't have been talking so damned loud,' Rob said to me. 'Stephen, I feel the right move is to apologize.'

'But you can't apologize.'

'Why can't I?'

'Because you're the insulted party. Only he can apologize.'

'Then what *can* I do?'

'Nothing—except send him a challenge.'

I might as well have asked him to play ring-a-ring-a-roses in the courtyard of the Bank of England. He became offensively British. He pointed out that he was a civilized Westerner visiting Romania to assist in the reconstruction of the country, that he had had enough fighting to last him the rest of his life and that he wasn't going to begin again on Romanian officers. So I shut up. I really was not sure what public opinion would be. One can't count on certainties in a time of social transition.

Rob stalked back to the ball-room and did his best to appear composed; but all he could manage was a fixed grin. He went home early in the open carriage which he had romantically retained for his private use during his stay in Bucharest. No doubt he was more patient with our absurdities when he observed himself jingling magnificently through the Romanian night behind a pair of black and lively horses like a baron in a whisky advertisement.

The next morning he felt like a plain business man with a headache, living in a cosmopolitan hotel full of other business men with other headaches. He did not want to see uniforms, horses, swords and the idle poor for the rest of his life. I don't suppose he even wanted to see Magda. He must have been sourly glad that he had an appointment with Mr Marguliesh. The world of Marguliesh was sane, and he, Rob, belonged to it.

Mr Marguliesh was his financial adviser and the correspondent of his London bankers. We all liked him. In the rush of little rats between money-lenders and the Stock Exchange, trying to profit by inflation without going to gaol, he represented a vanished world. His white waistcoat, his taste in cigars and his obvious integrity would have graced the City of London.

Marguliesh told me afterwards that he was shocked by Rob's appearance. He immediately rang for his senior bank servant—about eighty years old and liveried in chocolate and silver—who came with his keys of office and unlocked a cupboard in the walnut panelling. There was something in it to suit every mood. Brandy and ginger-ale was Marguliesh's prescription for Mr Tymson.

When Rob was half-way through his long, golden glass and they had discussed some sound and sober question of shipment against treasury bills, Marguliesh delicately referred to private problems.

'It's half past eleven,' Rob protested, 'and nobody who was at the ball is up yet. How on earth do you know?'

It was never any good putting that question to Marguliesh. He knew everything. It always seemed natural that he should. As likely as not he had the barman on his pay roll.

Rob cursed all primitive societies and finally asked him—assuming that he would have the same point of view as a respectable English banker—whether he would fight a duel himself.

'Fortunately,' said Mr Marguliesh dryly, 'I am not officially a gentleman.'

'Well, damn it, I'm not officially a gentleman, either!'

'Oh, my dear sir, the aristocracy of industry! We accept it at last. And then you were a lieutenant-colonel in the war. Of course there is always a doubt who is and who is not a gentleman in England. It appears to depend on education. Here the last thing one expects of a gentleman is education. But if you send this fellow a challenge you prove what you are.'

Rob asked if he had to be a bloody fool in order to be rubber-stamped as a gentleman. 'Yes,' said Marguliesh. 'And if you ever wanted to marry into the aristocracy, how much more smoothly things would go for her!'

He was our banker too—though that was a pretty hopeless task—and I know he was just as anxious about Magda's future as I was. But Rob had the Englishman's dislike of anyone suspecting his emotions. In spite of the civilizing influence of brandy and ginger-ale he denied furiously that he had any intention of marrying into the aristocracy.

'A challenge would also do no harm to business,' Marguliesh suggested.

'I think, if I may say so, that is rather a sordid way of looking at it,' said Rob—and he cashed a cheque and scowled his way out.

He lunched at his hotel in a furious temper, and after a long afternoon's sleep went down to the bar for some companionship. There he found Delorme and greeted him as his only friend. Delorme had been a comrade-in-arms. He was civilized, reasonable and only too willing to explain English customs to Romanians and Romanian customs to English when he didn't know much about either.

'The captain is expecting you to send a friend to call on him,' Delorme said.

'I wouldn't send my worst enemy to call on him.'

Delorme made it clear what he meant. Rob patted him on the shoulder and repeated that duels were a hundred years out of date. 'They have gone out even in France,' he said.

'I beg you will not repeat your *even* in France, monsieur,' Delorme replied.

Rob protested desperately that he meant that in the most gallant of countries only politicians and critics fought duels any more, and who the hell cared if they killed each other. But Delorme had gone.

Though I did not know all the details of that unfortunate day till afterwards, I guessed that Rob would be readier to listen. To my mind the solution was obvious. He should give full play to his taste for operetta, and go through the ridiculous, bloodless farce of a Romanian duel. Still, I only decided to intervene after I had run into Delorme dining alone and looking extremely Napoleonic and disdainful. He gave me the news, but was not prepared, he said, to discuss further my good friend, M. Tymson. He added that this was the twentieth century, but that British manners were sometimes enough to make one forget it.

After that I went up to Rob's room. He had taken refuge in his business correspondence and was not at all pleased when I pretended to think that he was clearing up his affairs. He said that a man of my intelligence ought to understand his point of view without having it explained all over again.

'I do, Rob,' I assured him. 'You object to bloodshed, but you will be delighted to put on the gloves with him, cut his eyes open and knock out his front teeth.'

'At least I shouldn't risk killing him.'

'Who's asking you to kill him? You surely don't think there is any risk in a modern duel? It's against the law, and nobody wants to be run in.'

'I don't understand,' said Rob. 'Then why bother with it?'

'Why bother with a carriage and pair when you could use a car? I do wish you'd believe that Magda and I are only trying to help.'

He remarked that he considered my influence very bad for

41

Magda—in a proprietary tone which was thoroughly promising—and then he said:

'But I don't know the drill. Would you yourself second me or whatever it's called?'

'Of course. An honour.'

'And what do I fight him with?'

'In principle you can choose.'

'Well, I did a course of bayonet fighting once. Can I have a go at him with rifle and bayonet?'

That should have warned me. I should have spotted that slow rising of fury to the brain which the English call logic. But I thought he was just being perverse.

'No, you can't! It has to be pistols, so that you can fire in the air if you wish.'

'What's the good of a duel then?'

'The point is, Rob, that he will fire in the air and so will you. But you can't count on it.'

'If I can't count on it, I'm damned if I do it. I should look a silly clot blazing off at the sky while he's aiming at six o'clock on the bull. If I'm going to fight him at all, I'll fight him square. How about swords?'

I insisted that swords were out of the question, but he knew that was not strictly true and kept on bullying me until I had to tell him what the convention really was.

'The épée is not used because people *will* get hurt with it. Only the fleurette is allowed. That's just a foil with the button off. But don't choose it, Rob,' I begged him, 'if you can't fence. You'll make it so hard for him just to prick you.'

'I'll make it hard for him all right. What about sabres, Stephen?'

I explained that sabres were not for society affairs. They were only used by brutally angry military men—who could keep accidents fairly quiet and be punished by court martial rather than the criminal law.

'Do you want to spend some years in gaol?' I asked him. 'Duelling is forbidden, Rob, just like drinking after midnight in England. If it isn't done decently, the police have to take action.'

'I don't give a damn,' he said. 'They started it, and they're going to get it. Sabres it is.'

'But how good are you?'

'Better than anything else. I used to do a lot of singlestick as a boy. You teach me the proper salute, and then I'll wade in.'

Wade in. Those were his words. I can hear them now. I was appalled at such bluntness in an affair which had to be handled with the utmost discretion.

'Look here,' said Rob, 'if you won't let me pick my own weapon I'll walk up to that captain and slap the face powder off his blue chin! Then he can choose machine-guns if he likes, and God help him!'

That silenced me. I had to agree to deliver his challenge. And, after all, if Rob could really use a sabre—singlestick meant nothing to me—it might for once be safer than the fleurette. The only concession I could get from him was that he would fence with me at my flat next day just to put my mind at rest.

I drove round to call on the captain and performed the formalities. His company was on guard duty at the Royal Palace, and the honour had gone to his head. So had the brandy which he and his chosen friend had been drinking, tapering off from the night before. Both those uniformed owls were sure that Rob had chosen sabres as a shrewd way of avoiding any fight at all. They called the bluff. Sabres would do.

Rob turned up at my flat the next morning. He was half angry, half pleased with himself. The hotel porter had seen him to the door with a deeper bow than he had ever given. His driver had attached a red, white and blue ribbon to his whip. The speed at which rumour travelled was amazing.

I gave him the time and place—on a river sandbank about six miles out of town at 12.30 the following day. The more usual hour was before breakfast, but the captain and his second wanted to avoid it on the grounds that the police would then be watching their movements.

'I suppose the captain is quite happy about sabres?' Rob asked. He sounded as if he felt he might be taking an unfair advantage, bless him! I put his mind at rest on that score. The captain was no master, but he had got through two rounds of the army championship.

We set to. Five minutes were enough to show me that nobody could possibly be less experienced than Rob. Somehow he had got German student duelling into his head and thought that sabre fighting was all cut and slash. His bucolic singlestick gave him the guards for that stuff. But I tell you he didn't even realize that the point of a sabre was meant for business.

'Your opponent can touch you wherever he likes,' I said, 'and I take it that will be painful but not vital. What terrifies me is that if one of those swipes of yours ever did by accident connect, you'd cut him clean in two.'

'Look here, I don't want to go to gaol,' Rob began, taking off his mask in despair.

It was going to be that or hospital, but I didn't say so.

'One of our foundry foremen was champion of Yorkshire at singlestick,' he went on. 'He told me that if you jump back and whack the ground you can get in again while the other fellow is wondering what you are up to.'

'He'd certainly wonder—especially meeting a lunatic for the first time.'

The trick was better than nothing. There was just a chance that,

43

with his reach and a twist of the wrist, he might get the point under the captain's sword arm. I refused to let him try it on me—I didn't want to spoil his confidence—but I made him practise the footwork and learn to lunge. Out! Whack the ground! And in like lightning! The slightest scratch was enough for the seconds to call it a day.

But the longer he practised it, the more I saw it could be suicide. I promised that if he would drop his damned British obstinacy I would tell Magda the whole truth, and that she would be thankful he had shown some common sense. That was as near as I had ever come to admitting she was all ready for orange blossom and London. He blushed slightly and asked me what I *had* told her.

Well, I had let her believe it was to be the usual pistols; and she was still chuckling at the thought of her Rob trying to keep a solemn face while he went through the absurd ceremony of loosing off a shot into the sky.

Rob at last left, still determined to educate the foreigner. I suppose he was conditioned by his long war service to taking useless risks with a sort of sulky anger. As for me, I was as near hysteria as a young man brought up to decent self-control can get. There was no power on earth which could now stop this folly but the police. And to let the police know the time and place of the meeting was the act of a coward, a man without honour, a really unscrupulous, unsporting scoundrel. It was far worse than cheating at cards or bribing a jockey to pull a horse.

I considered all possible friends who could help with advice; every one of them would assume that it was too late. At last I thought of Marguliesh. As he had said to Rob, he was not—officially—a gentleman. He was safely seated in the stalls of this detestable comedy and could see what the actors did not.

I drove round to the bank, and he had me shown into his office at once. He was very fond of Magda and Rob, and, I think, disapprovingly fond of me. He was horrified when he heard of sabres and took all the blame on himself. Given Rob's character, he ought to have foreseen, he said, what might happen.

I felt the disgrace so strongly that I had not even formulated to myself what I wanted him to do: to tell the police. I couldn't allow Rob to be killed or sentenced. Magda was deeply in love with him, and he was the only man of first-class character likely to come her way who wouldn't care whether she had money or not.

Marguliesh understood all that without my having to stammer more than two words of it. 'Just tell me the time and place,' he murmured, 'and forget you ever did.'

I pointed out agitatedly that the police were inclined to malicious gossip. If they let it slip that their information came from Marguliesh, everyone would guess that I . . .

'Don't worry about that,' he replied. 'It is often of great importance that information should not be traced to me.'

Of course. Brokers, the market, issues of stock—he could handle all that. But what about the police?

'A man such as I in a country like this,' Marguliesh said slowly in his melancholy way, 'is unfortunately compelled to have his agents everywhere.'

I told him the time and place of the meeting, horrified at what I was doing. He smoked half a cigarette and asked me a question or two. Then he said: 'There is a pleasant little tavern some two kilometres up river from your sandbank. I think you know it?'

I didn't dare ask him why he thought so. It was a rendezvous which I had found useful for a very private and sentimental affair.

'Be there with Mr Tymson a good hour before the meeting. Any conversation you have will be overheard and reported to police head-quarters.'

'But Rob and I will be speaking English,' I protested.

'The person who composes the report,' said Mr Marguliesh, 'will not think it worth while to bother with too many details.'

I called for Rob next morning at eleven. He was fiercely determined to appear normal. The only sign of nerves was in his language as he fumbled about the hotel bedroom looking for his matches. I told him that he wouldn't need any matches—which was hardly the best way of putting it—and then had to explain that I had brought some. I knew he would keep on lighting his pipe until his right hand was otherwise occupied.

It offended him to be looked after as if his thoughts were out of joint.

'Got the sabres?' he asked sharply.

'Yes—and a picnic basket with drinks for the party when it's all over.'

'Don't the other fellows do anything?'

I said they didn't. As a matter of fact they were bringing the sur-geon.

'What do we want to start so early for?'

'Just to get clear of the town in case the police suspect anything.'

'Blast the police!' he exclaimed. 'Slip twopence to the right man and he'll fix the police for you.'

These business men seemed to think alike. But in an affair of this kind it was not so easy. Police procedure was to give a polite and formal warning to principals and seconds. If that failed—and it was supposed to fail—the police tried to turn up when the duellists were already on the ground. That ended the quarrel, for the prin-cipals had already shown their courage, and nothing more was to be gained by firing in the air or very cautiously poking at each other with the fleurette. If, however, police were successfully avoided, a duel fought and damage done, the criminal law was enforced—not so heavily as on a pair of gangsters but enough for a sharp lesson.

I drove Rob to the tavern, where we sat under the willows along a backwater of the river and shared a bottle of white wine. There was a poor and respectable clerk entertaining his family in the garden and obviously above all suspicion—obviously, that is, unless one had a guilty conscience and began to wonder why he should choose such an hour on a working day for a family treat. He went into the back passage of the tavern where there was a telephone. I felt suddenly hopeful and, simultaneously, defiled.

We left soon after twelve. The track which ran along the river was full of pot-holes and cut by pebble drifts from the fast spring torrents. I doubted if the car would take it and allowed plenty of time in case we had to walk part of the way.

But the track gave us no trouble at all. We climbed the flood-bank. Below us were the hard sand, the blue swirl of the river and another car. The military men, coming direct from Bucharest, had evidently doubted the state of their track just as I did, and arrived early at the rendezvous.

'For heaven's sake tell me what I do!' Rob appealed. 'Do I say good-morning, or what?'

'You say a cheerful good-morning to his second, and bow very distantly to him.'

'And suppose he apologises?'

'Accept it quick! But he won't.'

The two officers in their best uniforms were strolling up and down the yellow sand, talking to an unhygienic-looking gentleman with a black beard and a black bag. Rob measured out his bows. He certainly appeared a most cool and formidable opponent. I suppose he was pretending to himself that there was a platoon behind him which had to be impressed.

It was only seventeen minutes past twelve. I went into a huddle with the other second, comparing weapons, complaining of the ground—anything to waste time, for I could see what he was going to propose. But the moment came when I could think of no more excuses. And the police would time their arrival for a minute or two before twelve-thirty.

'Delay is so embarrassing for our principals, M. le Comte,' he said. 'So shall we . . .?'

Rob and his opponent took off their coats and rolled up their sleeves. The surgeon wiped down the sabres with a swab. The seconds passed them on. When Rob faced his man I could see he was trying not to give him a nervous grin. The captain's face was set and pale. For all he knew, he might be up against a master. I expect he hoped he was. At least it would be a guarantee that he wouldn't be run through the liver by accident.

Rob performed his salute very well. The captain attacked instantly in a violent *flèche* which Rob by wild luck parried. He must have felt the experienced control of his opponent's wrist as the points slithered in tiny semi-circles against each other, and realized there wasn't a moment to be lost. He jumped back half a step, tapped the ground smartly with his sabre and lunged.

I closed my eyes, I think—a split second in which to imagine the captain dead, Rob racing for the frontier and myself in the dock for aiding and abetting. The mess in reality was bad enough, before the law and from a housemaid's point of view. Rob's hilt was within two feet of the captain, and the steel through him between shoulder and elbow. He was so appalled—the sensation of his sabre jarring on bone—that he hadn't yet noticed that his opponent's curved point had ripped up six good inches of his forearm. He apologized instantly, just as for some unavoidable foul in the course of a jolly game.

'But it is I who should apologize,' replied the captain with a startled smile, and held out his hand.

We seconds, overcome by alarm and relief and the unconventional behaviour of our two gladiators, fluttered incompetently round them. The surgeon lost his head and kept exclaiming that it was unprecedented and that the seconds must decide which of the two gentlemen should be attended first.

'Shove on a couple of field dressings, Stephen,' Rob said, twisting a handkerchief round his arm above the elbow, 'while he fixes the captain.'

The captain grinned at Rob and gave a deep sigh which made the surgeon bustle to his professional duty. But to us the sigh was plainly one of relief. Almost anything might have happened. As it was, the pair had only to keep their arms in slings and their mouths shut. I was the only person who knew we were not yet out of trouble. When Mr Marguliesh said that something would be done, done it was.

Naturally I heard before any of them the noise of a car roaring in second gear along the track. I held up my hand. The captain's second dashed on to the flood-bank and put his head over the top. He signalled back frantically that it was the police. Rob didn't understand the danger. I was aghast at the result of my crime and couldn't use my head at all. It was the captain who was inspired.

'Pretend nothing has happened yet!' he ordered.

I helped the pair of them on with their coats while they tried not to yell. The other second, back by now, wiped the sabres and laid them out ready for use. Then we hurled the surgeon's implements and bandages back into his black bag, and kicked sand over the clots of blood.

It was the colonel second-in-command of the national police who descended majestically from the flood-bank, followed by two lieutenants of gendarmerie. They were all gorgeously uniformed and medalled. A distinguished foreigner and a captain in a crack regiment, rumoured to be so brave and angry that they insisted upon sabres, deserved the best costumes in the wardrobe for the third act.

'Gentlemen,' said the colonel in formal French. 'I observe that I am fortunately in time to prevent a scandal.'

It certainly looked as if he was. Rob and I stood arm in arm, with his hand dripping into his pocket and my thumb gently compressing the artery. By heaven's grace the captain's point had skated alongside without puncturing it. The captain and his second, also arm in arm, fiercely patrolled their own territory of sand. The surgeon, in the centre, caressed his beard and seemed to be meditating upon the mysteries of his craft.

It was up to me. I played the exquisite young aristocrat, reluctantly handed over the sabres to the police, raised my hat and made a little speech—after which I returned hastily to Rob in case blood should begin to show through his jacket. The captain's second barked a few bluff words. The colonel of police saluted both parties and gave a third speech, exhorting gallant men and allies to compose their differences.

Rob and the captain, unable to shake hands, pretended to be deeply moved and kissed each other. It was astonishing how quickly that man could adopt local customs when they suited him.

'Gentlemen, I shall not intrude upon you further,' said the colonel—and prepared to make off with the confiscated sabres and his lieutenants.

'One moment, sir!' the captain's second very formally insisted. 'I trust, Count Stephen, that you do not consider that we gave information to the police?'

'I am as certain of your honour as of my own,' I replied gallantly.

The colonel poured some hasty oil on that lot of waters.

'Let me assure you all that we acted upon a report received only an hour ago from an entirely independent source. You will understand that it is our duty, detestable though it may be, to make use of such agents as we can find.'

The civil power swaggered away, and that was the end of it—except for some painful first aid and the welcome contents of my picnic basket. The affair was kept very quiet, but Rob thereafter was free of the country, the court and the regimental messes as few foreigners ever had been. Romanians adore a dangerous jest. It soon got round that he had never handled a sabre in his life except to learn the salute.

Magda practically did not speak to me at all until I had to give her away in church. She said that my behaviour had been unforgivable. So it was. But I never told even her why I thought so.

THE COOK-RUNNER

'I exchanged,' he used to say, 'a foot for a stomach. I have no regrets.'
He said it rather too often, perhaps, but that could be forgiven to so
jovial and so excellently served a host. And it was true that he had no
regrets. He looked contented. That, when you come to think of it, is a
rare quality in our contemporaries: to look contented, to give out,
even, a feeling of contentment.

The marked limp bothered him little—a deal less than if it had been
caused by gout or any of the other ills that befall a man in his late fifties who has been generous to his body and allowed his soul to sit in at
the entertainment. Devenor could afford to be generous. Between the
wars Romanian oil had so rewarded him that the loss of concession
and capital equipment was more annoyance than disaster. He was the
younger son of a younger son, but he had made more money than all
the rest of his distinguished family put together.

'Twenty years of merry life,' he would say. 'Twenty years of near
heaven. All very wrong by our present standards. All very immoral. I
was most certainly a parasite. Ah, but a parasite has duties!'—he
chuckled with ironical self-satisfaction—'And the most important is
to appreciate.

'To appreciate! Wasn't there a school of philosophy—in quieter
days—which maintained that nothing could exist unless there were
an observer to observe it? Well, there you are! The first duty of a
parasite is to observe and enjoy. And if he isn't around to do it, there
won't *be* anything to enjoy.'

His Romanian heaven had been in miniature, confined to a few
thousand individuals of, by international standards, quite moderate
wealth. They liked their women to be decorative and of a warm delicacy, and gave almost equal importance to their food. They were determined to enjoy the best of two traditions—the Parisian and the
Byzantine.

Their supreme achievement, the seventh seal of their culture of the
palate, was the Gradina Restaurant. It was unique. No kitchen in
the world, Devenor insisted, could give such a variety of fare.
Through its hundred odd years of life, the Gradina had collected the
most self-indulgent recipes of three empires—the Russian, the Aus-
trian and the Ottoman—and refined them by careful attention to

French craftsmanship. In summer Devenor had placed his stomach and both feet—all heartily intact—under a garden table, where he could look up from lights and linen and silver into the cascading branches of a willow. In winter he had his corner seat near the entrance to the long, narrow dining room that smelt freshly of tarragon and white wine.

The utility food of post-war London was hard to bear. It had deprived him, said Devenor, not only of nourishment but of ambition. What was the use of money when the utmost luxuries obtainable were an old goose or a slice of dead cow with the same gravy poured over both? True, he might have lived in Paris, but he had spent too many years in looking forward to retirement, his friends, his club and London, for him to return to exile gladly.

He dreamed of Bucharest as a man dreams of his once passionate enjoyment of poetry. Yet he was careful to distinguish the ingredients of regret: youth, freedom, women, food. Youth and freedom had gone beyond recall. Women—well, he had for them a tender and sentimental affection, as for a superb bottle that might at any moment be opened but had much better be left in the cellar to mature still further. There remained food.

For long he could get no news of his Gradina. Then at the club he met a diplomat, all fresh from his expulsion from Romania, who told him that the beloved restaurant was reserved for workers' recreation.

Devenor, still living with his memories, was almost turned into a communist on the spot. To open that supreme flower of luxury to any of the masses who could appreciate it—that, if you like, was a justification of revolution. He said so, and his generous dream was instantly shattered.

'A tenpenny lunch, old boy. Soup and one greasy course.'

Devenor used to swear that inspiration, there and then, had come to him. Very possibly it had. Shock is a stimulant. He retired behind his newspaper to think it out. What had happened to the Gradina's cooks—any of them who hadn't been commandeered for official banquets? Surely a Gradina cook must have the artist's horror of communism? Surely he would be glad to leave? Rescue was a duty.

From that moment in the club, Devenor, converted to the possibility of heaven, went at his task like any fanatical missionary. He saw the parallel. 'My intention,' he said, 'was to save two human souls from destruction. And I don't see that it matters a damn if one of them was my own.'

He had friends enough alive in Bucharest, and even a worthless and affectionate godson. Cautiously he wrote to them all, but received only a few picture postcards of greeting in reply. He tried for his Gradina cook through consuls and labour exchanges and refugee organizations and old pals in the Board of Trade. He told the truth and was laughed at. He told ingenious lies and was obstructed. At last he lost his temper with all this paper and politeness. It was plain that there was nothing for it but to have a look at the frontiers, and possibly do the job himself. It would be an occupation, a joyous return to his early days of adventure. He loved and understood Romanians, but all his life he had refused to take them seriously when they told him what he had decided was impossible.

He made no plans at all for his penetration of the Iron Curtain. It was impossible to make any. Romania might be visited by students or delegates who were prepared to wait six months for a visa, but Devenor, a former oil magnate, would have to wait for a revolution. As for illegal entry, that no doubt was possible to some lean and hardened desperado. Devenor, however, was neither hard nor lean; he was only desperate. He hadn't had a decent meal in his own house for five years, and worse outside it.

For a start he flew to Istanbul. He did not confide his business to anyone, least of all to Romanian refugees. He listened; he enjoyed his holiday; and never for more than ten waking minutes did he forget his objective. But he could take no action beyond the patient acquisition of large sums in Romanian and Turkish bank notes. He considered himself, he said, entirely justified in breaking the currency laws of his own and any other country for so worthy a cause. After all, had he intended to rescue a scientist or politician, his illegalities would have had general approval. It was not his fault that government officials could not see the superior importance of a cook.

He tried out, in imagination, many a plan. Most of them involved crawling through barbed wire, for which he was quite unfitted, or jumping overboard in darkness, which, though of buoyant belly, he intensely disliked. He was perfectly well aware that he might have to risk his liberty, but he wished to do so without avoidable discomfort. Finesse was his game, not youthful exercise. It was just a matter of waiting for an opportunity which would allow him to use his perfect knowledge of the Romanian language and character.

He had to wait a month. Not idly, he insisted, not at all idly. Hotel bars, obscure cafés, frontier villages, the docks—he frequented them all as assiduously as any spy. Then, in the course of one of his morning patrols, he found on an unguarded quay, awaiting shipment to Constantsa, the topmost section of a fractionating column. It was familiar, friendly, a section not only of steel but of the continuity of his life. He knew the refinery that must have ordered it, the route it would take, and could even guess at the accident which had made so urgent its delivery.

This gigantic cylinder of steel was labelled and scrawled with injunctions for speed—speed in handling as deck cargo, speed in unloading, speed in railing to Ploesti. The very written word 'Ploesti' comforted

him. Even in that tough and smelly oil town there had been a restaurant where the proprietor, if you gave him warning, would joyfully
attempt the standards of the Gradina.

To Devenor the cavernous, complicated tube was home. It
wouldn't be the first time he had explored the interior of a fractionating column. And he knew its journey so well—twenty-four
hours to Constantsa and, in the merry evening of capitalism, not more
than two or three days on the docks, provided his agent had dealt
generously with customs officers and stationmasters. Those minor
bureaucrats would certainly do a better job now—would rail the
column at once to Ploesti in a real Romanian panic, for fear of being
accused of sabotage.

He admitted that it was entirely illogical to treat a strange section of
fractionating column as an old friend, and that a journey inside it was
likely to be just the sort of adventure he wanted to avoid. Still, there it
lay—about to be transported into the heart of Romania like a prince's
private railway coach. It was even divided into compartments by the
bubble trays, with, as it were, a corridor down the middle.

Devenor bought an inflatable mattress and a hamper of nourishing
food. He entered the column through the manhole in what would be
the top when it was erected at Ploesti. The hole was large enough to
admit his stomach, but too small to light the recesses of the interior,
the forbidding labyrinth of trays and take-off legs and leads. The
other end of the section was shored with timber and effectively
plugged.

He took only water to drink. He prided himself on that. It was proof
of a disinterested missionary spirit. 'I thought,' he would say, 'that in
the heat I must expect as deck cargo even wine and water might
reduce efficiency.'

It *was* hot. He chose a part of the column which was shaded by
wood and sacking, but he could not avoid the heat of the Black Sea sun
on steel. He had lost pounds in his Romano-Turkish bath when the
cranes lifted him off the deck and dropped him on to the waiting railway truck. The drop was uneven. He used to protest, with professional indignation, that the fools must have strained every joint in
the section.

He anchored himself firmly in his corner seat between bubble tray
and take-off leg, while the great flatcar was violently shunted up and
down the yard. At last he felt himself moving purposefully in one
direction, and relaxed upon his mattress with all the self-satisfaction
of a traveller who had successfully cheated the customs.

'But I was frightened,' he admitted. 'Yes, sheer panic underneath.
There wasn't a minute when I didn't wish I had stayed in London.
Still, when the train started, I couldn't help feeling proud of myself.'

He looked cautiously out of the manhole. The flatcar was at the tail of the train with only the caboose behind it. On the platform of the caboose a sentry was settling down to sleep. He was glad to see that the Romanians still posted their unemployable military on trains to prevent pilfering. It was a comforting reminder that the national character had not changed.

The train rumbled over the Danube, and idled across the starlit Wallachian plain. Whenever it halted, Devenor, kneeling at the manhole, heard the dear sounds of his second homeland: the barking of dogs in distant villages, the sigh and swirl of the streams past their willows, the croaking of frogs. Frogs fried Colbert—that was the way the Gradina used to do them. He dozed uneasily until shaken up by renewed shunting. When that was over, he could not resist deep sleep.

The discomfort of his own perspiration awoke him a little before midday. He poked head and then shoulders out of the top of the column. He was in the shadeless, dusty marshalling yards to the south of Bucharest. So long as he drew no attention to himself, there seemed no reason why he should not walk out into the city. He did so, greeting with an air of genial authority the casual groups of railway workers who were munching their loaves in the open doors of unloaded wagons.

Devenor did not want to show himself in the centre of the city. There were too many people who knew his face and liked it well enough to cross the road with outstretched arms and a whoop of welcome. His tentative plan was to get in touch, as unobtrusively as possible, with Traian, a former headwaiter at the Gradina and a staunch friend. He wandered through the suburbs until he came to a garden café, dirty and barren, but large enough to possess a telephone.

Traian no longer had a number, but there was one in the name of Devenor's godson Ion. He was not at all surprised to find that Ion had not only ridden out the storm but provided himself with an excellent address. As an irresponsible youth of twenty he had had a police record of dangerous socialism. True, his opinions were a pose, adopted merely to annoy his intolerably correct relations at court, but those of his set who could have given him away were dead or in exile. Devenor was prepared to bet that war and revolution had only changed godson into an irresponsible youth of thirty.

'He treated me as if I'd just dropped in from the fields,' Devenor said, 'as if there were no reason in the world why I shouldn't be in Bucharest. He even sent his car round to the cafe for me. He just told me that of course he had a car—how the devil did I think he was going to live without a car?'

Over lunch in Ion's luxurious flat, this show of idle riches was explained. Godson was an undersecretary—for he had always enjoyed yachting—in the Ministry of Marine.

Devenor asked if he were a genuine communist, and got himself rebuked for indiscretion.

'My good Uncle,' Ion had said, 'you really must learn not to ask such frank and English questions. Do you suppose I want to be shot by your venerable side?'

The excellent lunch was entirely unreal. Devenor seemed to himself to have moved back ten years in time, and not at all in space. Bucharest was going on—at any rate in the flat of a government official—exactly as before. At street level the June air was thunderous as ever and, six storeys up, the geraniums of Ion's window boxes stirred in the light breeze. Devenor's favourite white wine was on the table and cool in the decanter. There were rather less cars on the boulevard below and paint was needed and the inhabitants were shabby—but no shabbier than in the early nineteen-twenties.

'I couldn't believe it was possible to be shot,' Devenor would declare. 'It was just as improbable as my godson being a communist undersecretary.'

Over the coffee he explained how he had arrived in the country and why. His godson followed the story with irreverent laughter and keen questioning. Then, at the end, he asked the most devastating question of all.

'Uncle John,' he said, 'how many of us would it hold?'

Devenor couldn't understand that at all. He asked Ion why in the world he should want to go to Ploesti by fractionating column instead of by car.

'Not Ploesti, Uncle. Turkey.'

'It isn't going to Turkey.'

'But why shouldn't it?'

Godson Ion accused him of becoming intolerably insular, of wholly underrating the lively genius of the Romanian character and the powers of the people's ministries. He ordered his godfather back to the column, insisting that it was by far the safest place for him, and told him to keep quiet and see what happened.

'But I want to talk to Traian.'

'You leave it all to me.'

Devenor disliked leaving anything to any Romanian, and especially to his godson; but there was really nothing else to do. Godson sweetened the pill by giving him an imposing button for his lapel, a basket of food and drink, and a car to return him to the outer suburbs.

The button aided bluff. He had no difficulty in returning to his comfortable and now well-furnished seat between the bubble trays. About six in the evening he heard a good deal of fuss around the column. The curved plates transmitted the sounds of the outer world like a telephone receiver. He could not mistake orders, arguments, excitement and the slapping-on of labels. At dusk a locomotive came to

54

fetch the flatcar and dragged it ceremoniously—like, said Devenor, a choirboy walking backwards before a bishop—along the loop line round Bucharest. The locomotive then steamed off, rocking and light-hearted, leaving the column on a remote siding in the middle of a belt of trees.

Devenor ventured out. He and his column were alone, except for the frogs and a nightingale, upon the soft Romanian plain. There was just enough light to read the labels on the car. They were even more urgent, menacing and precise than before; but the destination was Constantsa instead of Ploesti. The waybill in its frame at the side of the car was resplendent with new red ink and rubber stamps.

'It was quick work,' Devenor admitted. 'They have plenty of energy for anything utterly crazy. But it looked to me as if my damned godson had consigned us both to the salt mines. I very nearly cleared out.'

He didn't, however. He got back into his refuge and had a drink from Ion's basket, and then another. The effect was to make him less disapproving when Ion and a friend arrived, and shoved two suitcases through the manhole.

Uncle John was formally presented to George Manoliu of the Ministry of Mines, and was compelled by every convention of courtesy to refrain from saying what he thought. Indeed, he found himself in the position of host, extending with proper flowers of speech the hospitality of his fractioning column and showing the two undersecretaries to their rooms between the bubble trays.

Godson Ion and George Manoliu spread out their blankets, and arranged a third compartment for the subdirector of Romanian State Railways who would shortly join the party. Devenor began to think that his chance of escaping death or Siberia had improved. These two young men and the third to come, able to administer between them—at any rate for twenty-four hours—the refineries, the railways and the shipping of the State, presumably had the power to order the column to be returned to Istanbul, to move it at the expense of any other traffic, and to direct the same or another ship to stand by at Constantsa to load it. And from what he knew of Romania, communist or not, he was certain that the respective ministries wouldn't catch up with what had happened for at least the better part of a week. He said that while they were waiting for the subdirector of railways he would see about his cook.

'Don't bother, Uncle John,' Ion assured him. 'That's all arranged.'

He hoped that it was; but the more he considered the character of his godson, the more sure he was that in the excitement of organizing his influential colleagues there could have been no time for a visit to Traian or the Restaurant Gradina.

Ten minutes later the subdirector of railways arrived, with no baggage but a bottle and what looked like an official cashbox. He announced that in another hour they would be on their way to Constantsa.

'And my cook?' Devenor asked again.

'Look here, Uncle John, we'll write for him,' said godson Ion.

Devenor crawled out of the manhole, and from the safety of the outer air addressed the undersecretaries. He told them that he was going to get his cook, that if they wanted to stop him they would have to catch him among the trees in pitch darkness, and that if they left without him he would go straight to the political police.

'They're still accustomed to foreign exploitation,' he would explain. 'There was nothing, really nothing, that they could do with a determined Englishman, in a temper. No doubt they would be equally helpless with a Russian.'

Ion quickly related the fanatical resolution which had brought his godfather to Bucharest. His two friends were delightfully sympathetic, enthusiastic indeed. This penetration of the Iron Curtain merely to obtain a cook appealed both to Romanian pride and Romanian love of a jest. A plan swiftly emerged from the committee. It was for Ion and his godfather to call on Traian—who was still alive, and whose son might be the very man for Devenor—and then to catch the column in the marshalling yards or anywhere along the line to Constantsa.

Fortunately, the trust of the three functionaries in one another was not so great that they had entirely burned their boats. Each of them had kept a car and driver waiting on a dirt road, beyond the belt of trees, all ready for swift return to Bucharest in case of accident or treachery. Mines and Railways now dismissed their cars, and returned to the column in high spirits. As soon as the road was clear, Devenor and his godson drove off in the third car.

Traian had been the headwaiter at the Gradina for twenty years, and had retired shortly before the war. If Devenor had known his address, he would, he said, have gone to see him at once, and left his damned godson to the inevitable end of his career as a commissar. Traian was a man you could trust. In all the years of his highly civilized trade he had never lost his peasant integrity.

He lived exactly where he ought to live: in the old eastern suburbs of Bucharest, where the streets of white, single-storeyed houses preserved something of the character of an untidy and once prosperous village. At the back of a yard, where the dusty earth just kept alive a tree, a few flowers and a couple of hungry hens, they found Traian sitting under the eaves of his house in the melancholy idleness of the old. He looked ill-fed and disintegrating: otherwise he was the same Traian who had hovered for twenty years at Devenor's shoulder, whose middle-aged wedding Devenor had attended (and attended for a full riotous fourteen hours), whose retirement had been put beyond the reach of

56

poverty by the subscriptions of Devenor and his friends.

Traian and Devenor embraced with tears in their eyes. 'And why not?' Devenor insisted. 'Why not? Hadn't we known each other at our best and proudest? We embraced the splendour of our past manhood.'

The old man—aged by undeserved and unexpected hardship rather than years—had no fear of godson Ion. To him gilded youth, whether it was communist or whether its cheques were frequently returned to drawer, was gilded youth. He talked freely. His wife was dead. His son, Nicu, trained in the kitchens of the Gradina and destined—for the Gradina thought in generations—to be the next chief cook but one, was working in a sausage factory. Traian himself was destitute. He could no longer be sure that he even owned his modest house.

'The tragedy of communism,' said Devenor, 'is that the state won't help those who can't help themselves. Even so, Traian wanted me to take his son. Yes, at an hour's notice. Nicu was asleep inside, before going on the early morning shift. Yes, he begged me to take his son.'

Devenor, of course, turned the offer down flat. There couldn't be any question of taking Nicu's support away from his father. Like a couple of old peasants, they talked the problem out unhurriedly, with many mutual courtesies, while the precious minutes of the night slipped away. Godson Ion fumed with impatience. He told Devenor not to be a sentimental fool. He told Traian not to spoil the boy's chances. He was remarkably eloquent in pointing out that there was no future at all for Nicu in Romania, or for any man of taste and ability who hadn't, like himself, had the sense to join the party.

Meanwhile Traian's voice was growing firmer, and the ends of his white moustache began to twitch into life. Devenor remembered that Traian was only sixty-eight; he decided to take the responsibility of abducting father as well as son. He felt, he said, damnably ashamed of himself for shifting such fragile cargo, but, after all, that well-fitted steel cylinder was little less comfortable than a Romanian third-class coach. He ordered Traian into the column regretfully and decisively, as if he had been sending back a Chateaubriand for another five minutes on the grill.

'And look at him now,' Devenor invited, 'when he brings in the brandy! I have to let him do something, you know. Oh, and he'll take a glass with us, too—but I can't make the old fool sit down to it when there are guests.'

Traian's son was collected straight from bed, and packed into the car. He had no objection to any change, however immediate and revolutionary, so long as it took him out of the sausage factory and included his father. He was on his way to the marshalling yards before

57

he had really got clear of a nightmare that he was making his palate into sausages; his palate, he said, had appeared to him as a large, white lump of lard.

The column had left for Constantsa. So insistent were the instructions of Railways, Mines and Marine that the yardmaster had presented it with a powerful, fine locomotive of its own. That fractionating column was going to be on board by dawn, all ready to be returned with ignominy to the corrupt capitalists who had sold it. The yardmaster expected a pat on the back from the ministry. No doubt, when he got it, it was a hard one.

Ion's driver did what he was told without question; he knew what happened to undersecretaries' chauffeurs who talked out of turn. They crossed the plain like a pair of headlights on the wind, but always the column kept a little ahead—for at intervals they had to bump over rutted country roads to the railway, or show Ion's credentials to saluting police.

They caught up with their flatcar at last, halted in the sidings before the bridge over the Danube and now with a train at its tail. A more awkward place couldn't have been found for a return to the safe recesses of the column, but they had no choice. It was their last chance, the absolute last chance. One side of the cylinder was flooded by the arc lights of the yard, as if some monstrous camera were about to take a farewell picture of it; on the other side was much coming and going of officials, and of the sentries who would ride every truck across the Cernavoda bridge.

Godson Ion told his driver to return to Bucharest if he did not come back in half an hour. He did not seem unduly alarmed.

'Of course he wasn't! Of course he wasn't!' Devenor crowed indignantly. 'That dam' pup had a perfect right to go wherever he wanted. As for the rest of us, we were just a problem to be shelved.'

In ten minutes godson returned for Nicu, who went with him unwillingly. But there was no object in protesting against Ion's plans; he controlled their fate. Devenor didn't know what he intended, and couldn't make head or tail of his explanations; he was only rendered thoroughly suspicious by a lot of high-flown nonsense about the young clearing the way for the old.

Traian and Devenor occupied a patch of darkness whence they could watch both the car and the column. They saw the two shadows of Ion and Nicu dive under the train. Shortly afterwards they saw the sentries posted. They waited for five more anxious minutes. Then the train started, and they watched its red tail-light swaying down the track towards the bridge and the impassable Danube.

After a journey of two hundred yards the train stopped. Devenor was so angry that he marched Traian straight up the line after it. He intended, he said, to get hold of the sentry and consign the whole heartless bunch of undersecretaries to Siberia, even if he had to endure their company on the way.

The sentry was on the platform of the flatcar, just outside the man-hole. He was hidden from his fellows by the bulk of the column and the tender of the locomotive. Within the column there was the silence of steel; there couldn't be anything else from the moment the sentry was posted. That excused Nicu's behaviour. He dared not make sound or protest for fear of getting his deserted father into incalculable trouble with the police.

It was sheer anger which gave Devenor his inspiration. He informed the sentry that a man was hiding in the fractionating column, and told him to winkle the fellow out with his bayonet while he kept him covered.

'I knew my Romanian soldiery well enough to risk it,' Devenor said. 'An air of authority. A little mystery. And they'll do what you tell 'em. There was the button, too, in my lapel—that seemed to impress him. I can't tell you what it was. I meant to ask Ion. But thereafter I was rather painfully occupied.'

As soon as the sentry was inside, Devenor put his head and shoulders after, and gave his orders. They were obeyed on the instant, and with only one quick rumble of sound. That unfortunate sentry—no, no, now living peaceably in America—was buried under desperate politicians leaping from the corners of the bubble trays. Then Devenor told his graceless godson to put on the sentry's uniform and take his place on the platform.

'Dam' play actor! He stayed on guard till the cranes hoisted us off the Constantsa water front, without anyone suspecting him of worse than obstinacy, and then managed to slip inside. That was that. They discharged us on to a deserted wharf at Istanbul, and all seven of us just walked out through the gates. Or rather, six of us walked. I was carried by Nicu and the sentry.' At this point it always pleased Devenor to expand and beam and wait for questions.

'No,' he would answer, 'nothing dramatic—no police, no bullets! Just sheer clumsiness. After the sentry had been nobbled, Nicu came out onto the platform of the flatcar, and I got down in order to pass Traian up to him. It was a bit of a strain on us two old gentlemen, and I couldn't pull my toes clear of the wheel when the train started. Nicu grabbed, and pushed the rest of me inside the column; but all the medical supplies we had were oil and wine, like the good Samaritan. Well, at my age, a foot is far from a prime necessity. But Nicu! Don't you agree that for me, without him, now, life would be inconceivable?'

HUNGARY

TELL THESE MEN
TO GO AWAY

Miss Titterton was so ashamed of being put inside—as she believed it was now called—and so uneasily certain that she must have committed an offence that it was very difficult to persuade her she was not a criminal. Even the Family could never quite restore her faith in herself.

In the nineteenth century the Family—Miss Titterton always pronounced the word with a coronet over the capital F—owned some five hundred square miles of Hungarian soil; by the twentieth this inheritance had been reduced to fifty. Neither chaperones nor husbands could control the females, and no racecourse, marriage, cabaret or casino was safe from the males. The only hope for the future of the Family and its estates was, their lawyers said—and the Emperor graciously supported the recommendation—an English governess who could inculcate a sense of discipline into the infant generation during the formative years.

The choice fell upon Ellen Titterton. Not for a moment did she feel unworthy, but she could not explain it. She had no connections with Nobility or Higher Clergy, and was far too truthful to claim anything but humble birth and a sound education. Though she was never allowed to suspect it, her appointment was simply due to the fact that she had been the fourth candidate to be interviewed. Her prospective employer, the Countess, had languidly remarked that, whether or not English governesses had the inhuman virtues ascribed to them, they were a dying fashion, and nobody could possibly be expected to endure conversing with more than three of them in quick succession.

Miss Titterton settled into the nursery wing, and was immediately adored by her charges. She had never, my dears, felt the necessity for any harsh discipline. At any rate she trained the characters of two generations of the Family with such success that they could without effort appear imperturbably British: a quality which in later life impressed their bank managers and allowed a presumption of innocence in such divorces as were sadly unavoidable.

When Ellen Titterton was sixty-five, the Family, who all loved a generous gesture, pensioned her off and presented to her a gay, distinguished, little doll's house just off the main street of their market town. She had as well enough savings of her own—she never seemed to spend any money except on felicitous presents to the children—to impress local society with her independence, and she earned a trifle of income by giving delicately efficient English lessons.

She was slim, straight, respected and as reasonable as ever. She had no special enthusiasms. She did not occupy herself unduly with priests or pets or worthy causes, content to contribute the graces of etiquette to her little circle of maiden aunts and major's widows. She read and recommended; she played the piano well; she left the proper cards upon her friends on all the correct occasions. The society which Miss Titterton ornamented was exactly that for which Providence and a Victorian girlhood had prepared her. She was also grateful to Providence for a basic training in languages which allowed her to speak Hungarian with a hardly noticeable accent.

In 1938 the Family saw what was coming and removed themselves to London. They could not persuade the beloved nursery governess to accompany them. At her age, she insisted, she did not chose to be uprooted. As she had always told the children, when one has made one's bed one must lie on it.

Her confidence was justified. Nobody thought of interning her when Hungary entered the war on the German side—or, if anybody did, the proposal was rejected as a waste of time and money. She continued to live her miniature social life and comforted herself by the thought that there was no quarrel between her two countries. It was a mere accident of diplomacy that Hungary had become an enemy nation. The Germans are so self-willed, my dear, though very musical of course.

When German base units were stationed in the little town, the social decencies were eased for her by her friends. Should some veteran German officer be invited to coffee, it was understood that Ellen Titterton must be warned. If, in spite of this, she came face to face with the enemy her dignified bow was a satisfaction to all concerned. It apologized so exquisitely for the fact that international differences prevented any personal relations.

The Germans found great difficulty, Miss Titterton said, in distinguishing between allied and conquered territory; she would have thought it could have been explained to them. So she was puzzled—but still charitable—when a German army truck, half loaded with furniture, called at her house. Out of it stepped an officer and six SS men.

The officer saluted and asked if he might be permitted to inspect the house. Miss Titterton realized that the visit was official, not social, and that her distant bow would be out of place. She followed the high, black boots from room to room and back to the front door. There, on her own doorstep, she was bluntly informed that, since the only occupants of the house were herself and her little dainty-aproned servant, she did not need more than two bedrooms. No doubt she would be glad to make a free gift of the furniture of the other to some suffering family in the Ruhr which had been bombed out.

Miss Titterton did not approve of this method of collection. Giving to the Hungarian troops she understood—and to hospitals, bazaars, all the scores of war charities. Very willingly she played her tiny part, for after all the Hungarians were not in action against British troops. Even if they had been, it would have made no difference to her pity.

She replied to the demand that she was very sorry, but she could not give up her furniture. That third bedroom, unused and spotless, was specially dear. It was the dream of her retirement that some day one of the Family would come to stay with her.

The officer showed his army authority—German Army—to remove furniture—Hungarian furniture—and regretted that he had no alternative. He ordered two men up the stairs. They seemed to Miss Titterton rather brutal and large, but she reminded herself that removal men had so much heavy lifting to do. All the same, she was outraged. She took the rational but extraordinary step of telephoning to the town police for protection.

The Family could never find out what had happened at the other end of the line. The police, who knew all about the Herrenvolk's requisitioning, could only recommend prompt obedience. Why they took any action at all was beyond conjecture. It may have been that they wondered if the SS was being impersonated by some band of ordinary, less efficient criminals; it may have been that they were just weary of being ignored. Whatever the reason, Sergeant Bacso, sword, pistol, moustache and all, paced round the corner of the main street and halted in front of Miss Titterton's house.

The dressing-table had got as far as the front door. It could go no farther, since Ellen Titterton, drawn up to her full height, was standing in the doorway. She neither protested nor fluttered. To get the furniture out she herself would first have had to be removed to the army truck, stiff and dignified as a piece of Victorian teak.

Sergeant Bacso was also of an older generation. He and Miss Titterton knew of each other's existence and reputation, but had had no dealings together. For Miss Titterton police were like plumbers—necessary and useful but required only in unpleasant emergencies. For the sergeant she was part of a closed world to which emergencies must not be allowed to happen. That at first was the only common ground.

The Family knew Bacso well—far from a hero and not the sort of man to interfere with his own comfort. He was gorgeous, bumbling, incoherent, and harmless as an old turkey cock. He gobbled at Miss Titterton and Hitler's SS. While he recovered from the shock of this forcible collection of free gifts.

The sergeant was not at all the modern policeman with a probation order in one hand and a tax demand in the other. He did not think of himself as representing the arbitrary benevolence of the State; he was just the protector of the haves, however humble, against the have-nots. Not a very worthy ideal. But, such as it was, it absolutely prevented him from pointing out quietly to Miss Titterton that a private individual should not argue with the SS. For Sergeant Bacso property was property.

He drew out his notebook and formally asked Miss Titterton whether she was or was not willing to present the furniture of one bedroom to the Reich. She replied decidedly that she was not. He took down her statement, closed his notebook and put it back in his pocket.

The SS men were grinning at him as if he were a circus clown in policeman's uniform. He had a wide-open escape route from the deadlock if he merely pointed out that Miss Titterton was British and that he washed his hands of her. The Family doubted if it ever occurred to him. He was used to thinking of her as one of the town's old ladies. The only officials likely to remember her nationality off-hand were those of the former British Legation where she appeared once a year for the party on the King's Birthday in some astonishing confection twenty years out of date and carefully pressed and ornamented.

Having decided that his customer's complaint was justified, Sergeant Bacso pulled his splendid moustache and awaited an invitation to act. He got it.

'Sergeant,' said Miss Titterton, 'is it not your duty to tell these men to go away?'

It was a gentle inquiry rather than a command. But there was no disobeying. Miss Titterton had developed her confident manner through taking over two generations of spoilt children from dear old peasant nannies who—regrettably but so very naturally—had no idea at all of discipline. Her voice was sufficient. Unlike the SS she had never been compelled to use corporal punishment.

Sergeant Bacso settled his gleaming shako on his head and joined Miss Titterton at the front door. What really bothered him was not so much standing up to a detachment of the most conscienceless thugs in the German Army as giving orders to an officer. Hungarians of his generation had a very great respect for officers.

He saluted and apologized with every second sentence, but he was firm. Miss Titterton's furniture could not be requisitioned without payment, and it was not going to leave her house until he had referred the matter to his superiors.

By this time a small crowd had gathered. They probably did not cheer, but looked as if they wanted to. The two SS men who were still carrying the dressing-table put it down. Their comrades stood by the truck, lounging and contemptuously interested. The unconscious arrogance of an old lady and a town policeman had surpassed their own.

The officer called them to attention and began to storm at Bacso. The foaming, emphatic German was a little too fast for the sergeant, but not for Miss Titterton—though there were words the meaning of which she preferred to ignore. She stopped the flow with a slight gesture of her hand and remarked that in the great days of the German Army the officers she met were always gentlemen. Women had been slung across the street for less. But Miss Titterton's rebukes were always unanswerable. That phrase 'the great days' made any violent retort extremely difficult.

The SS were almost about to climb into their truck and visit other free contributors. Afterwards, of course, they would have returned and had the furniture of the whole house off her. But for the moment they were on the defensive. They were back in school with the copy-book maxims of truth, courage and good manners.

Sergeant Bacso, triumphant and peaceable, invited his country's allies to accompany him to the police station; he meant that he was only too willing to refer the question of Miss Titterton's bedroom to higher authority if they would be good enough to come with him. But the SS officer, ready for any excuse to reimpose himself on the situation, pretended to believe that the sergeant was threatening arrest. He nodded to his bullies around the truck who intimidatingly strolled forward.

Bacso in a noble access of Magyar defiance drew his pistol. The illusion of civic law and order was destroyed. By resorting to violence he immediately removed himself from the fantastic world which Miss Titterton had created.

It could easily have been his last act; but the Herrenvolk, relieved of unwelcome memories of civilization and back in their familiar environment, decided that he and his pop-gun were merely comic. They disarmed him and, according to Ellen Titterton, deprived him of his nether garments. She was reluctant to give details. Good manners were as needful as always even if you young people chose to call them inhibitions. It appeared that the SS detachment had hustled Bacso round the corner and launched him into the main street by a kick on the bare backside. He had the sympathy of the whole town, but it was recognized that he never would get over the humiliation, never be so professionally fierce and polished again.

Miss Titterton's respectability, too, was gravely compromised. The police came for her at once, and the local magistrate with them. In spite of being a distant cousin of the Family and a frequent visitor—a highly-strung little boy, she remembered, who had been so unnecessarily afraid of the dark—he would not hold any conversation with her and would not listen. He bundled her off to his court under the eyes of the SS, and promptly gaoled her for insulting glorious allies and creating a disturbance. A common gaol it had been, among common criminals. She had been very glad to see how well the poor women were treated. She was sure that she had been allowed no special privileges beyond permission to decorate her cell with curtains and chintz covers and to invite selected prisoners to coffee. Their moral education had been sadly neglected, and she hoped that her influence on them had been for the good.

Miss Titterton felt that it was very forgiving of the Family to rescue her and fly her back to London immediately after the war. When they explained to her that prison had been the only way of preserving her from a quite certain concentration camp and the very possible attentions of the Gestapo, she tried hard to believe them. But in her experience, she said, justice was always done. She was afraid it stood to reason that she had deserved her sentence—perhaps for not taking enough care with the unruly member, my dear. It was very kind of them all to accept her disgrace so light-heartedly.

THE PICKET LINES OF MARTON HEVESSY

My dear Joe:

It's good to hear that at least one government has had the sense to put a round peg in a round hole, and that some small part of the security of the United States is in your hands. And thanks for kind words. My memory is that we learned from you, not you from us. But that we should both have this impression is probably what Eisenhower wanted.

So Marton Hevessy has given me as a reference. I have no reason to believe that he was ever a communist. I must confess, however, that his father always said he would end in jail. He used to say it lovingly, if you see what I mean, for he was very proud of Marton; but he was afraid, like any other father, lest his son's nonconformity should draw upon him the resentment of the herd.

First, here is a solid fact to reassure you. In old days any Budapest bank would have given Marton Hevessy a tiptop reference. From a banker's point of view—I'll come to mine later—he was an honourable, enterprising commercial man who had built up his own business from nothing. Industrial design, it was. If you invented an ingenious electric shoe cleaner, for example, you called on Hevessy to give it the form which would most appeal to the public—though once in a while he would turn out a design so preposterously imperial that it would have won a gold medal at the Exhibition of 1851. That was the aristocrat in him; he considered it his duty to set standards, not to accept them. The Hevessys are a very ancient family, and Marton cannot help looking like one of his ancestors. I don't suppose that so much tall, audacious elegance has ever been to him anything but a handicap.

What do you know of Marton Hevessy? Joe, it's like a question set in an examination paper. State shortly what you know of Don Quixote.

I can guess what sort of answer you want: some little definite sentence which will enable you to stand up as a supporter of the traditional liberalism of the last hundred years. I wish I could slap it down on your desk; but I am not in the confidence of the Almighty. I cannot imagine Marton—so rounded, so passionate a European—as a contented American unless one of his unpredictable loyalties were

69

engaged. I think it has been, but that is for you to judge. None of his friends could ever foretell how he would react to any new landscape of humanity, though we had absolute faith that the personal expression of his emotions—when, as it were, complete, varnished and framed—would be just as satisfying as his notorious gesture in defence of Sarita's religion.

You've met Sarita Hevessy, of course. I am certain that it was she, not he (for the one time he never appealed to his friends was when he was in trouble), who told you to refer to me. I can imagine her facing you across the files on the table, all fragrant with common sense and her very great love of her husband. You refused to be impressed by all that beauty, didn't you? You kept a professional poker face, and reserved judgement. But your first impression was right. She's gold from the heart outwards.

Sarita! So un-Hungarian a name may have made you uneasy. Her family were Sephardic Jews, who chose to remain behind at Budapest when the Turks retreated. Reverence for their religion sat pretty lightly on her and her family. They were refreshing and agreeable citizens of the capital. And Budapest was an Eden, you remember, where nobody bothered, until Nazi and Zionist had coiled themselves around the Tree of Knowledge, how host or guest elected to walk with God. If Marton had married Sarita five years earlier than he did, she would merely have mentioned—between casual drinks, perhaps—that she supposed she was a Jewess if she was anything, and left it at that.

In 1938, however, there was a tough crowd round the Tree of Knowledge. They ate the apples and threw at each other those they couldn't digest. Marton despised the lot of them, and took action. He wasn't a man to address a public meeting or write a letter to the press; his revolt was personal. He told Sarita that before he could allow her to honour him with her hand in marriage he would become a Jew.

Sarita protested. She was a most capable and tolerant child, and she tried to laugh Marton out of this misplaced loyalty. Still, she was Magyar all through—for her family had loved and lived and drunk their wine and ridden their horses on Danube banks for five hundred years—and as a Magyar she couldn't help being impressed by irresistible extravagance of gesture on the part of her lover. Marton had put himself in the class of those Hungarian magnates who ordered from Nice a special train of flowers merely to pave the courtyard for the entrance of a bride, or built a Cinderella's glass coach that she might be carried to a single birthday picnic in the forest.

She wasn't conceited. She didn't think that she was worth such fantasies. She never suspected that any good citizen of Budapest would have been ashamed of his ignorance if he couldn't tell to a visiting provincial the name of that golden arrow flighting down the Corso, with the chestnut hair and the velvety warm skin of Magyar horse and woman. No, it wasn't any sense of her own value that made her give way to Marton's insistence. It was just the glowing unnecessariness of any such sacrifice at all.

The Hevessy marriage was near perfect—as soon as Sarita had managed to stop her husband's sober visits to the synagogue, which were embarrassing to everyone but himself. She didn't prohibit, of course. She just knew how long Marton needed to tire of any of his exciting perversities. Moral for a policeman, Joe!

On which side did he fight? But what a question! Hasn't Sarita told you that he is the most loyal man she ever met, that the key to his whole character is loyalty? He's a Hevessy and a patriot, and of course he fought for Hungary against the hereditary enemy. Marton went off to war with Russia as a dashing captain of cavalry. A little elderly for the part, perhaps, but for youth he substituted enthusiasm—or as much of it as his hatred of Hitler allowed.

Ah, but what happened to Sarita, you'll ask. Isn't it easy to account for Marton's communist sympathies? Didn't the coming of the Russians save her from an extermination camp? No, it didn't. Even the most rabid Hungarian Nazis would have thought it ridiculous to pester Hevessys, however they might describe their religion on a government form.

What do you know of Marton Hevessy? Well, I can answer for him in the post-war years. Siege, slaughter and Russian occupation looted from him everything movable, including, we thought, his romanticism. Just to feed his wife and children and remake his business were tasks of knight-errantry valiant enough even for him. He succeeded, and he was content. He wasn't a worker to be bullied, or a capitalist to be ruined. He was a specialist; and whether he designed for private clients or for the State, his living was secure. Sarita was a little sad. She found herself married to a sober, tranquil professional of industry. He even used to spend free evenings with his lawyers.

I am surprised that these unusual absences did not worry her, especially since he avoided all discussion. Still, his character appeared to have changed. She might easily have thought him obsessed, like any other solid citizen in his middle forties, by some dull and technical affair such as patent rights. And lawyers are indestructible; they continue to function under the milder forms of communism so long as there is any private property left in the deed boxes.

No, there was nothing to arouse a wife's suspicion until Marton began to take an interest in history. History, he insisted, would judge their period as one of necessary but too drastic reforms. It was the duty of a loyal citizen not to allow all the links with the past to vanish. For example, the Hungarian Nobility should not be forgotten. Whatever its sins in the past, it might again—in a hundred years perhaps—be needed.

I expect that at first Sarita merely listened from one tolerant little ear, and received these magnificent lectures with a proper pleasure that her husband was enjoying his dinner. It was hardly tactful to point out that in the ten years of their marriage she had never heard Marton allow to the hereditary nobility any value whatever.

He held his great-grandfather to be disgracefully typical of the whole class. Great-grandfather had lost every cent of the Hevessy money at cards, and was left with nothing but an entailed estate which he couldn't sell. He returned his estate and barony to the Emperor with a request—and a model it was of dignified Hungarian prose—that his Imperial and Royal Majesty should be pleased to pay the Hevessy debts and save the Hevessy honour. He then dressed himself in full regalia and galloped his favourite hunter over a cliff, with the reins—so far as *rigor mortis* permitted an opinion—still lightly grasped in his left hand. It was a death in style which should have appealed to Marton, but did not.

So when Marton's sudden passion for aristocracy grew and flourished before as well as after dinner, Sarita at last took it very seriously and connected it, quite rightly, with the mysterious visits to his lawyers. She couldn't help assuming that her disappointingly sober husband was engaged in some crazy plot to restore the old régime and—though no doubt preserving the motherly smile on her delicious face—she panicked. She began, all unknown to Marton, the long series of intrigues and letters and pullings of gossamer wire by invisible hands, which were to take the Hevessy family out of Hungary and into your office files, Joe. She should have remembered that Marton's revolts were always personal and unlikely to draw upon him the wrath of governments—even communist governments—but her haste was forgivable. Of every four men she had known in 1939, at least one must have been killed by politics. That omits, of course, those who were killed by war.

While Sarita was worrying herself sick over State trials and searching the papers for news of any arrests which could possibly lead to her own circle, Marton, I have no doubt, preserved an exasperating complacence—until one evening, in the midst of a terrifying week of militant communism on the march, he came home from the office and kissed Sarita's hand with gay, exaggerated deference and addressed her as Baroness Hevessy.

She was. That was his business with the lawyers. He had been proving to the satisfaction of the High Court that great-grandfather, when he so flamboyantly paid his debts, had a son two years old, the existence of whom, in all that dignified excitement, he had omitted to mention to the Emperor. Consequently the Imperial and Royal action was void. The entail could not be broken. The barony could not revert to the Crown.

There was nothing at all that Sarita could do about it. The case was simple and, for the courts, a joyous holiday from legalizing the dictates of dictators. The lawyers had all gone to work with immense professional zest to settle a claim that was satisfyingly constitutional and wholly useless. Beyond a shadow of doubt Marton and Sarita were Baron and Baroness Hevessy.

Their friends—and believe me, Joe, every one of them will be grateful to you for giving him the chance to speak—were as delighted with Marton as at his solemn circumcision. I am told that even hardened communists took a careful look round and laughed. There is still a wry sense of fun in Budapest.

I can hear you remarking sternly that he doesn't call himself Baron Hevessy. But of course he doesn't! The title was only for use in reddest Hungary. It was his personal protest. He wouldn't dream of using it in a country where it might be of some use to him.

I don't know how Sarita got him to leave his (in spite of everything) beloved country when her schemes came to fruition. My personal opinion is that the government unofficially expelled him. He was too well known in low cafés and high, and his exquisite, unpunishable gestures might have started a fashion. However that may be, there they are in your hands—Sarita, Marton and the children.

He had a good job in America, too, you say regretfully. It must have been, if his employers bothered to make him declare whether he had ever been a communist or not. And so he refused to answer, did he? And Sarita refused to answer for him. God, there's loyalty for you!

Well now, Joe, I admit these questions have to be asked, for one can't run a great country with gloves on. But at the same time I know what the effect would be on myself if I were asked to declare my politics as a condition of employment. I should answer like a wide-eyed sheep, and be ashamed of myself afterwards for not having had the guts to tell the questioner to go to hell.

But then, I am not a citizen in the magnificent class of Marton Hevessy. Nothing on earth would induce me to become a Jew in a swarm of Nazis, or to provoke confession-forcing commissars by creating myself a baron, or to pass myself off as a possible communist in the America of 1951. What courage the man has for doing the right thing at the wrong time—the wrong time for his own personal benefit, that is.

Joe, what do *you* know of Marton Hevessy?

ROLL OUT THE BARREL

Margit was an island like the rest of us. In the set of complicated currents she kept her shores intact only by loyalty to what was best in herself. She had not much else to be loyal to.

She was a Hungarian peasant who had earned her lonely living as a servant in Budapest ever since she was fourteen years old. Social democracy and a husband with a bit of land—those were her desires, political and personal. Towards the present régime she was dully neutral, for it snatched away with one hand what it gave with the other.

She took pride in her skill, and as much in her employers as they permitted. For the last six months she had worked for a middle-aged consulting engineer, respectable and law-abiding. He seldom laughed, and his ready smile seemed to spring from a natural courtesy rather than any personal interest. He left no doubt, however, that he appreciated her cooking, and that was enough for Margit.

She used to day-dream—failing a better subject—that he had asked her to be his wife, though any woman could see that he was dedicated to something, perhaps the memory of a former love, more distant than marriage. The dream never lasted longer than the washing-up of two plates and a coffee cup.

Margit knew very well that she hadn't the beauty to revive a dead heart. All her mirror told her was that she was squat and thick and brown; it could not reveal that her eyes were gay and that she moved with light feet and a provocative swing of the skirt. That touch of gallantry had been born of the czardas danced in the village of her girlhood, and was kept alive by the barrel of excellent wine in the kitchen.

The barrel was a present from her brother, who had inherited the little family vineyard and contrived to hold back enough of the harvest to supply himself and her. The rest went to the State cellars for export. Margit was puzzled that wine should have become so scarce and expensive. In the days before the war a generous employer would no more have thought of reckoning up what was drunk in the kitchen than of counting the potatoes.

So Margit treasured her hundred-litre barrel. She wasn't a heavy drinker. At the moderate rate of a big glass for lunch and another for supper, there was only enough to keep her morale more gay than grim for about two hundred days. The barrel, too, was a symbol. It brought into the worried city a sense of solidarity with her village—a spiritual rather than political class-consciousness. She felt for her hundred litres the welcome that a business woman would give to a hamper of flowers from the garden of her first lover.

Some of her treasure, of course, she had to share; but that, too, was joy. She was enabled to be gracious and to indulge the aristocrat that lived in her peasant heart. So, when she received a visit from the well-dressed gentleman who had recently begun to sit outside the café at the corner, it was hospitality rather than fear which made her draw a jug for him.

She knew what he was. Among the humble there was unspoken alliance for the recognition of secret police. The porter of the block, who that very day had been ordered by the well-dressed gentleman to give him a weekly bulletin of information, had dutifully kept the secret, but handed out broad hints to chosen friends.

The policeman in Margit's kitchen was a very superior specimen of the breed—not at all the type which normally collected information from porters. She greeted him with the politeness reserved for a class above her own, and hovered hospitably over him.

'Good wine, this!' exclaimed the gentleman from the café at the corner, stretching his legs under the table. 'Is your employer rich?'

'My brother sent it me,' she replied. 'It has nothing to do with the master.'

'And what does he drink himself over there?'—the visitor jerked a thumb towards the narrow passage which led, through a faintly delicious atmosphere of spices and onions, to the office and dining-room of Margit's consulting engineer.

'Whatever he can get, sir.'

'And plenty of it, eh?'

The visitor, determined to be a democrat, pinched her playfully. Margit's reception of the compliment was cold. She knew from experience that her rotundities were eminently pinchable, and she did not—for example, with the porter—take offence. But the caress of her visitor was incorrect; he made it appear a studied gesture rather than an irresistible temptation.

Margit dropped her best manner and answered him with a rough frankness. That was one good thing about the present régime. You needn't—if you belonged to the proletariat—bother with ceremony when you didn't feel inclined.

'How can anyone get plenty of it?'

'Complaining of the régime, are you?'

'Listen, I'm a peasant! Better off, worse off? I don't know. Wait and see—that's what we say.'

'What about the visitors here? Is that what they say?'

'Do you think I've nothing to do, cocky, but crawl up the passage and listen at the door?'

The visitor gave a hoarse chuckle, into which Margit's wine and pleasant, broad accent had injected some sincerity. 'We come from the same district,' he exclaimed. 'I see that!'

'Every district has some black pigs among the white.'

'That's the end, sweetheart,' he said—quite tolerantly, but as if the inevitable time had come to exchange good-fellowship for his normal business attitude. 'Sit down!'

Resignedly she sat down opposite him at the kitchen table. He represented the limitless power of the State. There was no need for him to explain or threaten, and they both knew it. He drew from his pocket three photographs of the same man: full face, right profile, and left profile.

'Have you ever seen that one?' he asked her.

'No.'

'Have you ever heard the name of Istvan Sarvary?'

'No. Who's he?'

'An enemy of our country, my girl. A revolutionary and war-monger. And at last I'm on his track. Look at those photos, and take your time.'

Margit obeyed. The police photographs were clear, glossy prints, upon which every detail could be seen. The subject looked like an unwashed criminal, hollow-cheeked, sneering and obstinate. She did not recognize the face. Then, in the left profile, she noticed the man's glasses. They were round, old-fashioned, and of heavy tortoise-shell, and there was a home-made repair just in front of the left ear, where the rivet or binding had been wrapped in some soft substance to prevent rubbing.

A possible identity for Sarvary at once occurred to her. Yet it was so unlikely that there was no sudden start of recognition in her eyes or mouth for the trained interrogator across the table to leap upon.

'You are interested?' he suggested.

'You told me to take a long look.'

'And what do you see?'

What she saw in the eye of the mind was a drawer in the consulting engineer's dressing-table, and a pair of old glasses with the left bar wrapped round by a neatly sewn strip of wash-leather. Could they be the same glasses? Was it possible for a haggard, clean-shaven man with dark, wavy hair to turn into her employer with his well-rounded cheeks, his straight white hair greased firmly back, and his white lux-uriant moustache which looked as if it had been over his mouth for the last thirty years?

Then there was his nose. The man in the photograph had a strong, fleshy nose, quite ordinary. Her employer had a Roman nose with a marked and distinguished hump on its bridge. The shape of it, she remembered—almost with a giggle—seemed to change in hot weather. No, of course it was unthinkable. Her kind master could not be a man wanted by the police, a barbarian trying to bring about another war.

'I've seen someone like him,' she said at last.

She couldn't tell how much her face had given away. Something, yes. The keen peasant game of buying and selling was in her blood. She knew, from the parallel of the market-place, that her hesitation had been too long and that she must explain it.

'Who?'

'The new notary of our village.'

'They have a queer breed in your village,' he remarked contemptuously. 'Stop fooling, girl! When did this man come to see your employer?'

'Never.'

'Then what was he doing—the person whom you thought the photograph resembled?'

'Our notary? He makes too much money at home to come to Budapest.'

The visitor rose from the table and brutally dominated her eyes.

'If you hurt me, I'll scream,' she threatened. 'They know I'm respectable here.'

'Hurt you? My dear, we don't do that sort of thing. I'm just going to give you time to remember.'

The gentleman from the corner café strolled impassively across the kitchen and turned on the tap of the barrel. The thin, fast stream of wine hit the tiles with a neat splash.

Margit shrieked, and leaped for the tap rather than for him. At once she made brutal contact with her chair again, arms bruised, bewildered by the dexterity with which she had been flung back.

'We like wine in our district, don't we?' he said. 'Barrel full?'

'Yes. Yes, sir,' she begged. 'Nearly full.'

'Then it will take about ten minutes to empty it. Plenty of time to talk.'

The purple and pink foam that had jumped from the kitchen tiles subsided, and the lake of wine deepened and spread.

'Please, sir! Please!'

'But, I shall be delighted to turn it off when you've told the truth. A pity for such good wine to be wasted! I should say your brother's is a rather stony soil facing south,' he replied, talking with an exasperating slowness.

'It didn't remind me of the notary. I swear it,' she sobbed, the big tears richocheting off her apron into wine.

'Ah? Of whom, then?'

'Nobody. I was impertinent. I've never seen the face before.'

'And the name Istvan Sarvary? Have you never heard it? Or over-heard it, perhaps? Think now! That's a generous tap you have there.'

'No, never! Never, sir! I've never heard of it.'

The words were loud and incoherent with grief. The lake of wine found out an imperceptible slope and began to run towards the passage. At the door it deepened to a quarter of an inch, and the colour changed from a pink transparency to black with red reflections.

'He might have come here without you knowing it?'

'Yes, yes, of course he might,' she answered eagerly.

'You're not sure that you haven't seen him, then?'

'No. How could I be sure?'

'Then we have only to take a little step further. Look! I'm just going to shut off the tap. Tell me when it was he might have come here—that's all I want to know.'

Margit was utterly muddled. What he invited her to say sounded so reasonable. Why on earth was she letting her wine run away when she had only to tell him a date, a movement, her crazy suspicion, any-thing? Yet—she didn't tell lies.

She opened her mouth and nothing would come. All the inhibition of the Christian Europe that had made her stood in the way. Had she been asked outright whether her employer could be Istvan Sarvary she might have answered that at least she had wondered. Might have. But there again, standing at the gate, was all the loyalty of a feudal system that had vanished and left nothing but its good behind.

'I can't tell you. I don't know.'

The interrogator kept the barrel running.

'Won't little one, not can't! Won't, you mean.'

She heard the front door open and shut as her employer came home.

'Good heavens, what's all this?' he exclaimed.

He bounded up the passage on the track of the wine, and caught the visitor with his hand still on the tap.

'Margit, your wine! What's all this?'

Margit's face was bedabbled with tears. The gentleman looked confused and guilty.

'Tap leaking?' the consulting engineer asked.

'He turned it on,' she sobbed.

'Friend of yours?'

'No, no, no!'

'Well, then—ah, I think I understand! But, my dear sir, if you had anything to ask, why didn't you come to see me? I know everyone in the building and my reputation is sound, I hope. No good telling you I'm a party member—too old, for one thing. But what I always say is, they're doing fine work for Hungary. Example to all Europe, eh?

We're both patriots, aren't we? Well, there's the bond. Now you put me through the hoops in any way you like.'

Her master was so friendly and natural that Margit at once put out of mind that imagined identity. After all, there was more than one pair of mended spectacles in the world. And then his nose! You couldn't alter a nose that God had made.

'What do *you* know of Istvan Sarvary?' the visitor shot straight at him.

'Sarvary? Why I thought he was abroad. Don't tell me the swine has managed to get back to Budapest?'

'He was a friend of yours, was he?'

'No, he wasn't. Far from it! But you've come to the right shop, my dear sir. I'll answer all your questions. We can't have men like Istvan Sarvary about. Margit, there's nothing to drink in the house. May we borrow what's left in the barrel? I'll make it up to you. We'll try to get something as good as yours.'

'You're generous,' the gentleman sneered suspiciously.

'You think so? I'll tell you how it is. I don't want the State to show pity. Try the dogs, shoot them, exile them, put them to work! They're expendable, aren't they? But a little woman like this—well when she gets in the way, the State can't help it and mustn't show pity. Never! But chaps like you and me are free to do what we can. That's what I say.'

Margit didn't agree at all with this view of the State, but she assumed it was politics and over her head. If a man with a good heart accepted cruelty, it meant nothing and was just words.

The man from the corner café took Margit's employer a little aside, and warned him of something in a low voice.

'She? Oh, I don't think she could have seen him. But you never know. Well, if there's anything at all, you'll get it out of her. Better methods than wine taps, eh?

'Now let's sit down. It must be seldom that you get a real hot tip straight from the horse's mouth and a jug of first-class stuff to go with it. If you don't mind me saying so, I've watched the scent of that wine making you more human every minute.'

The visitor grinned, then pulled himself together with military solemnity and declared that he had no time for gossip.

'This is going to be worth your while, captain. I'll tell you for a start one man whom Sarvary is likely to be seeing—his wife's cousin. You didn't know that, did you? And you're in charge of the investigation.'

'Not yet,' the visitor admitted, 'but I shall be. It's every man for himself in the police, and I like to wait for the best minute to put in my report. Now you help me, and I won't forget you. What would you say if I told you I'm on to a connection between Sarvary and this very house?'

'Your very good health!' exclaimed the consulting engineer, raising his glass. 'Is that so? Well, well, now let me see! First of all I'll fix up my Margit, and then I'm with you. I can't have such a cook upset,' he explained. 'You can't expect a little artist to work without a drink in her heart. Look here, sweetheart, here's an address! You go there and tell them to deliver another barrel of red this evening. And you must need a rest after all this. Take the afternoon off if you want to.'

He scribbled a note and gave it to Margit. She had never seen her employer so cordial. She was hurt that he had never smiled at her as genuinely as he was smiling at this filthy crook from the corner café, and hurt, too, even if she were to be compensated, that the pair of them should calmly sit down and drink up the rest of her wine. She said to herself that it was unfeeling. Just unfeeling, that was all. Not even enough to excuse a toss of the head.

'But I can't stop long,' the visitor protested. 'I don't want to take my eyes off this street.'

'Splendid! Splendid! It's good to know that our safety is in your hands. But why not telephone one of your sergeants and tell him to check all movements in and out of this house in your absence? A good chance to see whether he knows his job! He won't know you are here and you can watch him through the curtains.'

Margit put her kerchief over her head and went out, leaving the two to their sly grins and good-fellowship. It was just like men, she thought, to sit down and souse on somebody else's wine and pretend they were catching enemies of the State. It didn't make any difference—townee or peasant, consulting engineer or communist, they were all the same. Wine and pinching people where people were roundest and sacrificing the helpless.

She delivered her employer's note at the address he had given her. It was a cheerless, obscure, commercial office without the heartening smell of liquor or the noisy group of customers welcome to try out many more vintages than they ever meant to buy. Well, nothing was sold any longer as, traditionally, it ought to be sold.

She called on a friend who might have comforted her, but wasn't in. Boozing, too probably. Then she idled away the afternoon in public gardens and at a public meeting. After two hours she went home. It was all very well to tell her to take the afternoon off, but who would get the supper, she would like to know.

Her employer was asleep. The gentleman from the corner café had gone. Neither of them had made any attempt to mop up the lake of wine and its meandering streams, so she set to work on the kitchen. She forced herself (for she was economical) to dip a fine white cloth in the deepest pool and to squeeze it into a glass in case the wine should be still drinkable. It certainly wasn't. She was ashamed and determined to clean her floor much more thoroughly than usual, especially after chopping meat.

Then three hefty men brought up her new barrel. They did not talk much, and they would not accept a drink. They weren't at all like the delivery-men she used to know. The three rolled away the old barrel down the passage. She wondered what wood her brother was using for staves. But perhaps the barrel seemed so heavy because the delivery-men didn't get enough to eat. That must be it. In these days they made criminals into policemen and boys of good family into porters. After that, all the tides of complication receded from her little personal island.

There was a flurry of nervousness when some police came to inquire about the gentleman from the corner café, who, it seemed, had disappeared. Her kind employer told her not to be frightened by them but to describe her interrogation just as it had happened.

'The only thing I shouldn't say if I were you, Margit,' he warned her, 'is that the man stayed on a little here after he telephoned his sergeant that he had gone. We don't want him to make trouble for us when he turns up again, do we?'

So Margit said nothing at all of that, and the police found the incident of the wine tap so comic that they paid very little attention to her. She disapproved of their behaviour. It was typically masculine and insensitive. But—taking the rough with the smooth, as she put it—she couldn't complain. The new barrel of wine did not carry in it the love of a brother, but at least she would be able to taste, whenever she sat down to her meals, the remarkable generosity of her master.

SPAIN

WATER OF ITURRIGORRI

The SS *Capitan Segarra* rested her five thousand tons of patch-painted black iron against the Bilbao dockside, heeling over wearily against the piles as the ebb tide slipped down river from under her. The fenders crackled and creaked. Capstans, spurting steam, chugged into their ragtime rhythm. The discharge gang swarmed over her, like hungry flies on an overweighted beast of burden.

She had to be emptied that day, for she carried a perishable cargo of crated Canary bananas. The dockers tore it out of her, racing against the fresh heat of the early morning. They were dressed so much alike that they gave the impression of a squad of soldiers; black *boina* on the head, wide red sash at the waist, blue trousers and rope sandals. Only in their shirts was there variety; they were of many shades of blue, mauve, yellow and green.

Apart from the bustle around the *Capitan Segarra* the riverside was still. It was a public holiday. The ships moored stem to stern along the wharf were dressed with flags. Here and there a watchman sat under the shade of a tarpaulin contentedly occupied with the rolling of one cigarette after another. The three *txistulari* marched along the waterfront—a drummer, a piper, and between them the leader of the band playing a drum with one hand and holding a pipe to his mouth with the other. The citizens, lying late in bed, were awakened by the gay Basque melodies which proclaimed a fiesta.

There was a halt in the discharge while the men below took the covers off another deck. Juan el Viruelas thrust a great hand into his sash and drew out tobacco and cigarette paper. He was a burly, pock-marked man with an expression of disgusted kindliness.

'Where's El Pirata?' he asked.

'I told him to come,' said the foreman.

'You told him? I spit on his mother! He's the man to lift these crates. Why isn't he here, *capataz*?'

'Who knows?' answered the foreman, turning away with the haughtiness of the petty official who has risen deservedly, but recently, from the ranks.

'He's still in the Sevillana,' said the oldest of the dockers.

He was nicknamed 'El Cura'—the priest—from his hollow cheeks, his blue chin, and his body emaciated by the forced fasts of poverty. It

85

was still useful, like an old rope worn thin.

'What the hell is he doing in the Sevillana?'

The Sevillana was a house of ill-repute. A chorus of stevedores explained to Viruelas what El Pirata was doing there. Juan el Viruelas burst into a stream of profanity. It was interrupted by a sharp bellow from Evaristo, the crane mechanic, forty feet above their heads: 'Stand clear!'

Viruelas leapt aside, and El Cura took up his post facing him. A sling of six crates thumped on to the ground between them. They became twin parts of a machine for loading porters, a four-handed engine which swung up each crate from the ground and lowered it precisely on to a human back bowed to receive it. As they bent down to lift the last of the sling, a hand loosened the sash round Viruelas' waist. When he heaved, the coils loosened and slid. He grabbed at his falling trousers, leaving one corner of the crate without support.

'Mind!' shouted El Cura.

Viruelas's hand stopped half-way and flashed back to the falling crate. His trousers fell around his ankles. The riverside shouted with laughter.

'I spit in the milk!' exclaimed Viruelas—it was his oath when he was really angry. 'Who did that?'

'El Pirata! El Pirata!'

Juan el Viruelas lowered the crate to the waiting back, wound himself into his sash, and turned on El Pirata.

'You want me to kill you?' he stormed.

El Pirata swayed on his feet like the high round funnel of a tramp steamer in a gale. He was six and a half feet tall, broad in proportion, and lordly drunk. He was bred a deep-sea fisherman, not a labourer. Though of age to succeed his father in the command of the family launch and to raise a third generation of sons within the thick, sea-silencing walls of the family cottage, he had chosen to taste the freedom of the townsman. He came to Bilbao to scatter his wild oats more magnificently than they might be sown in Arminza; neither the single tavern nor the chirruping sisterly girls of that little village offered a field for the exuberant harvest he desired. Manual labour he detested. It was too easy and too poorly paid—an insult to his manhood. But there was no alternative. He could not read or write.

He was pure Basque, and his great head was rich with the marks of race: grey eyes, and dark, straight hair; a full-lipped hearty mouth; a long hawk's nose whose chiselled fineness contrasted with the heavy curves of the high cheekbones. There was a kind of devil-may-care pride in the very flesh. His *boina* dripped gallantly over one ear. His sash was vivid crimson and wider than the ordinary. He wore gold rings in his ears and an orange shirt. Because of his dress they called him 'El Pirata'—the Pirate.

'Come on!' said El Pirata. 'Come on, Viruelas!'

'You're drunk!' remarked Viruelas disgustedly; he had no intention of fighting El Pirata, but had meant to satisfy himself by all the dramatic preliminaries.

'And what then, Juanito? And why aren't you drunk too?'

'Because he's a decent fellow,' interrupted the foreman.

'Is today a fiesta, *capataz*?' asked El Pirata, trying to get him into focus.

'*Si, señor,*' the foreman answered with exaggerated politeness—he too was feeling a grievance at having to work on a public holiday.

'Why?' asked El Pirata.

'How why?'

'Why's a fiesta?'

'God knows,' said the foreman.

'No,' replied El Pirata. 'So's to get drunk the night before. That's why's a fiesta.'

He hiccupped wildly and slapped the foreman on the back.

'But I'm a man of my word, that's what I am! I say I'm coming to work. I come to work.'

'You can't work like that.'

'You, what do you know?' retorted El Pirata. 'Stand out of the way there, *capataz*!'

El Pirata attacked the sling that had just descended. Without help he swung a two-hundred-pound crate on to his back, carried it away, and stacked it. He dealt with all six as quickly as Viruelas, El Cura, and the gang of porters. Then he pushed El Cura aside and took his place with Viruelas. The two grinned at one another. Evaristo stuck his oily head over the edge of his box to admire the two muscular backs whose pace he would follow.

'*Olé*. El Pirata!' he cheered.

'*Olé*!' answered the gang.

There was no shade. The white sun smote upon the white concrete of the wharf. Particles of straw mingled with the dust that spurted up under the wheels of the loaded waggons; the dry mixture stung into the throats of the workers. Paint blistered on the *Capitan Segarra*'s rails, and the distant piping of the *txistulari* died away in the heat. The men worked swiftly, savagely, thirstily. Then, a little after eleven: 'Water of Iturrigorri! Water of Iturrigorri!'

A girl's voice called the words, rising and falling on the melancholy minor scale of a pedlar's cry. Between the calls she blew a little horn which echoed along the deserted waterfront.

'La Rubia! It's La Rubia, I spit on her little body!' cried Viruelas affectionately. 'Bless the girl! Who'd have thought she'd be here on a fiesta?'

'She's a comrade!' shouted El Pirata. 'She's a worker! I say so! I, El Pirata!'

'You think a lot of her,' grumbled Viruelas, almost accusingly.

'I think a lot of—a lot of . . .' El Pirata paused. Whenever he stopped working, the scene of his labour whirled round him; he waited for it to be still. '. . . a lot of soli—solidarity!'

La Rubia came round the bend of the wharf into sight. She was seventeen, but no taller than a girl of ten. Yet all her fully ripened body was built to scale; she was a perfect miniature of a woman. La Rubia had only two garments—a blouse pulled tightly down into a skirt of sacking. Her fair hair was laden with dust; her feet and legs were bare; her face was dirty. A piquant dirty face it was: snub nose, grey Basque eyes, a high, wrinkled forehead, and a flower of a mouth that the effort of scraping a living out of the docks had hardened into a downward curve at the corners.

She was a virgin—there wasn't a docker on the wharfs of Bilbao who had any doubt about it—but apart from that she was much as the other waterfront women, haggard and strident workers continually with child, their own wombs serving them as an inspiration for rough humour. La Rubia was brazen and foul-mouthed as they, for she had walked the docks during half her short life; but, unlike them, she was accustomed to respect. The dockers had petted and protected her as a child. When she became a woman she demanded from them the same consideration; she enforced it with blistering language and a total lack of sentiment. Her power was easily held, for she was loved because of her trade. La Rubia was a water-carrier.

She was the only water-carrier in Bilbao. Indeed, she had invented the profession for and by herself. She supplied a demand which the numerous riverside taverns would not satisfy. For a *perra chica,* the smallest Spanish coin, she sold a pint of water with a squeeze of lemon and a sprinkling of sherbet.

At her side walked a donkey towing a little cart to which was lashed a thirty-gallon barrel. The barrel had been filled at the spring of Iturrigorri. To the true Bilbaino that water was worth its price without the lemon; the very word was cooling—the very thought of Iturrigorri, where a full stream of icy water dashed out of the mountainside into a sunless pool overhung with ferns. La Rubia kept up the illusion. The barrel was decked with moss and greenery, and over it waved fronds of bracken freshly picked from the hillside. Between the donkey's ears was fastened a tall fern like an ostrich plume. The little beast resembled its mistress; it was diminutive, very dirty, and it would stand no nonsense.

She came abreast of the *Capitan Segarra* and blew her horn.

'*Agua de Iturrigorri! Agua de Iturrigorri!*'

'*Hola,* beautiful!' shouted El Pirata.

The daily competition of badinage between La Rubia and El Pirata was the delight of the wharf and of the contestants themselves.

'Whom are you calling beautiful, son?' asked La Rubia aggressively, drawing herself up to her full height of four feet six inches.

'He's drunk,' said Viruelas.

'Shall I tell you where he was last night?' asked El Cura.

'You, what do you know?' answered El Pirata, with a shade of anger in his favourite expression of disdain.

'Of course he's drunk,' La Rubia said. 'Last night was the night before a fiesta.'

'She knows me, the little one!' El Pirata exclaimed delightedly. 'How she knows me!'

La Rubia's cheeks flushed under the powder of dust.

'There are many like you,' she replied, implying that she took no particular interest in El Pirata.

She turned away to attend to the customers who crowded round her. Her hard fresh voice dominated the rattle of the discharge.

'No money, El Cura? Drink, man! Pay me next time! . . . You wish it were wine, Juanito? Water for thirst and wine for pleasure! . . . Mind your hands, *capataz*! They are walking where they shouldn't . . . *Hola*, El Pirata, why don't you come? Are you so drunk you can't see the barrel?'

'I see it,' said El Pirata. 'I see it, *salerosa*! But I don't want a wash.'

He plunged a hairy hand into his shirt and searched among the objects next to his skin. He used his shirt as a general pocket. It hung out over his sash in lumps, each of which represented a personal possession. He drew out a bottle of beer and, closing his mouth on the neck, wrenched off the cap between his teeth. The gang shouted their admiration. They never tired of this trick.

'He's stronger than the devil!' El Cura exclaimed.

'*Quiá!*' said La Rubia contemptuously.

El Pirata felt vaguely that La Rubia was not impressed. He zigzagged toward the barrel, swept her into his arms and held her above his head like a child, with his hands upon her hips.

'*Bruto! Bárbaro!* Let me go!'

She grabbed a wisp of black hair and wrenched it out of his scalp. Those of the gang who stood idling slouched swiftly on to El Pirata. The sullen wrath of El Cura deepened the wrinkles of his face. Viruelas bristled, and dropped his hand to the knife hilt that protruded from his sash.

El Pirata lowered La Rubia to the ground and looked at the circle of furious faces. He did not know why they were angry with him; he was at peace with everyone when he was drunk. His mind struggled to gain some concept of what was happening in the exterior world. One emotion chased another over his bewildered, mobile face. Viruelas pulled out his tobacco-pouch instead of his knife; it was impossible to quarrel with a man like that.

At last El Pirata understood what he had done.

'It was a joke,' he said perplexedly. 'A little joke, that's all! Pardon, *señorita!*'

He turned to the men around him.

'Look!' he said. 'I didn't mean to touch her. I just picked her up. Just picked her up . . .'

He paused. El Pirata had no means of expressing fine distinctions. He knew that he had not meant to insult La Rubia, but it was hard to explain.

' . . . Picked her up like . . .' He sought desperately for an example.

He swayed toward the cart, slipped off the traces, and drew the donkey from the shafts. Then he put his shoulder under its belly and heaved. The donkey shot up in the air. A hand on each flank, he held the little beast above his head and grinned. He had explained himself—his mates would understand that it was just his desire for violent action which had made him lay hands on La Rubia. The donkey kicked wildly. A foreleg landed in the pit of El Pirata's stomach. He crumpled and dropped.

'*Ay, mi madre!*' shrieked La Rubia.

She punched the donkey with her horny little fists, while Viruelas pulled his unconscious friend clear of its body.

'He bought it,' said Viruelas.

'He didn't!' stormed La Rubia. 'He didn't! You drove him to it—you, *hijo de perra!*'

'I wanted to protect you,' said Viruelas feebly—devil of a little girl, why did she blame a man for what was her own fault?

'Juanito el Viruelito wanted to protect me!' cried La Rubia, mocking him hysterically.

'I spit in the milk! Did you like him to insult you?'

'What's that to you?'

La Rubia dropped on her knees beside El Pirata, weeping over him. '*Se ha muerto mi hombre!* He is dead, my man! He is dead! My man is dead!'

Her hands and lips fluttered desperately over his body and the red patch on his scalp where the lock of hair had been.

'Carry him into the shade, Juan,' said El Cura.

There was no shade, but Viruelas understood. He pushed the fighting La Rubia aside and carried El Pirata behind a pile of rails where the two would be out of sight. Feeling the big man's heart, he was not greatly concerned about him. He knew El Pirata's resistance, he had seen him knifed, stunned, run over, and partly fed into a concrete-mixer.

The discharge went forward; thump and rattle of derricks; smell of rotten bananas; eternal lifting and stacking. While the last crates were being collected from the corners of the hold and carried to the waiting sling, Viruelas strolled over to his friend. He was snoring. His stupor had apparently merged into a healthy sleep. La Rubia stood near him, her face stern and streaked with a mud formed by dust and tears.

'He'll live,' she said.

She looked at Viruelas appealingly. There was something else she wanted to say, but could not say it. Her helplessness was new to her and startling. She had never been shy in all her life and did not recognize the sensation for what it was.

'I won't tell him,' said Viruelas, understanding her trouble, 'but I can't stop the others telling him.'

'Then amuse yourselves well!' answered La Rubia bitterly: she knew that she would lose her standing with them. '*Adiós*, Viruelas, and thanks!'

'*Adiós, chica!*'

She harnessed the donkey and walked away.

Half an hour later the last sling came up out of the hold. The men put on their jackets, looking amazedly at the high stacks of crates with which their labour had covered the wharf. Finding El Pirata asleep, they laughed and went on their way. Viruelas woke him up, intending to see him home. He was sober and thirsty. He picked up a quart can which La Rubia had left under a mat of green leaves and drained it.

'Was she angry with me?'

'To me,' replied Viruelas casually, 'it appears that she was not.'

They spent the afternoon together in the garden of the Bilbao brewery, but El Pirata could learn no more from Viruelas about La Rubia's behaviour.

Next morning the gang were down in the hold of the *Capitan Segarra*, loading her with iron rails. They had been at work for some minutes when El Pirata strolled up the gangway. He considered it his right to be late if he wanted to be. As he was the hardest and strongest worker of the lot, no foreman ever disputed the odd minutes with him. He looked down into the hold, waiting until the rail which was being lowered into position should be clear of the ladder.

'Here's El Pirata!' announced El Cura, catching sight of him.

'How's your girl this morning?' asked the foreman.

'Where does the donkey sleep?' shouted Evaristo, leaning out over space.

'The ugly have all the luck,' grumbled another.

'Leave the riverside in peace, pirate!'

'For him the flower of the wharf, eh?'

El Pirata stared down on to the upturned, mocking faces. 'The world has gone mad,' he remarked cheerfully.

'Only one is mad, and that's a girl,' growled Viruelas.

'What girl?'

91

'He doesn't know the name of his own *novia*,' said the foreman.

El Pirata did not. He clambered down into the hold and began to work. His mates gave him no peace, but he bore the running fire of comment in good-humoured silence; it was only by listening that he could find out what had happened. He thought at first that they had unearthed some joyous tale of his exploits in the Sevillana, but it was soon clear that the *novia* whose affections he had won was La Rubia.

'Bet you're the first man she's ever kissed!' said El Cura.

El Pirata was startled out of his pose. 'She kissed me?' he asked.

'She thought you were dying,' Viruelas explained.

'Assuredly she kissed you,' said El Cura. 'I saw it. Several times.'

'May your eyes rot! And to think I couldn't kiss her back!'

'Pity the girl hasn't got a brother,' Viruelas said.

'What in hell does she want a brother for now?'

'He'd cut your guts out.'

'You, what do you know?' replied El Pirata, shrugging his shoulders.

The grabs jingled and clicked as they fastened on to another rail. In the moment of silence before the crane and its pulleys purred into life La Rubia's voice floated down into the hold.

'*Agua de Iturrigorri! Agua de Iturrigorri!*'

El Pirata hitched his *boina* over the other ear and swaggered. El Cura winked at the skies. Evaristo caught the wink and translated it correctly. With the rail suspended in mid-air, he switched off the current.

'Hoist away!' shouted the foreman.

Evaristo climbed out on to the platform; with pretended concern he poked an oil-can into the maze of pulleys.

'Cable's jammed!' he answered.

The men who were working in the hold came up on deck. La Rubia and her cart were alongside the ship.

'Here's your *novio*!' the foreman said, digging El Pirata in the ribs.

La Rubia spat. 'There's no man on the wharf who can call himself my *novio*!' she answered.

'Wish the donkey would kick *me*!' exclaimed the foreman.

'Are you set on it being the donkey?' asked El Pirata, using the provocative second person singular and drawing back his foot.

'*Santisima Virgen!* Do you think you're fighting for a woman in the Sevillana?' La Rubia snapped.

El Pirata ignored the rebuke. The foreman had already stepped back into the crowd.

'Viruelas, El Cura, you don't understand,' he said simply. 'I'm going to marry the girl.'

El Cura took the remark as a joke and wanted to share it. He cupped his hands round his mouth and shouted up: '*Oiga,* Evaristo!

El Pirata is going to marry La Rubia!'

'And drink water!' Evaristo laughed.

'But since I tell you I am going to marry her!' roared El Pirata.

'Marry me? Me?' La Rubia murmured, frightened for the first time in her life by the overbearing masculinity of her customers. 'I—I'm too small.'

'And what does a fisherman want with a big wife?' replied El Pirata. 'You, I can carry you out to the boats like this!'

He leaped from the deck to the wharf, and caught up La Rubia in his arms so that her head was on a level with his own.

'He's going to fish for sardines and use her as bait,' the foreman suggested.

'*Cabrón!*' screamed La Rubia.

She writhed in El Pirata's grip and sprayed the whole wharf with insults. She leaned her body over his confining arm as if it were the edge of a pulpit and cursed them all to hell.

El Pirata held her fast and smiled. He was not worried any longer because his mates chose to have a bit of fun. He was thinking of the hanging nets and the boats and the swell eddying over the slipway of Arminza. Why hadn't he asked her to marry him before? He'd only been waiting for such a girl—hadn't his father said that a fisherman couldn't make money without a wife? She was very small, yes! But she could sell fish and hold her own with the wives of Arminza. *Dios*, she could do that! ('Be quiet, *chica*! Have you no shame?') Oh, these women! Didn't she understand that the wharf was laughing at him, not her?

'You, El Cura! Doesn't she deserve to be married, or what?'

El Cura had not looked at the question in that light. He was just contrasting their figures and enjoying the fun of it. 'Yes, man! Of course she deserves it!'

'She's worth more than El Pirata,' said Viruelas.

'You, what do you know?' answered La Rubia disdainfully.

The foreman slapped his thigh.

'Good girl!' he shouted admiringly. 'Good girl!'

The feeling of the gang swept into sincerity. The great male still stood before them with his little woman tucked up in one arm, but they were no longer figures of fun. La Rubia had stood up for her man. She had dared to protect him—and in his own words. They were real; they were mates, those two. They had put on the dignity of Roman matrimony. The men crowded round El Pirata, slapping him on the back, showering La Rubia with barbarous compliments.

'*Olé*, La Rubia! *Olé la agua de Iturrigorri!*' they shouted.

THREE OF CASTILE

They were big, worn men, still young if one looked closely. They had not come any great distance—some twenty miles on various battered wheels and four more on their feet—but in time they had travelled much farther: out of black industry and back to boyhood in the green and silent valleys on their own high border of Old Castile. They were three dockers from the wharves of Bilbao, proud of their strength, since they had nothing much else to be proud of, and dryly aware that they were only willing animals whom society would feed reluctantly when that strength was gone.

It was a public holiday. The Cock, the Monk and the Fly, starting out with a vague intention, unexpressed, of getting well rid of the port and its roaring Basques, wandered south-westwards into the mountains, accepting any casual friendships and casual transport which offered the objective of still another tavern. A rolling walk over the soft summer dust landed them, with a brand-new evening thirst, in the village of Agudas. The dark Rioja was cheap. Each of them trickled half a litre of it straight down his throat.

Dancing in the plaza had begun, but was half-hearted; so the arrival of strangers was a welcome event, though very properly disguised by the contemptuous glances and pretended laughter of the girls. Many of them were partnering each other, for marriageable youths left the remote village early for the towns of the Ebro or the iron foundries of Bilbao.

El Mosco—the Fly—effected satisfactory introductions. He was persistent. That was how he got his nickname.

They were three excellent little girls: fair-haired and muscular, modest with their rotundities in front and glorying in those behind. They crowned the day. No denying it. They belonged to the hills as irrevocably as the dockers' usual girls—when they could afford any—belonged to the rubbish dump at the back of the power station.

The Cock—*el Gallo*—full of a momentary ambition for all he was not, took refuge in imagination.

'Tomorrow,' he announced, 'we are off to Cape Town.'

He was tall and graceful, with straight, black hair; and it was natural for him to provide the touch of romance which his appearance promised. Normally he had the shyness of the athlete, and preferred

94

that his routine of physical labour and drink should not be complicated by women. But, once supplied with those desirable and ex-
plosive comforts, his reactions were incalculable.

'Are you a sailor?' his girl asked.

'I? I am the First Officer of the *Artxanda Mendi*. And my friends
here . . .'

El Gallo hesitated while he examined them through the noble haze
of wine and affection. The Monk—*el Fraile*—suggested respectability.
He was broad, snub-nosed and looked as if he might make a humorous and kindly husband. His immense fore-arms and responsible face
at once provided the right profession.

'My friend is the Chief Engineer. And this other is his Second.'

'It is a big ship?'

'Neither too big nor too small, like you who are as high as my heart.
Five thousand tons. And to think we sail tomorrow!'

'I have never been on a ship,' said the prettiest of the three girls,
whom *el Mosco* had annexed, 'nor have any of us.'

'Then come and see one! You shall all go down the river with us and
we will land you with the pilot at Portugalete.'

'It is not certain we sail tomorrow,' said *el Fraile* giving him a kick
under the table. 'It could be next week. The captain told me.'

'Tomorrow at midday!' *el Gallo* shouted. 'Nothing is more certain!'

And certain it was. At noon, or soon after, the *Artxanda Mendi* would
go down the River Nervion on the first of the ebb. For three days their
gang had been loading her with iron rails, awkward and dangerous in
the slings.

The Cock's fantasy was possible. If he had ever learned to read
easily, what he claimed could have been true. There was no class difference of speech and little of dress to give him away. A ship's officer
who had drifted up to Agudas on a public holiday, homesick for his
mountains and looking for simple fun in a village square would have
worn, like the three dockers, a beret and a bright single-coloured shirt
buttoned up at the collar without a tie. Trousers of blue cotton were
improbable, but not to the innocent.

The Monk and the Fly caught the infection. When they had listened to themselves long enough, they believed themselves. Ship's
routine, at any rate in harbour, was second nature to them and they
had drunk with enough seamen in their time to be familiar with
foreign ports. Girls and men were charmed by these technicians of the
sea returning so genially to the haunts and ways of their youth.
Agudas was turned into a paradise of free wine, continually re-
appearing in the empty jug.

A little before midnight the three dockers danced their way to the
main road. When they awoke in a dry ditch and peered over the edge
of it at Bilbao and the steep valley of the Nervion, they retained some

vague memory of a sympathetic acquaintance who had given them a lift in his ox-cart and discharged them above the town. It was seven in the morning. They walked automatically down to the port gates and checked in for work.

Since they could hold their liquor and had slept on clean weeds they were not in such a nightmare condition as the rest of their gang unloading the *Florinda*, round from Vigo with general cargo. Their heads were beyond being disturbed by the rattle of derricks, the startling coughs of steam capstans and the stench of the dried cod which powdered them with nauseous grey dust. They lowered their backs for loads and carried them. It was easier to work than not to work. In the next berth lay the *Artxandra Mendi*, hatches closed, heat shimmering above her orange funnel.

At ten o'clock there was a break. *El Gallo* looked in his pockets. 'Any money?' he asked.

El Fraile belched in answer.

'And you, *Mosco*?'

The Fly ran nervous hands over his spare, wiry body as if he were cleaning his wings. As a forlorn hope he looked for a lost copper coin in his shoes. 'Nothing.'

'We were robbed?'

'Perhaps in our sleep.'

After an interval for thought the Monk remarked: 'We spent it.'

'Women?'

'We were in the mountains!' the Fly protested virtuously.

'Haven't we enough for a bread?'

'Nothing.'

'Women!' the Cock complained. 'Without doubt!'

'There were not.'

'But there was dancing.'

'Perhaps. It was a fiesta. What I would give for coffee and a bread!'

El Gallo shook his shining black crest and stirred it with his fingers. 'We could not have been dancing alone,' he said.

'You were. On the road.'

'The road from where?'

'Agudas!' shouted *el Mosco* triumphantly.

'It comes back to me,' said *el Gallo* as one recovering a dream.

'And nothing would content you but to be mate of that black bitch there!'

'It's true I have imagination.'

'You should be on a newspaper!'

'What are we to do if they come to the ship?' asked *el Fraile*, wrinkling the leather of his anxious clerical forehead which had also fitted the part of chief engineer.

'They won't.'

96

'Won't they? Look at it, man! All three together with leave from their mothers! Why not? Why shouldn't they come? A ride in the ship, and off with the pilot. Nothing more reasonable. In their best clothes and all pinti-painted!'

'It won't be the first time we've made a date with women and not turned up,' the Fly reminded them.

'But they are not women!' roared the Cock.

'True. They are not, so to say, women.'

'We must see the First Officer,' said the Monk seriously.

'And how the devil are we going to see the First Officer? Whoever heard of three dockers calling on the First Officer? And if the foreman catches us looking round the cabins of the *Artxanda Mendi* . . .'

'He knows very well that we are honest.'

'Perhaps. But he knows we could have no honest reason for being there.'

'The mate is bound to go on shore. We might catch him.'

'Knock off!' the Cock ordered. 'All three to the gates!'

'And how do we eat?' asked the Monk, foreseeing the certain result of deserting their gang in the middle of an urgent job.

'Eating has nothing to do with it,' the Cock replied. 'This is a point of honour.'

He rose from the pile of straw on which the three were reclining, hitched his beret over one ear and approached the foreman.

'We're off,' he said, 'with apologies. A private affair, *capataz.*'

The foreman looked up into the impudent face, hollowed and etched by dissipation and hunger.

'If you want a drink, *Gallo*, get it! Back in ten minutes, and I say nothing!'

The fly searched his usually fertile brain for a convincing excuse. He was too tired. He could think of nothing but an aunt's funeral. It would not do.

'I'll tell you the truth, *capataz*,' he said. 'We can't help it.'

'An affair of delicacy,' the Monk explained.

'I spit on your delicacies! Listen, *Fraile*, you are a responsible man! I know that none of you three has a peseta after a fiesta. Do you want to starve? If you let me down now when we have to empty the *Florinda* I must make up the gang and there'll be no work for you for a week.'

'We could work in the holds,' *el Fraile* suggested to his companions. 'They won't see us there.'

'Who won't see you? What's up? A little trouble with the police?' the foreman asked.

'Them? They don't mix it with me!' the Cock crowed, and turned to the Monk. 'You—haven't you got any sense? It's not a question of being seen or not being seen. We have to meet a certain person at the gates.'

'True,' answered *el Fraile*. 'I had forgotten. Our excuses, *capataz*, but there is no remedy.'

They slouched off, responding with quite unnatural politeness to the threats and curses of the puzzled foreman. Outside the gates they leaned wearily against a truck and watched the brisk traffic of men who had breakfasted—clerks, seamen, agents and customs officers.

They had not long to wait. The First Officer of the *Artxanda Mendi* strolled out through the gates. The hatch covers were on and he had time for a last taste of the shore before the turn of the tide. He had the same gallant build and colouring as the Cock, though shorter and not so gaunt.

'No hands wanted,' he said automatically as the three approached him, and then recognized them as belonging to the gang of labourers who had loaded his ship.

'What do *you* want?'

'A word with your lordship. Nothing more,' said *el Fraile* with most formal courtesy.

The First Officer was held by his air of solidity. 'Well? But it's no good coming to me with complaints. See the agent of the Line!'

El Gallo was silent. Face to face with the man he resembled and might have been, he was shy.

El Mosco started to talk. Even by walking on there was no getting rid of him. The mate was reminded of the persistence of touts on the Buenos Aires waterfront.

'*Bueno, hombre, bueno!*' he said at last. 'But come to the point! What the devil do you three want?'

'A favour,' *el Gallo* replied bluntly. 'A favour that we have no right to ask, being poor. But it has nothing to do with work or money.'

El Gallo's dignity had stopped the mate in his stride up hill from the river. He met the docker's eyes and turned impulsively across the street into a wine shop.

'Sit down! I am listening.'

The Monk began the tale of their *romeria* through the villages and put over very well—though more by tone and gesture than any richness of vocabulary—the beauty of the dusk and of Agudas.

'So, you see, what with the wine and so sympathetic a society—but no doubt you have done the same yourself.'

The First Officer had. 'Three cups for the gentlemen,' he ordered. 'And what then?'

'It so happened,' the Cock confessed, 'that in the enthusiasm of the moment and without the least disrespect to yourself I said I was the First Officer of the *Artxanda Mendi*.'

'Man! But there's no harm done! No doubt with a little study of navigation you would be as good as myself.'

'If it was only that! But this exaggeration—I told it to three girls.'

'I had already guessed as much.'

'And these gentlemen, my friends—I swore that *el Fraile* here was Chief Engineer and *el Mosco* his Second.'

'Without asking so much as by your leave,' added *el Fraile*.

'You didn't deny it,' *el Gallo* accused him.

'One might as well deny God Almighty to a priest.'

'I see that the situation got out of hand,' said the mate sympathetically. 'But what does it matter?'

'If it was only that!' repeated the Cock. 'It's that we invited the girls to visit the ship.'

'And to go down river as far as the mouth,' the Fly wailed dramatically.

'They are very pretty, very well brought up,' said the Monk in his most fatherly manner. 'We cannot think of them going back to their village in tears and saying they made the trip to Bilbao for nothing.'

'If it depended on me, *amigos*, you could receive them on board dressed up as admirals! But the captain would object.'

'We weren't going to propose that! No! Something much less! Would it be possible for your lordship to say that the officers have been changed, that we had to go to Cadiz by the first train this morning?'

'And that we explained the matter to you, and begged you to entertain them?'

'But you don't have to see them again!' the First Officer laughed.

'I know,' the Cock agreed. 'And if they were women I wouldn't mind ditching them. But they are three decent little girls of our own sort.'

'A point of honour,' the Fly explained.

'Of delicacy,' the Monk corrected him.

'They have never been on a ship, you say?'

'You would not believe how excited they were!' said the Cock. 'And the eldest is already seventeen.'

There was a moment's silence. Never to have stood on a deck seemed to all four men as astonishing as never to have ridden in bus or train.

'You will take another cup?' the Fly invited.

That had to be said. He could only pray that an unknown proprietor would give credit.

'I have to be on duty. So if you will excuse me . . .'

'When you return from Cape Town then.'

'With great pleasure when I return from Cape Town. Well, *amigos*,' said the *Artxanda Mendi*'s mate, getting up, 'the foreman will be waiting for you.'

'We are not working today.'

'But the *Florinda*?' asked the First Officer, who had observed how his companions wolved the little saucers of *entremeses* which came with the wine. 'She is in need of a full gang and another if they could get it.'

'It was more important to see you.'

'You are from Castile?'

'From Old Castile.'

'Don't worry. I will do what I can.'

The Cook, the Monk and the Fly crossed the bridge over the River Nervion and aimlessly plodded down the road opposite the wharfs. Without work or any spirit of holiday rest they had time to feel their tiredness. They did not go far—a safe distance down stream from the *Artxanda Mendi*—and then climbed the steep hillside. They found an uncomfortable nest among the rocks from which they could look over the roofs of the narrow belt of houses.

It was the top of the tide. There were rolling clouds beneath the surface of the river as the fresh water coming down from the mountains stirred yellow sediment. The *Artxanda Mendi*, which had seemed a mere slab of iron among the tracery of cranes and masts and signal gantries, was suddenly in the middle of the stream—a graceful black and white arrow aimed straight at them until she turned to port on to her course for Portugalete and the open sea.

She came abreast of them, and they heard the four clangs of the engine-room telegraph as the First Officer rang from Dead Slow to Slow Ahead. She was gallant with house flag and code flags saluting the yard where she was built. A new Spanish ensign flared red and yellow over the wake. On the bridge were three more bright patches of colour, so close together that they were probably holding hands in alarm at so many strange men so very occupied, with no time for more than swift explanation and the occasional warm word of courtesy.

El Fraile sitting motionless, hands clasped round his knees, watched with paternal approval.

'They are there!' shouted *El Mosco*. 'All three of them! On the bridge!'

El Gallo lay on his stomach with his head on his arms. He half turned for a single glance.

'Of course they are there. Let me sleep, *Mosco*! I am hungry.'

THE PEJEMULLER

They were so angry that they entirely missed the point. Their voices were hoarse with fury, and gasping for insults as for breath; so that, at the end, they never knew whether they had witnessed an atrocious crime or a supremely chivalrous act of deliverance. The little Andaluz was equally capable of either.

That fairground was no place for creatures compounded of fire or, perhaps, of water. Magnificently earthy was the crowd of tall Basques: farmers, fishermen and townsmen full of the vigorous Rioja wine which rooted them to their soil and gave to their good-humoured spirits the cruelty and luxuriance of trees, overshadowing all but their own kind. The spirit of the Andaluz was rootless and extinguishable as a flame.

The town was two fields distant from the turbulent circle of lights, and that was far enough for the calm of deep stone wall and murmuring plaza to have lost their influence—more especially since few respectable women were at the fair. The sea was only a lane away, but lying unobtrusive in its summer silence. Bounded by the darkness of a ring of oaks, the fair became an individual world with its own repetitive pattern of life, gay in the clinking of glasses and money, the clattering of hoop-la rings and balls, exasperated by the clarion music of Spanish roundabouts, the cries of showmen and the popping of the shooting galleries.

Paco Igarzábal and Salvador Aguirre strolled tolerantly along the outer aisle of booths. They were well dressed, but showed their solidarity with fellow Basques by wearing *boinas* on their heads and no ties around their collars; only by an air of patronizing joviality did they reveal that either of them could have bought the fair and fairground.

They had visited the Six-Legged Calf and the Hairy Woman. They now halted outside the booth of the Mermaid, feeling in massive pockets for small change. The entrance was not painted with any of the exciting monsters that decorated other booths. It was surmounted by a large, severe and well-lettered placard, announcing PEJEMULLER AUTÉNTICA (Genuine Mermaid); it added OF CANARY ISLAND WATERS—as if there were different and no less authentic breeds of mermaids from other waters.

Paco and Salvador entered the booth and joined the half-dozen men who were standing on the dusty turf before a curtained recess.

The mermaid's proprietor, seeing that there was now a quorum, closed the stretched canvas door. He was a little fellow with slender, flaring nostrils, thin lips and pointed chin. He looked more like a clerk than a showman, for he was dressed in neat-shabby black. A drooping bow tie, though only a length of black tape, suggested the minor intellectual.

He delivered no advertisement, seeming to trust in the rarity of his exhibit. He turned out the central light, drew apart the curtains and said *Señores, look*! in a tone of modest pride, as if wondering that to him it had fallen to catch or make or care for the mermaid.

The glass tank was some five feet long. The top was open, so that the customers could see that it was brimful of water. The sides and the back were hidden by a stucco of pebbles and marine growth, some real, some painted. A faint green light illuminated the *pejemuller*.

Her body to the waist was that of an undernourished girl of twelve, the breasts just forming. From the waist down she was conventional fish. The tail was a marvel of its creator's artistry, for it sprang from the skin in little, irregular scales, leaving no definite line at which the sceptic could declare it to be attached. The scales grew larger over the full and powerful curve, sliding upon each other sleekly and naturally, then lessened as they passed, as imperceptibly, into the smooth membrane of the flukes.

She lay supported on one thin arm, facing the customers. Her face was yellowish, and small even for her dwarfed body. The eyes were pale and expressionless. The sandy hair was long and sparse, and so tangled among the rock and seaweed at the bottom of the tank that it could not be said to float, or not to float. She breathed, sometimes violently, but no bubbles came to the top of the water. Her only other movement was a slight and graceful swaying of her flukes. This she performed as if it were a drilled duty, now forgetting for too long an interval, then offering an extra wave or two to show repentance.

Paco Igarzábal leaned upon the rope which divided him from this phenomenon, and gave himself up, with a lusty pruriency, to close examination of its anatomy. He was a wholesale grocer and he best appreciated life when it was delivered in good coarse truckloads. He and his friend, Salvador Aguirre, were boon companions whenever they were not engaged in making money. They played billiards together on two evenings a week; they went to the bulls together, and they visited the stews of Bilbao together. The chief reason for their friendship was that they did no business together.

Salvador was a man of some education; that is to say, his system of book-keeping was up-to-date; he could carry on the correspondence of his timber yard in correct Spanish; and he did not believe in God—though not, of course, a declared atheist, for that would have been to identify himself with the enemies of timber merchants. He was immensely busy within the limited area of his interests, and his workmen called him the wood-louse.

Salvador twisted himself this way and that among the onlookers in order to examine the tank from various angles. He apologized importantly and continually, and at last delivered his opinion.

'I will tell you how it is done,' he said. 'There is a glass sheet which runs away from us diagonally—' he belched and had another shot at the word '—diagonally across the tank from top to bottom. Thus, friends, you see an unbroken sheet of water, but the mermaid is in an empty compartment.'

'Then how does she breathe?' asked a fisherman. 'There would be no air.'

'She is wholly immersed in water,' answered the showman, the Andaluz. 'The *pejemuller*, gentlemen, does not, as I have myself observed, breathe like a Christian. She admits water into her body through a system of gills.'

'But where?' roared Paco. 'Where does she keep them?'

He suggested several possible positions.

'*Caballero!*' protested the showman abruptly. 'Be decent! She can hear.'

The *pejemuller* showed no sign of hearing. She waved her tail in languid response to the enthusiasm of the world outside her tank.

'But can she understand?' asked Salvador Aguirre with a precise little smile. 'She seems to me to be an idiot.'

'She understands as much as you,' replied the Andaluz with a show of courtesy.

Paco shouted with laughter, and slapped his friend on the back.

'I say it is a little girl,' declared Salvador, his wrinkled face working with an excited obstinacy that hid humiliation. 'I say that the tail is of coloured scales of mica, and that diagonally—'

'It is a *pejemuller*,' interrupted the showman.

'It would not be your daughter, perhaps?'

The face of the Andaluz burned and went white as ash.

'It appears I am among brutes,' he said.

'And whom, *señor*, do you call brute?'

'Since you have said, *señor*, that I would exhibit my daughter . . .'

'Man, I said there was a diagonal and—'

'There is no diagonal.'

'There is a diagonal.'

'You know as much of diagonals as of your father.'

'You lie!'

'Stupendous bastard!'

Paco Igarzábal swayed forward his big frame between the two smaller men.

'Let us see, friends! Let us see! What is this? Are we going to kill one another for a little difference of opinion? This gentleman says that there is no diagonal and that, by logic, the *pejemuller* is a *pejemuller*. My companion says that there is a diagonal, and that the gentleman is perhaps exhibiting his afflicted daughter.'

The Andaluz leapt at him, just as Paco expected—for he was never one to miss a chance of sport. Paco grabbed him by the opening of his black waistcoat, and held him at arm's length. The Andaluz twisted and stamped, answering the renewed insults of Salvador, who was kept back by Paco's other arm.

'Let us see!' repeated Paco. 'A little calm, gentlemen! All this for a diagonal, that can be settled in a moment!'

'*Hijo de puta!*' hissed the Andaluz.

'Big names!' Paco answered, unaffected. 'How much will you take to show us the tank?'

'More than I paid for your mother,' the Andaluz retorted, and spat in his face with a clean trajectory parallel to the arm which held him.

Paco Igarzábal barked with anger and flung him to the ground. Onlookers crashed down upon the struggling men, trying to separate them. The tank rocked on its trestles and spilled water over the edge. The mermaid held her pose, ceasing only, since no eyes stared at her, to move her tail.

At last the tumult of bodies cohered into two groups. The fisherman, huge and benevolent, held the Andaluz. Paco and Salvador were surrounded by the rest of the onlookers, all counselling prudence at the tops of their voices. Not a word could be distinguished in the uproar. The tent heaved and shook as passers-by pushed down the door to listen to so magnificent and delectable a row.

Paco was now more angry than Salvador—if indeed there could be any choice between two men who were living in a fantasy of rage—but, seeing himself surrounded by fellow townsmen who were wont to respect him for his supercilious calm, he choked on his stream of oaths and shouted at the Andaluz in a voice that quivered with the effort of control: 'Listen you! This is to end all argument. I will buy your mermaid and your tent! Understand?'

This astonishing offer brought silence. The Andaluz seemed to recoil as if his spirit were about to leap into passion beyond the reach of all humanity. The fisherman who held him tried with sincere simplicity to conciliate.

'Sell him the mermaid at your price, friend!' he said. 'Don Paco has money. And thus—in peace!'

'Ten thousand pesetas,' offered Paco.

'I am a *caballero*,' answered the Andaluz, each word a slow, reluctant gasp of pain. 'I carry this vile trade among brutes who have no upbringing, but I am a *caballero*. You have called me a liar. You have said that this unhappy thing is my daughter. Now you think that for your money—' his voice rose to a scream '—Where, among whom am I? Ay, my pride! My shame! *Cabrones!* Must I show you what it is to have a heart?'

He fell upon his knees, and the fisherman, not knowing whether this unexpected limpness was a mere feint or the illimitable appeal of a defeated soul, rested a light, embarrassed hand upon his shoulder. The Andaluz dived beneath the rope and flung himself at the nearest trestle. The green light went out. The tank thudded on the ground, and the water flopped in two solid masses against the canvas of the booth. The plate glass tinkled and crashed as the Andaluz flailed it with the trestle.

Men fumbled for the switch, heaving and swearing in the corner where the showman had turned off the central light. No one crossed the rope to enter that shadowy hell where a spirit translated its devastation into the material.

White light glared. At the back of the booth stood the Andaluz, the trestle in his right hand, his left around the waist of the *pejemuller*. She clung to him with her arms round his neck, pitiable as a shivering monkey. She was even smaller than she had seemed in the tank; her tiny yellow head was against his cheek, but the glittering tail did not reach his knees. Except that she clung to what she knew, she was not human.

The Andaluz walked through the tent and over the prostrate door. He still held the trestle in his hand, but it was no fear of physical violence that parted the crowd of powerful Basques. He passed under the harsh lights of the roaring fairground, blood and filth upon his face, clothes dripping water. He walked proudly. What march, what music of sunlit trumpets he heard, that too was accepted by the onlookers. They followed.

He took the lane to the sea, where, beyond the circle of trees, only the softness of the night gleamed on the black and changing mirrors of that marvel which flapped against his thigh. He strode over the rock and down to the boat-slip. The ripples of the Atlantic, inch-high, hissed as they parted over the descending stone.

'God guard thee, little friend!'

He loosened the thin arms from his neck, and flung the *pejemuller* into the night sea. She took the water cleanly, rose once and went under, her tail seeming to flick the starlit surface.

'And now—leave me in peace!' cried the Andaluz.

He stumbled away across the rocks, unnoticed, uncared for. The crowd were arguing, shouting with a recrudescence of anger, gaping into the darkness for another sight of the *pejemuller*.

In the morning, when they wanted the Andaluz, he had gone, leaving behind him only the debris of the tank, impossible to reconstruct. They understood that he had flung away his living for the sake of his honour; that was no thought foreign to any of them, except perhaps to Salvador. But what it was that he had flung away neither high-tide mark nor the passing of the months disclosed.

TECHNIQUE

The curtain flopped on to the dusty boards. The crowd roared for more. *Una mujer estupenda*—a stupendous woman! So the playbills called her, and so she was. The crowd hammered on the tables and shouted at the fallen curtain to give them back their Isabelita. There were three tiers of them in the music hall: on the sawdust-covered floor the labourers from dock and market and factory; a yard higher on the surrounding dais, where the drinks were a little more expensive, the minor employees of commerce, the sailors with money to spend; in the gallery of boxes, the *capitalistas*—moneyed youth, shopkeepers, travelling salesmen, a foreigner or two.

They were roaring jovially now, but at times they could terrify. What they shouted for they got—the management saw to that. And, since there was no limit to what they might shout for, it was up to the lonely woman on the stage to dominate them. She must be, as Isabelita put it, a Danielita in a den of lions.

Even when the lions were out of hand, the true artiste knew how to tame them and harness their undisciplined ferocity to her own triumphal car. A jest would do it, a swing of the hips, a laugh of provocative contempt. And above all, a girl had to hold them with her eyes. Isabelita had no trouble with them, though even if she had danced like Argentina herself it might not have been enough. A Spaniard among Spaniards, she understood and loved her audiences. Her triumph was not only that of a consummate artist; it was that of the orator who masters a potentially hostile crowd.

The blue curtain drifted irregularly up into the wings. The stage was empty. The click of the castanets began behind the backdrop and the orchestra followed the rhythm with accompaniment more conscientious than they would ever have given to the human voice. Isabelita believed in making the lions hungry before they were fed. She showed them an arched instep; she showed them the flounce of a skirt; she showed them a hand. The quick rhythm of the castanets stirred their hair with a pleasurable wind of expectation. Then she was there. She was not a very lovely woman. A plump body she had, and blue-black oily curls swinging free around the white neck. But her eyes glittered. The mouth smiled distantly, ironically. Every movement of the little feet travelled upwards through her whole body. Even

106

the flower behind her ear was alive.

Isabelita's art was perfect. The Madrid professor who taught her was as exacting as the priest of a complex religion. His ritual of shawl, heel, hip, skirt and hand was unvarying and established by the experience of centuries—a highly conventionalized technique for expressing a limited number of simple emotions that could be understood by any human being. Intellect played but a small part in his and Isabelita's style, yet such were the dash and precision of performance that the dancing was intensely exciting. There was no suggestion of inhumanity. A girl was not a bird, a machine, a flame, an abstract thought. A girl was a girl; and it was in this that Isabelita excelled.

She beckoned to her lovers. She fled from them. She led them over strange cities and seas to high adventure—for the desire of her truly seemed high adventure when she danced. She raised them from their seats with a swing of her shawl and flung them back again with a flick of her skirt that had all the salaciousness of a bawdy jest. She shook the golden brandy in the glasses with the rattle of her impatient heels, and stood motionless except for the swift hands that wove a belt of clicking, tempestuous music around her waist. Then, with a great sweep of her panelled skirt, she sunk before them in a foam of white lace and raised her eyes once. Isabelita's glance at her audience was a masterpiece of irony. It asked: 'My lords and masters, have I pleased you?' And it added: 'God help us, what shameless dogs!' It touched a chord of humour common to every man in the house, and they thundered back their enthusiasm.

Isabelita slipped back into the public dressing-room. Being the most highly paid artiste, she had a curtained corner of it to herself. The crowd yelled for a second encore. There were only a thin curtain and a canvas backdrop between the dressing-room and the audience. The applause came through, not in the muffled waves of a theatre, but loud and ferocious, with every exclamation distinct.

Isabelita sighed happily. 'You see, Maruja,' she said, 'it's worth the trouble to learn to dance.'

'They always like the classical stuff,' answered Maruja, 'if the woman can put it over.'

'It's not classical if she can't,' said Isabelita proudly. Isabelita always danced for her audience as for a lover. She considered that a step without a definite glance at a definite member of the audience was not a step at all. Being almost illiterate, she could not analyse her art, but what she unconsciously knew was that, in her particular style, technique without personality was not technique at all.

The audience roared incessantly.

'Won't you give them another encore?' Maruja asked anxiously.

'No! If they want more, they can stop for the second show.'

'A little more. Just for a minute,' pleaded Maruja.

'*Chica!* Are you in love with the manager?' asked Isabelita reproachfully.

'I can't go on—not with them in this mood,' Maruja said desperately. 'I can't! You must understand—I can't!'

Maruja's act, the next on the bill, was a simple one. She came on with a large Teddy bear and sang songs to it. As and when the lions roared for her to do so, she removed garments. If they were yawning after a full meal, they allowed her to depart with some remnants of modesty. If they were hungry, she got off the stage with the Teddy bear only. Again, it was a question of domination. When Maruja was swift in repartee and outrageous in speech, when she made the audience feel definitely inferior to her, the act was not in the least brutal; it had a certain Rabelaisian piquancy quite devoid of nastiness. But the trouble was that Maruja was a very pretty girl. The act should have been put on—and usually was—by some motherly old soul with an abominable body and a sergeant-major's voice. If Maruja could not tame the rows of males in front of her, she became merely a shrinking girl; the bottom fell out of the act; everybody went home feeling a little ashamed, and the management cursed.

It was impossible for Maruja to go on until the audience were in a quieter mood. Isabelita gave her a comradely spank.

'I'll cut them down to shape for you,' she promised.

She ran on to the stage and put her head through the slit in the curtain. The house greeted her with a wild wave of applause.

'Thank you, children,' she said to them. 'I will give you one little one. And then no more! Shall it be a *jota*?'

'*Jota! Jota!*' roared the house, and each one found individual expression for his admiration. 'What you will, Isabelita!' . . . 'Let us see your pretty feet!' . . . 'Beauty! My tripes move when I see you!'

Isabelita talked to them through the curtain while she changed. She lifted the mantilla and slid off the foaming skirt. The dresser handed her the Asturian peasant costume. High heels to low slippers—flowered bodice to the generous bulge of the country blouse—no hesitation! She threw the two halves of the curtain away from her with both hands and was on them with the fury of the village dance, feet leaping to the imaginary skirl of bagpipes. One could smell the hills and the winds off the Atlantic.

It was over in two minutes of wild action. The audience stared, mouths half open, amazed at her agility.

'*Ya!* And don't follow me home!' said the country virgin. 'I'm going to be married next week!'

She vanished, and the crowd shook itself loose with applause and laughter. Cigars were relit and glasses drained.

Isabelita was radiant. She swung into the dressing-room hand on hip, acting for herself, enjoying her own force and humour.

'*Ay!* What utter children are men!' she cried. 'It is we who count for something in this world—we, *chicas!* Get in, Maruja! By God, they don't deserve to have a wench like you to look at!'

There was one girl who did not join the group around Isabelita. She sat by herself, making up, and every now and then looking at the triumphant Isabelita with curiosity. She was a slim, bronzed German. Isabelita, the Latin, was white as ivory, for she kept carefully out of the sun. The fair-haired Northerner was golden-brown from the midsummer beaches of the Baltic.

Primitive and essentially coarse, Anna thought. She was a little contemptuous of Isabelita's triumph. She resented the brutality of the audience and she disliked the whole business of intimacy with them. She had in a muddle-headed way adopted a theory of dancing—that, since the art of the dance was universal, beauty of movement was alone enough to hold any audience. It seemed to be as true in Spain as anywhere else, for her act was watched in respectful silence and greeted with moderate applause. Actually, it was puzzled applause. The patrons on the floor, who were essentially polite when an act did not conform to the recognized conventions of impoliteness, felt that applause was expected; so they gave it.

The lions roared. Maruja ran into the dressing-room as naked as the day she was born and thoroughly happy. She had given of her best—plenty of spirit and an instant of flashing physical beauty—and it had been appreciated. Anna was shocked. She had no false modesty, but her body was to her a religion. Athletic and good to see, she danced with only a short sarong. She had little interest, however, in admiration for herself as a woman; she wanted admiration for her movements, and to have those movements properly seen, for in her way she was an artist. She belonged to the cabarets of capitals, of Berlin and Paris and Warsaw, but what she had to give was not yet good enough for the capitals—therefore the tour of provincial music-halls in Spain.

Isabelita and Maruja went up to the stage box reserved for artistes, hung their shawls over the balcony, and ordered drinks. Maruja had seen Anna's act for several nights. To Isabelita, just come from San Sebastian, it was new.

'How is she?' she asked Maruja.

'I do not know,' answered Maruja. 'She can't dance and she's a lady and she's very indecent. I do not understand her.'

Anna had the lights lowered for her act. She set a small cruse of burning oil in the centre of the stage and around that she danced. The lithe limbs moved beautifully and naturally, but style was wanting. As music she preferred one of the Indian Love Lyrics. She had evidently studied rhythmic dancing, free expression, sun worship, and heaven knows what. The lamp dance represented a Vestal Virgin watching the sacred flame. Had it been just a shade better, it would have been very good. But to Isabelita, trained in a hard school, it was nothing at all, and, as Maruja had said, it was indecent. For why expose yourself to no good purpose? The customers didn't even yell.

The three tiers of males stirred unhappily as Anna danced. The Spanish prudery was awakened—a prudery depending entirely on environment. There was no sentimentality in it, for Anna neither suggested purity nor reminded her audience of carefully guarded sisters and daughters. But she was out of place—discordant though not irrelevant, as if her almost naked body had suddenly flashed upon a bevy of travelling salesmen exchanging stories on that very subject. The floor customers hesitated to sip their drinks—this from a sense of economy, since liveliness was not at the moment called for. The *capitalistas* were bored; their glances strayed around the hall, coming to rest at the box where Isabelita and Maruja sat.

To Anna, too, Isabelita was important. She watched Isabelita, not consciously seeking approval, but interested to see what the reaction of the star would be. The patrons, Anna hoped, would be moved by the romance of her golden body prowling catlike around the lamp, of the studied—but false—gesture with which she loosened the wreath around her forehead and let fall her veil, of the clean line from wrist to hip as her uplifted arms worshipped the flame; but she desired her sculptural poses and the long patterns woven by her bare feet to be suggestive to the star. She had little respect for Isabelita's art, but a measure for Isabelita's success. Success, sweet anywhere, had an even more notorious glamour in the world of the Spanish cabarets. Triumph was peculiarly triumphal. So, when Anna glided from the stage to the accompaniment of the usual modest applause, she had a glance for Isabelita, a comradely glance which asked for approval and return.

Isabelita's eyes were otherwise engaged. She was arranging a carnation behind her ear. Her movements parodied with rare humour and all the skill of plump arms trained to the limit of expression the gesture of Anna undoing her veil. Anna's look did not rest long enough to catch Isabelita entertaining herself; she saw only indifference. But the patrons in the opposite box, watching those eloquent arms as the curtain fell, guffawed with the loud relief of men just come from church or boys from school. It was the end of the first show. The house began to empty.

Anna was utterly homesick as she dressed: a false homesickness since she had no real longing for the office in the stuffy provincial town to which she had once been tied. But, being out of harmony with her audience and her environment, she felt gloomily alone. She did not expect a rousing welcome such as that given to Isabelita and the handful of other popular artistes; she did not even want it. She prided herself that here in Spain her art was for the few. She wished the music-hall to lead not to the gallant atmosphere of bullfighters, grandees and the best champagne, but to the concert hall. She would not admit that she had come to the wrong shop with her wares, but she felt that the Spanish market was very foreign to her. Even the memory of a German provincial office was a refuge.

'Why can't I throw myself into it?' she sobbed—and then to herself, unconsciously recalling the gentle accents of her father: 'Thou must, little one! Thou must!'

She draped a green Manila shawl over her shoulders—a concession to Spain—and went up to the artistes' box.

The *capitalistas* strolled back and forth along the horse-shoe gallery, looking for friends and empty tables in the boxes. The workers were rapidly refilling the tables on the floor with the brusque and purposeful movements of men who have only the smallest silver coin to spend and mean to spend it to the best advantage.

Isabelita and Maruja casually made room for Anna. Maruja was in the box at Isabelita's invitation. The star always invited one or more of her humbler colleagues. Otherwise she and Anna, being the only two dancers with any pretensions to art and a living wage, would have occupied the box alone.

'It wasn't bad, my dear,' said Isabelita kindly, 'But of course your dance doesn't mean enough.'

'It isn't meant to mean much, except just beauty,' Anna replied. And then, anxious not to appear rude: 'It's another art, quite different from yours.'

Isabelita was a little startled at the other woman's assumption of equality. Her first impulse was to snub Anna, but she vaguely realized that they were not on common ground, and so, with Spanish good sense, set out to define her position.

'There's only one art,' she said firmly. 'Learn and train, and train and learn, and then, if you have it in you, you can dance; and if you haven't it in you, you can't dance. My professor said he could teach me to hold my heels together, but only the good God could teach the blood to run in them.'

Her swift heels rolled a faint tattoo on the hard floor. It pleased her. Without moving from her seat, indeed hardly moving at all, she let hands and shoulders, eyes and head, dance to the demon drumming of her heels. The little gem of art ended in ten seconds. It was a mere epigram translated into movement; yet it had a beginning, a middle, and an end, all three polished, inevitable, and full of humour.

'I think the blood runs in you if you would let it,' Isabelita went on, 'but you haven't learned and trained yet.'

'It's an entirely different technique,' said Anna.

'*Ay de mi!*' laughed Isabelita. 'It's no technique at all! Have a drink, frigid one, and I will teach you how to dance!'

'I would rather,' Anna said, 'that you taught me how to handle the men upstairs.'

When the two shows were over, the girls had to entertain at a not unpleasant little cabaret above the music hall. They were paid for their attendance and they received a liberal commission on such champagne as they could persuade their escorts to buy; in return they permitted them immediate caresses and exaggerated hopes. Isabelita was thoroughly used to this epilogue to her dancing. It was unavoidable in most of the halls she toured. She undertook it with vivacity, and if surrounded, as she often was, by admirers who had deliberately come upstairs to compliment her and buy her supper, with enthusiasm and much good-fellowship. Anna, accustomed to the sentimentality of the German cabaret, disliked the franker spirit of the Spanish and was unable to handle it. Her request to Isabelita, while an obvious attempt to change the subject, was quite sincere. To the star, however, it seemed that Anna had refused point-blank her offer of help and contemptuously asked her for information that any harlot could give as well.

'It is easy,' replied Isabelita.

'But how?'

'I do not know. Laugh—drink—be respected! With me they do not go beyond the bounds of what can be permitted.'

Anna was exasperated. She had already heard Isabelita rebuff too personal a compliment with a bawdy joke. She had seen her cut up an overwhelming amorous advance with laughter. Anna herself had attempted this method. It had repelled advances with too much success; the customer had paid his bill and gone home without a word. Yet this crude, plump dancer, utterly unable to analyse the secrets of her own power, could allow herself the haughtiness, licentiousness, and humanity of a medieval queen.

'It's like dancing,' said Isabelita. 'One must know how it is done. There is no second-best.'

'If it comes to the worst, one can always break a glass.' suggested Maruja humbly.

'Little fool, it should never come to that!' laughed Isabelita.

'But it does sometimes,' Maruja sighed.

'Lord, what a child! Look, Anna! I will show you what Maruja is talking about.'

Isabelita picked up a tall goblet, holding it by its short stem, and tapped it three times on the corner of the table. At the third tap the goblet smashed, leaving a long, spear–headed sliver of glass attached to the stem. 'That will frighten any man,' she said, 'but why one should want to frighten a man I do not know.'

112

Anna fingered the glass weapon curiously. 'Did you ever use it?' she asked Maruja.

'I once tried,' admitted Maruja. 'But the glass broke in the wrong place, and he was very kind and tied my hand up and after that we were lovers.'

Isabelita gurgled with deep laughter. Her laughter was like a bell under water. 'You would, Maruja!' she cried. 'You would, little angel! And it's so easy to break in the right way! Look!'

She picked up glass after glass, collecting them with swift snatches from her own box and the box behind her, smashing them cunningly on the edge of the table, and laying in front of her a row of deadly little irregular instruments that might have been made for a Dresden china surgeon. The waiters hastened in from all sides.

'I pay, sons!' exclaimed Isabelita grandly, throwing down a twenty-five-peseta note. '*Quiá!* It's dead here! The *caballeros* must have something to look at until I dance again!'

The musicians were already tuning up, warbling like a gaunt and hungry roost of black-backed birds before the dawn should bring them to such fullness of melody as they had. The places left vacant by those who had stopped only for the first show had new tenants. The smoke and laughter thickened. Men passed and repassed the back of the artistes' box, exchanging pleasantries with Isabelita and her companions.

Isabelita preferred to receive her court after she had danced and not before. 'Let us go and change,' she said.

The three gathered their shawls around them, smiled at the floor and the gallery, and filed out of the box; then through the artistes' door, and down their dirty staircase to the dressing-room.

The second show, like the second act of a play, developed the atmosphere created by the first. It was more intimate and less superficial. The entertainers remembered that the second house had dined well. They were also mindful that those of the *capitalistas* who had been sufficiently attracted by the romance of the performer would afterwards go upstairs to the cabaret to explore the reality of the woman. The singers of couplets thought more of the words than of appropriate and improper gestures. The dancers asked the electrician for less, and more entrancing, light. The guitarist, who had a wife and family to support and gave his regular and automatic best at every performance, changed his greasy black tie for a clean one.

The lions were good-humoured—hungry, but playful. They insisted that the singers of the more outrageous couplets should suit action to word and permit the den a full view of their delights; they were complimentary to the dancers; they entertained each other with their remarks; and they felt a generosity reflected on themselves when the Conde de Urdiales, who sold automobiles and was an amateur of music and women, vaulted on to the stage from the box opposite the artistes', crowned the guitarist with a velvet brassière left behind by the preceding turn, and covered the bottom of his Cordoba hat with silver.

When Isabelita's number was reached, she was a little drunk. She had not taken enough alcohol to render her careless of her surroundings, only a single golden glass of manzanilla which intensified and quickened the current of sympathy between stage and floor. She was of Spain rather than in it, of her audience rather than performing before them. The reaction of the audience was ecstatically physical. The nerves of their spines shivered in sensuous pleasure under the music of her fingers and the beat of her heels. The tradition of Rome and of Africa in the classic dance expressed the desires of those cells of Rome and Africa which had been passed down from womb to womb into the bodies of that living crowd. Isabelita filled the sordid hall with a concentrated essence of Spain—of pageantry and bulls, of village fiesta, of wailing song under moon-glare on white wall and yellow rock; precise and delicate images of savagery and passion. The three tiers of males talked, applauded, drank and behaved more or less as at all other performances, but their dreams as they watched her played over their love of the race and its unknown destiny, inspired by the art rather than the shape of woman.

To Anna in the dressing-room came also this communal current. The music, the rhythm of Isabelita's heels and castanets, the swinging of her skirt seen from the wings, were much the same as they had been at the earlier show, yet they had intenser meaning. She, like everyone else in the place, was a little drunk on Isabelita's single glass of manzanilla. That glass of good wine in the stomach of a consummate artiste had commanded, inevitably, the response of five hundred men and a few women eager for any emotional experience which would lift them out of their daily lives.

Isabelita entered the dressing-room silently and with tears in her eyes. The applause thundered and thundered from the hall. The audience, released from her spell, were impatient with their own hands because, crashed together, they could not make more noise. Maruja, the following turn, they hardly noticed. She was wise enough not to call any lasting attention to herself. She crooned rather than sang to her Teddy bear, and what the words were nobody knew or cared. The stream had not passed her by, but she did not attempt to swim on it. She knew she was good to look at and was content. So, while they collected their thoughts, were her audience.

While Maruja was still on the stage and three minutes were yet to go before Anna's turn, the manager came into the dressing-room. His usually kindly face glowed with annoyance through a carpet of unshaven bristles.

'You must put more on, Anna,' he began. 'I told you—'

'Why?' she interrupted curtly.

114

'Why? Because I have just been fined by the civil governor for permitting your indecency.'

'Indecency! How dare he! And the others—look at them! Oh, how
dare he! How dare he! *Schweinerei!* . . .' She broke into a torrent of
hysterical German, her Spanish unable to deal with the rush of
anger—the first genuine emotion she had felt in Spain.

'For the love of God, shut up!' The manager was almost weeping.
'They'll hear you out in front!'

'I do not care if they hear me down the river!' shouted Anna. 'The
damned, dirty civil gov—' She felt a soft hand clapped over her mouth
and turned in fury.

'Sh-sh, *chica*!' said Isabelita, holding her. 'Do not be indiscreet! *Ay*,
and I thought you Northerners were cold!' she added with gentle
humour. 'If only you could show such passion in your dance!'

'Oh God, what do any of you know about dancing?' Anna cried, her
voice breaking with misery.

'Well, to you it may not seem much,' answered Isabelita with an air
of finality as of one not wishing to argue. 'Shall we go to the box,
Maruja?'

The child Maruja, just come from the stage, slipped an evening
frock over her head and followed Isabelita wonderingly. It seemed to
her to be the moment when rival artistes began to throw plates at one
another, yet she could imagine neither of these goddesses indulging in
such vulgarity. Conscious of storm clouds, she did not know what
lightning, if indeed any, would follow. She fled after Isabelita, her
pretty head still struggling through the opening of her frock.

Anna slowly and deliberately took down a scarf from her peg and
wound it about the breasts that had dared to offend the civil governor.
The suppressed anger of the Northerner possessed her. It was in perfect harmony with the sultry atmosphere of emotion. She strode out
of the wings, slinking forward on long, golden, slender legs without a
trace of the temporary malaise she had felt on former occasions. The
crowd, to whom a rumour of the civil governor's action had come,
received her with applause in which was a note of pity. Not that they
disapproved of the governor; they considered that for the dignity of
his office he could have done nothing else. Anna's act, to them as to
him, had been vaguely indecent. Still, there was the eternal pity of
the Spaniard for the human being that had to earn its bread in spite
of the arbitrary and ever-interfering preventions of the law.

The passion in Anna's heart gave her for the first time a feeling of
intimacy with her audience. Insult and outrage had shattered the
detachment with which she had always gone through her series of
moderately pretty movements. Possessed by a berserk demon which
had to be exorcised by violent action, she hurled herself into the
music. 'Give the swine something they can understand!' she shouted

115

to herself. 'Oh, give them something they can understand!' She tried, but her dance had fury without form. She challenged comparison with the wretched posings of the early turns. She even attempted some stock tricks from the Spanish dances, recollections of the easy grace of Isabelita. It was incredibly bad—burlesque without humour. It was hysteria, the negation of all art.

Isabelita, watching from the artistes' box, was disgusted by such a profanation. She had utterly lost the regal pity with which she treated the failures of her fellow-performers. Twice offended by Anna, she was now hard and insensitive. She caught the expression of the Conde de Urdiales in the opposite box and giggled. He was watching Anna with blank amazement—with the absurdly puzzled expression of a man who has drunk rather too much and suddenly been transported on the magic carpet of another's unaccountable emotion into an unintelligible world.

Rising to her feet, she began to imitate Anna's dance within the confines of the box. A touch of her hand produced a slight dishevelling of her glossy hair which suggested Anna's bob. She pinned a hastily folded table napkin across her flowered bosom. A bottle on the table represented the sacred flame. Her shawl became a wickedly funny veil. With every exquisite movement of her body she pretended delirium and inefficiency. Anna raged on through her dance, knowing nothing of the parody until she saw the eyes of the pianist flash up to the artistes' box. She looked at the audience; up to that moment she had felt them, but only seen them as a blur of faces. They were all looking away from her and up to the box. They were not laughing, but an uneasy grin seemed to dominate every face. She followed their eyes to Isabelita, gay, careless and imitating her.

Anna signalled to the musicians to stop at the end of the bar and walked into the wings without another glance. The audience clapped feebly. They had not laughed, nor had Anna wept. The tension in that hall was terrific. The mood of exaltation aroused by Isabelita's dancing had never descended, and on to it came the impact of a hysterical woman on the stage and a wild act of comedy at which none could laugh outright. Only Isabelita, insolent and triumphant, neither realizing the supreme effect of her own performance nor heedful of her later cruelty, was insensitive to the storm of suppressed and conflicting emotions that she had raised.

Miguel de Urdiales signalled across to her and to Maruja to meet him in the cabaret. The house emptied. The sweepers began to pass between the tables brushing together the sawdust and cigarette-ends.

Anna was quite calm as she dressed. She was alone in the dressing-room, for the rest of the girls had already gone upstairs. The sweat dripped at intervals from her armpits and ran down her golden sides. It was cold sweat, not the pleasant warm dampness of exercise, and

116

she vaguely wondered at it. She was not thinking of Isabelita or of her uncompleted berserk mood. Indeed, she was not thinking of anything at all. She gave exaggerated importance to every motion of dressing, and talked to herself aloud in trivial little exclamations. She took particular care over her make-up for the cabaret and was astonished at the brilliance of her eyes and the stillness of her face. She put on a straight white frock that well showed the athletic and lovely lines of her body.

She was remote and calm when she walked into the cabaret. Those few of the customers who had not patronized the music-hall and did not know who she was assumed her to be some frigid and self-sufficient tourist waiting for the husband or friend who at that moment was depositing his hat and coat.

Isabelita and Maruja sat at a table near the door with Miguel de Urdiales and two of his friends. They needed a third woman to complete the party.

'We must invite her,' said the Conde de Urdiales.

He heaved his tall figure off the low, gaudily upholstered bench. Youth and dignity concealed a slight unsteadiness of the feet. He approached Anna courteously. She bowed and walked silently before him to the table.

'Sit here, *chica!*' said Isabelita genially and with a little remorseful smile, patting the chair next to her.

Anna thanked her and sat down.

'A barbarian, the civil governor!' Isabelita went on. 'But do not mind, Girl! We all admire you and will make you at home. Isn't it so, *caballeros?*'

The three men vied with each other in paying compliments to Anna, who accepted them pleasantly and remotely.

'I behaved badly,' admitted Isabelita with regal frankness, 'but it did me no good and it did you no harm. We shall be friends, I know it.'

'I am sure of it,' replied Anna gravely.

Her mind was still running on trivialities; they occupied it so thoroughly that she had not given a thought to her surroundings. The cold sweat still trickled down her sides. She was able to contemplate Isabelita quite calmly, even to admire, very distantly, as if it belonged to a complete stranger, her superb good nature.

'And you, little flower'—Isabelita turned to Maruja—'you say nothing. What is it?'

'I am afraid,' answered Maruja simply, with a little shiver of her naked shoulders.

'*Que va!* Everybody is sad this evening except me. Let us drink, Miguel!'

Miguel de Urdiales poured her a glass of champagne and then filled the other five glasses. Isabelita drank hers, tilted back her chair, and, with the air of a merry queen to whom all things must be permitted, propped up her bare legs on the table. They were beautiful so, the blue veins and muscles stretched tight beneath the round knees.

'Will you dance?' asked the man on the other side of her.

'Not yet. Let the place wake up a bit.'

To anyone entering at the moment, the cabaret would have seemed fully awake. The high stools at the bar were each supporting a man. The tables were fairly full. The orchestra blared over a cheerful undertone of voices. But Isabelita loved an extravagant communal spirit. She liked to see flowers thrown and much outrageous jesting and the whole house dancing a *jota* in the middle of the floor. She didn't much care for foxtrots, but she enjoyed a solo with the rest of the cabaret playing the chorus around her.

The Conde de Urdiales began to speak German with Anna. She was hardly aware that the language had been changed, for her disjointed thoughts had been running in German. Isabelita's attention was attracted.

'Speak Christian, Miguel!' she laughed. 'The good God made it to talk to women in. And Anna speaks so well.'

'She does indeed,' agreed de Urdiales. 'She learns amazingly quickly.'

'*Ay de mi*!' exclaimed Isabelita with mock sorrow. 'I wish she would let me teach her to dance!'

The mists very suddenly cleared away from Anna's brain. She was back at the point where she had stopped the orchestra. Hatred and fury overwhelmed her—against Spain and the civil governor, against Isabelita. Above all, against Isabelita. Her fingers caressed the long water goblet in front of her. She turned deliberately to de Urdiales.

'You see,' she said slowly, 'I have not the training. You must learn and train and train and learn'—her voice rose to a scream of misery and passion. 'You must learn to drink and laugh at men and insult women! You must have technique. . .'

She smashed the goblet so swiftly that not one of them had time to think what it could mean. Then she drew the glass knife with a single powerful cut through vein and muscle across the underside of Isabelita's knees.

The men tried to hold her, but could not. She was away from them, away from the doorkeepers, and out into the street, running, running. She did not know whether they were after her. She was not trying to escape. She ran from the blood. She ran because running stopped her thinking what she had done. Her feet, undirected by herself, took her to the port, and there they found her in the morning exhausted by weeping and asleep upon a pile of crates marked 'Hamburg'; they sent her on board the ship with them, for Isabelita had said that she would make no charge against her.

SECRET POLICE

He was shabby even for a passenger who had worn for two weeks the same creased suit of semi-tropical clothes down in the immigrant accommodation of the MS *Patagonia*. He was aware that he had aroused the fury of a large and nationally important shipping line. And his passport was out-of-date.

'If you would be so good as to accompany me to my office, sir . . .' the Port Security Officer invited.

Mr Bernard Vasey came willingly enough, accepting a chair and a cigarette in the manner of a man who had a clean conscience and was superbly indifferent to his appearance. He managed it by forcing himself to remember that he was more accustomed to give orders to minor officials than to receive them.

'My passport is sufficient proof of British nationality,' he said. 'I am under no obligation to have it stamped merely to land in the United Kingdom.'

The Port Security Officer made no comment except to ask why he had not had his passport renewed by the nearest British Consul to his place of residence.

'He was seven hundred miles away.'

'Why did you not attend to it at Pernambuco before you embarked?'

'Because the *Patagonia* was due to sail.'

'Would you care to account for the fact that when the *Patagonia* called at Vigo you endeavoured to remain in Spain illegally?'

'Any complaint from General Franco?'

'After you had paid your fare at Pernambuco you had little or no money left. Yet when you were forcibly escorted on board by Vigo police it would appear that you had acquired a considerable sum.'

'I won it at cards.'

Bernard Vasey was conscious that his answer sounded weak. He felt embarrassed about that card session. He feared that he might be looking guilty and tried to regain the initiative.

'Inspector, you have undoubtedly been asked to grill me by a very angry shipping line,' he said, slightly raising his heavy eyebrows, 'I question whether you are not exceeding your duty. And in any case you will not uncover any criminal activities.'

119

'Your third-class cabin was filled with flowers, bottles of wine and other articles of value,' continued the Security Officer, unmoved.

'I declared them.'

'Where did they come from?'

'From friends.'

That seemed to shut him up. There was, after all, no reason why a poor third-class passenger should not have rich friends. What about students? But now this obstinate official, after drawing a blank with his nonsense about money, was off again.

'I see from your passport that you were in Cuba shortly before the revolution.'

'I was. A holiday. Why not?'

'Your political sympathies are left-wing?'

'My political sympathies vary, Inspector. From a business point of view I like to be on the winning side. On the other hand, the sight of desperate poverty does occasionally . . . Oh Lord, I see! Cuba! Has something been passed to you by our consul in Vigo?'

'I cannot disclose sources of information, sir.'

Mr Vasey was at last perturbed. He had not returned to his own country for some years. To judge by newspaper reports—though he told himself that they always exaggerated—it was less free and easy than it had been. Possibly there were ways in which officials could make themselves quietly unpleasant to suspected communists. He was confident that he could remake a satisfactory future for himself, but perhaps not easily with a question mark against his name.

'I shall have to explain,' he said. 'I'm afraid I didn't think it essential. To start from the beginning: having been offered a free air passage from up country to Pernambuco . . .'

'By whom?'

'By Brazilian police. Politics, not crime. My God, not what *you* mean by politics! It was just that I was aware of certain disreputable secrets in the private life of our newly elected State Attorney. I had no intention of spilling them, but he couldn't take the risk. You wouldn't take it yourself, Inspector, if you, for example . . . well, I mean . . . well, of course such a thing is quite unthinkable.

'On arrival at Pernambuco I had just enough money to buy my passage home. The voyage dragged, as voyages do when one is unable to use the bar. Fortunately third-class passengers are provided with free wine at meals. An insurance, no doubt, against the scandal of suicide.

'When the *Patagonia* called at Vigo two days ago, I resented my poverty more than ever. I had an old and precious friend in that city. His true name and responsibilities I shall conceal. Let us call him Don Alonso.'

'If I am to give any credence to your story, sir, I shall require names and addresses.'

'Well, you won't get them!' replied Vasey, his spirit momentarily restored by the thought of his old friend.

'Together with professions and descriptions,' the Port Security Officer went on, ignoring him.

'I'll be delighted to give you a description if it's any good to you. Eyes brown and generally laughing. Nose classical. Let me see! Yes! About my size. Short upper lip. Mouth thin and mobile. But since you aren't likely to meet him all you need know is that his charm and efficiency have very rightly promoted him to a position where he is below the Lieutenant-Governor of the province but considerably above—if I may say so without offence—the Port Police.

'Dressed as I was and so obviously destitute I refused to go ashore and call on Alonso. I contented myself with leaning over the rail and unkindly watching the importunities of guides, curio sellers, restaurant runners and taxi drivers as they attacked the first-class passengers.

'The noble people of Spain, Inspector, despise foreigners in the mass; from such pitiable objects one may extract money without demeaning oneself. But when a foreigner presents himself as an individual he is considered to share the common sorrows of humanity. In remembering that I began to feel ashamed of myself.

'I saw that all through this morning of melancholy sulking I had been putting pride before friendship. Alonso had never hesitated to call on me in days when he had nothing but a horse of doubtful ownership and the clothes he rode in. That was in Nicaragua. Though an alien, he could not resist dabbling in politics. At the time it seemed to me folly. But when he returned home to Spain his experience proved invaluable.

'This debate within myself went on far too long before warmth and decency overcame the unsuspected Joneses in my character. I did what little I could to improve my appearance and set out for Alonso's office. Fortunately it was hot enough to carry my coat, and my shirt was clean.

'Even so, the porter was not impressed and conducted me to a waiting-room where the applicants for government attention were of the humblest. But my card at least was of virginal whiteness. I had some hope that it would reach Alonso's desk. It did. Do you know the Spanish people, Inspector?'

'No, sir. They give very little trouble.'

'I only asked so as to know how much I must explain. There's a grain of truth in most of the exaggerations, good or bad, which everyone has heard about them, and I think many of these myths derive from the splendour with which they give their hearts when they give them at all.

'Alonso shot out of his office sparkling with exclamations of welcome. He cleared up the affairs of the day with the decision and efficiency of a Spaniard in a hurry, and took me out to lunch. I had wasted too much time in hesitation. It was then two o'clock and the *Patagonia* was due to sail in the early afternoon.

'From the terrace of our restaurant we could see her clearly—a fine twenty-five thousand tons of speed and luxury moored at the Ocean Quay. At quarter past three her siren roared a warning, and I regretfully pushed back my chair though we had only reached the fish. Alonso told me to sit down and stop fussing. The ship, he said, would not leave till after four. I assumed that he was in a position to know.

'There was now time to tell him something of my future plans and my sudden and disastrous expulsion from Brazil . . .'

'Would you care to repeat those facts to me, sir—very shortly?'

'I would not, Inspector. To you as an Englishman my story would appear most unlikely, whereas to Alonso it was obviously and instantly true. You are accustomed here to politicians who do not take their profession seriously enough to be corrupt.

'We had reached the comfortable stage of the cigars when the Agent of the Line joined us in the restaurant. He had been waiting for my friend at his office and had only just discovered his whereabouts. He begged Alonso to intervene with the Chief of Customs who was holding up the *Patagonia* on a serious and complicated charge of inaccuracy in the ship's manifest.

'Alonso provided him with coffee and a brandy, and asked for details. It appeared that crates of sheet rubber landed at Vigo did not correspond to their proper weight and description. The Customs suspected them of containing arms. They had been shipped from Pernambuco.'

Bernard Vasey looked at the Port Security Officer and was satisfied by his reaction. His account of the agent's irruption into lunch was quite true except for one detail. The crates had in fact been shipped from Rio. But he had noticed that his interrogator was allowing his attention to wander; it was essential that he should be convinced that every word was worth the hearing. For that reason Vasey deliberately injected the mention of Pernambuco, and was gratified to watch the expressionless face across the desk become even more expressionless.

'Alonso at once sprang into action, eager as always to help the underdog in any clash with officialdom. He cursed the Customs and said that they were inclined to see bogeys under their beds; their informants were the dregs of the port and notoriously unreliable. He implored the Agent not to be impatient with his country's bureaucracy. It must be allowed to look ridiculous sometimes. That was the price a business man had to pay for orderly government. He could not intervene, but—since the matter could be said to concern the security of the State—at least he had the power to order the political branch of the police to investigate at once; they would see that the ship was not delayed a moment longer than was necessary to clear up this ridiculous rumour.

'I was sorry that my friend should be drawn into all this, but it was luck for me. When the Agent had left and Alonso had made a long telephone call to his office, we drove to his delightful bachelor home on the shore of the inner harbour where we passed an hour or more with a swim, cool drinks in the shade and the exclamatory conversation of old friendship. I was no longer anxious when I heard the distant bellowing of the *Patagonia*, for Alonso was in continual touch with her. He said that there might even be time—knowing the Customs—for us to dine before the ship sailed. Anyway, he had asked a few friends out to meet me.

"Meanwhile his valet had been giving skilled attention to this suit, still spotted by the mildew of the rain forests and the nourishing soup of the *Patagonia* . . .'

'You said this friend of yours was about your size, Mr Vasey?'

'Near enough. Slightly broader shoulders and less backside.'

'Why did he not lend you a coat of his own for this party?'

'That, Inspector, would have been an indelicacy. It would have shown that he had noticed and was ashamed.

'I was about to speak, I believe, of the party. There were two girls and one man. I will describe the man first, distinguishing him by the name of Juan. He had some connection with the family, and was undoubtedly a political boss and Alonso's protector in high places. He must have been in his early fifties and looked it, though at the moment on holiday. He was a formidable fellow, somewhat like a frog—yellow and wrinkled, with bags under his eyes. It was clear that he had often heard of me from Alonso.

'The girls were charming. When Spanish women get away from mother, Inspector, they are inclined to increase the distance rapidly. Frasquita was a poetess in a small way and descended from everybody who had ever mattered. Her real claims to distinction, however, were delicately physical. Luisa was a secretary in Alonso's office. To the simple taste of a wider public she might have appeared a trifle severe in type. But a tiny waist and high intelligence amply compensated for what I may call her white-collar qualities . . .'

'If you would come to the point, Mr Vasey. I am quite ready to assume that there was a mixed party.'

'I fear my story is still some pleasant hours away from its point, Inspector, but I will pass over them as quickly as I can. Meanwhile let us not forget those twenty-five thousand tons of *Patagonia*, frantically calling on the British Consul for help, radioing her home port and subject to the inquisitions of what liberals call a police state and authoritarians a benevolent dictatorship. To make matters worse, the *Patagonia* cherished in her luxury suite the Managing Director of the Line, impatient as any other tycoon returning from holiday.

'In order not to delay the ship, Alonso had cut right through all red tape and simply ordered the dubious crates to be hoisted back on board; they could be unloaded, after giving the customs time for reflection, two weeks later when the *Patagonia* called again at Vigo on her outward voyage to the Americas.

'I am surprised that the Line did not accept that very reasonable solution. Perhaps it wished to, and couldn't. The Managing Director may have been determined to impress both his wife and his captain by a display of obstinacy. The Customs may have complained that Alonso had no right to order any such thing.

'However it was, we had another visit from the distracted Agent. Alonso was once more as helpful as a civil servant could be. He waived all formalities and said that of course the crates could be unloaded again if the Agent could rustle up some dock labour to handle them at that late hour. No doubt a foreman and a gang could be found in the taverns. He guaranteed that the Port Authority and the Workers' Syndicate would have no objection. He offered the assistance of his police. Everything possible would be done to help the *Patagonia* out of the mess which those nitwits who called themselves Customs Officers had made.

'I could not help feeling sorry for the ship, Inspector, though my interest in her, as a mere passenger in the slave hold, was limited. All those first-class passengers, those pointedly virile officers in white and gold, those state-rooms with private balconies, those lounges and bars which my imagination—for I hadn't seen them—clothed most gloriously with panelling and tapestries! All that urgent cargo for which you here had booked the cranes, the labour and the transport! When one thinks of the expense of it all and the charges for demurrage, one asks oneself—at least I do—whether the Line should not have handed over some vast guarantee and cleared the ship. But Latins can be difficult when they stick to the letter of the law.

'It began to look as if I might be able to stay to dinner, though in Spain that meal is seldom taken before ten. Meanwhile the five of us settled down to a game of poker . . .'

'Assuming that your story is true, Mr Vasey, how did you sit down to poker with no money in your pocket?'

'Alonso financed me, Inspector. I had flatly refused to take a loan from him or any assistance whatever, for I wouldn't have him think that I had come ashore for that purpose. But I could hardly sit watching the game like an empty juke-box. Politeness compelled me to accept a stake.'

'It was at this game that you claim to have won?'

'I did. At the time I put it down to being somewhat more sober than Alonso and Juan. I now think that unlikely. Indeed, I am regrettably certain that Alonso had arranged that they should lose to me whenever it could be done without arousing my suspicion.

'That was all the easier since our rules were complicated. The two ladies were playing strip poker when they lost and for money when they won. It worked out to the general satisfaction. Luisa, for example, holding a full house against Juan's four twos raised him with all her cash winnings and continued to raise him on the alternative terms. Since she was a respectable secretary, the position, though not without its piquancy, was embarrassing. On the next hand, we all threw in to her pair of kings, and thenceforth could reasonably consider her heightened colour to be due to Alonso's flow of liquor.

'I had just cleaned up a jack-pot of fifteen thousand pesetas and the poetess was looking charmingly like Botticelli's Aphrodite—a picture, Inspector, but you will have found variations of the same theme on confiscated postcards—when Alonso was called to the telephone. He came back folding and unfolding his hands—his favourite gesture when life was getting him down—and said that we should have to leave to catch the *Patagonia*. He apologized to me and to us all. When I asked him why the devil he should feel it was his fault, he replied that the fact was . . . but this is so important that I will give you the ensuing conversation in direct speech, translating freely but with scrupulous accuracy.

' "The fact is, Bernardo, that she can't sail till I allow it,' " he explained, "but I have now run out of excuses for holding her. And here we are sitting down to a really promising evening with dinner nearly ready! Why do British Lines have to be so infernally correct that one can't get anything on them?"

' "The hell they're correct!" Juan said (he must have been a brilliant administrator—he didn't even have to stop and think). "I understand that there is a passenger missing from the *Patagonia*."

' "That wouldn't stop her sailing without him," Alonso replied.

' "We should have a case if he were a very undesirable immigrant. Have you ever been a member of the Communist party?" he asked, turning on me fiercely.

'The bags under his eyes were frightening. They filled out when he was interrogating a suspect. I said I had nothing to do with communism. For the moment I took him quite seriously. I was still trying to adjust myself to the revelation that all the *Patagonia*'s troubles had been engineered by Alonso.

' "Have you ever been in Cuba?"

' "Not since Castro. I was there a few weeks before." '

' "A few weeks before!" Juan exclaimed. "Did you hear that, Alonso? He is probably responsible for the whole thing. We can't have a dangerous revolutionary of that sort loose in Spain. Hold the ship until the police find him!" '

' "I still don't see how I can, Juan." '

' "Have they reported a passenger missing?" '

' "No, they haven't." '

' "Deliberately permitting the escape of a political, Alonso?" '

' "It demands the closest investigation. I will hold the captain personally responsible. Or should it be the purser?" '

' "Damned if I know! Let Port Police sort it out!" '

' "What about the British Consul, Juan?" '

' "What about him? Order someone with imagination to call on him at once and whisper Cuba loudly! Tell him that it is absolutely essential that the fellow be found and put on board the *Patagonia*. We don't want to have to shoot him. Your deal, Frasquita, and remember what Bernardo told you about never drawing to the middle of a straight." '

'Inspector, it was dawn when the police found me wandering in the sort of street to which a drunk would naturally gravitate. After repeatedly embracing me, Alonso and Juan had turned me out of their car on to the pavement. They apologized for the unavoidable indignity and assured me that the police had orders to treat me with respect when I was picked up. In fact they continued to apologize in such loud voices that windows were opening and I had to beg them to drive off before they were compromised.

'Five minutes later I was asked for my papers by two unpleasant individuals in plain clothes. They arrested me triumphantly. I was hardly treated with respect. Firm but genial contempt for an intoxicated barbarian was the general tone. From the police station I was marched on board the *Patagonia*.

'There under the British flag the flow of language was regrettable. The jurisdiction of ship's masters is extensive, but they do not take advantage of it, Inspector, to prosecute their officers for public obscenity. My cabin door was locked upon me and only opened when we were safely at sea. That was well into the morning. Naturally the Port Offices had to open before the ship could be cleared.'

'Very interesting, Mr Vasey. And the presents?'

'Oh, the presents! Yes, the presents. I can't help feeling that without them the Line might never have recommended that you should grill me. They would have written me off as just another irresponsible drunk who had missed his ship and aroused suspicion. But the presents were the last straw.

'Just before the *Patagonia* sailed, they had all been deposited in the First Class, outside the Purser's office. Such delightful baskets! Such ribbons in the red and yellow of Spain! The Purser naturally assumed that they were intended for the Managing Director of the Line, and delivered them to his state-room. So when the director had read and with difficulty believed the name to which all this film-star loot was addressed, insult was added to demurrage.

'My cabin was unlocked to admit a procession of grinning stewards who deposited the stuff on the opposite bunk, fortunately empty. Alonso must have ordered the lot well beforehand, but I have no doubt at all that it was Juan, still in an expansive mood and with the hangover yet to come, who insisted on the cards bearing the inscription: Comrade Bernardo Vasey, from his international admirers.

'May I catch my train now, Inspector?'

ENGLAND

TWILIGHT OF A GOD

Sir Matthew's eyes were keen and humorous as those of a robin waiting by the spade for worms, and shielded from the sun by enormous pepper-and-salt eyebrows. Only a man whose former work and present hobby were connected with the ground under his feet could have permitted such luxuriant growth without ever finding it inconvenient.

The contractor's temporary fencing sagged as he leaned his weight on it, watching the clearance of a building site in the main street of his village. Fifteen feet below him the open jaws of a scoop had just begun to crunch and lift a pile of debris. Without the least hesitation he squashed the fence to a negotiable angle and charged straight down the slope of rubble and broken brick. The scoop clanged shut a yard from his right ear.

'Closish shave, that, guv'nor!' said the dry, weary voice of a foreman from the lip of the excavation.

'Miles to spare,' Matthew Fowlsey answered cheerfully, cleaning the earth from a tile which he had rescued.

'Didn't stop to think, did you, what would 'appen to me if your 'ead was in the truck?'

'He knows his job,' Fowlsey said, pointing to the crane cabin. 'He could take your hat off with that scoop without spoiling your parting. So could I.'

'In the contracting business yourself?'

'No. Oil. Before I retired.'

'Don't wonder they wear tin 'ats on the job. Wotcha got there?'

'A Roman tile. I thought I saw two Ds scratched on it. And I did.'

'Writing, like?'

'With the point of a sword, perhaps. I don't think he could have cut so deep with a stylus.'

'Ain't come across a two-inch grease nipple with a screw thread, 'ave you?'

Fowlsey retired under his eyebrows and searched the ground beneath the crane. 'Here it is,' he said.

'Cor! I was lookin' for that little bastard 'alf an hour last night.'

Matthew Fowlsey returned home with his tile and was greeted by his wife with a cheerful cry that lunch was ready. Assuring her that he would not be a moment, he retired to his study. The slow revelations of his soapy water, solvents and acids were more interesting than the shouted appeals which he automatically answered. Lunch could wait.

Three-quarters of an hour later he appeared in the dining-room carrying the tile. 'Muriel! My Muriel! Vagliodunum! It is Prior's Norton, my dear. I picked this up from a hole in the main street. The grafitto of a legionary! Roughly translated, it means "God Rot Vagliodunum!"'

'If Vagliodunum is Prior's Norton, Matthew, I entirely agree with him,' Muriel said, and left the room.

There was a cold mess on the table which had been a soufflé, and a stew on the sideboard which he recognized—though it was now glazed with cold grease—as a very creditable shot at his favourite Persian dish. Darling Muriel! Damn—and she wouldn't cool down till evening!

Ever since Fowlsey discovered a gold coin of Alexander the Great in the stomach of a Caucasian wild goat he had realized that archaeology was the ideal hobby for a mining engineer—though at the time his interest had been in the goat's diet. He polished his classics and mastered the scripts, ancient and modern, of the Middle East till his opinions aroused as much curiosity among dons as prospectors. Always more fascinated by discovery than finance, he had retired with a knighthood but only a comfortable pension. He was thoroughly happy. Living in Prior's Norton was a new experience—perhaps, he admitted, a little too new for Muriel.

Sir Matthew washed up the dishes, picked roses from the garden and deployed upon his wife that charm which, in pursuit of his hobby, had always overwhelmed authority from Ministers of Culture to headmen of villages. Having won her smiling permission to invite Charles Kinsale over from Oxford for a couple of nights, he picked up the telephone and dictated a long wire.

Kinsale's reply was uncompromising but satisfactory: DON'T BELIEVE A WORD OF IT BUT SHALL COME FOR MURIEL AND SAUSAGES.

'Charles believes in nothing,' Sir Matthew complained, 'but the Later Roman Empire and his own belly.'

'That makes him very easy to entertain, my dear.'

The Prior's Norton sausages were unique. They lent themselves to grilling rather than frying and were temperamental at that, but Muriel—aided by the advice of Miss Mallaby who kept a tea-shop on the main street—had brought the art of cooking them to perfection. Friends from more spacious days angled for invitations to a meal as if the Fowlseys were still cossetted by a host of native cooks and houseboys.

Charles Kinsale arrived early the following afternoon. After complimenting Muriel with lengthy eighteenth-century politeness he was dragged off impatiently to the study. He was a much younger man than his host, but lacked the air of youth which irradiated Sir Matthew. When he made a definite statement it was so, and a waste of time to try to prove it wasn't.

'I have looked up everything known about Vagliodunum, Matthew,' he said modestly. 'The site is unidentified. According to the Antonine Itinerary it should be about eight and a half miles south of here.'

'That site has been excavated.'

'Really? By whom?' Kinsale's voice rose to an academic falsetto of disbelief.

'It's in the middle of a brickfield,' said Fowlsey.

'Very well, Matthew. Quite. But that does not help us. Now, I agree that the scribbler on your tile was Italian. So there is a possibility—we can put it no higher—that he was a soldier. All he tells us is that he disliked Vagliodunum. He does *not* tell us that Vagliodunum is Prior's Norton.'

'Yes, he does. Soldiers curse the place they happen to be stationed, not the place where they were stationed before.'

'Is that fact or conjecture?'

'Fact,' replied Sir Matthew boldly, aware that there might be exceptions to this rule but that this was not the occasion to elaborate them.

'I will make a note of it. Now, I have another scrap of information for you. There is a fragment of a fourth-century geographer dealing with Roman Britain. It is believed by Hasensohren—who is sometimes inspired—to come from an Alexandrian commentary on the earlier geography of Marinus.'

'The Marinus who was also used by Ptolemy?' Sir Matthew asked, scoring a point.

'Quite. The text of the fragment is corrupt. Vagliodunum is a possible but not a very likely reading. But whatever town he is talking about had a considerable Temple of Mithras—for goodness sake don't jump to conclusions, Matthew!—two hundred paces to the right of the cross as you come from the south-east.'

'That would put it under the church,' Fowlsey exclaimed. 'The market cross is the Roman cross-roads. Come on! Let's go!'

Prior's Norton lay in a shallow, green valley between limestone hills. Its main street, running over well drained gravel above the stream, had been constantly used by man from palaeolithic hunters to the excavators of the hole where Sir Matthew had found his tile. The lane which crossed it at right angles, charging straight down one slope, over a paved ford and straight up the other, was Roman and nothing much else.

Kinsale, protesting, was led over the ford, by a white, wooden footbridge and up to the main street. To their right were the manor, the church and the vicarage; to their left, the village shops. Sir Matthew introduced his distinguished friend to the vicar, who politely pretended to have heard of him.

'Kinsale has some fascinating evidence that there is a Mithraeum under the church.'

'I am here,' Charles insisted sternly, 'merely in the hope of wealth. Sir Matthew's luck is fantastic. When it was his business to look for oil he found antiquities. Now that he is free to devote himself to archaeology, he will certainly strike oil. But there is no more chance of a Mithraeum under your church, vicar, than under my college.'

'A Mithraeum?' said the vicar. 'Well, I suppose it might be here if anywhere. So many churches are on the sites of older temples. Mithras—now, let me see . . .'

'Of Persian origin,' Kinsale expounded. 'The giver of life—intermediary between God and man. Like other mystical religions, Mithraism was very popular in the army and with old ladies. Baptism was by bull's blood. Some form of Mithraism might well be our religion today but for the accident that Christianity was better suited to the political system of Constantine.'

'And no doubt to other purposes well,' said the vicar. 'I remember now. It was a religion of great beauty. Perhaps it helped to prepare the way. Well, if there was ever a Mithraeum we ought to find some trace of it. The church is built on bed-rock, and we can get at the foundations.'

They could—just. But the space was less than five feet, too low to walk and too high to crawl. Fowlsey was enjoying himself on hands and knees; so, apparently, was the vicar. After half an hour of examining rock under the light of their torches Charles Kinsale, weary of repeating that all the chisel marks were medieval, considered that the vicar might have warned him what he was in for. It had possibly been tactless to mention Constantine, let alone the old ladies.

'So what do you think?' asked Fowlsey, when they returned to daylight covered with dust and cobwebs.

'That you should join the Boy Scouts, Matthew. No doubt they have a badge for proficiency in archaeology. Have you perhaps a clothes-brush, vicar, before we venture upon the main street of Sir Matthew's Vagliodunum?'

'You know, I'll tell you what happened,' Fowlsey said. 'Your geographer got turned inside out. Vagliodunum was a garrison town.'

'What the devil has that got to do with it?'

'He might have been dining in mess. Come on, they say, you're off in the morning but there's time to visit our Mithraeum and kill another bottle with the flute girl afterwards. Now, there's a round hill on each side of the valley, and both look reasonably alike. He wouldn't know which was which after dinner. When he said two hundred paces right of the cross, he meant left.'

'You are too inclined, Matthew, to judge our ancestors by yourself.'

'And a very good thing, too!'

'That would put it under dear Miss Mallaby's tea-shop,' said the vicar.

'Or under the Dog and Lobster. We'll pace it out.'

'Matthew, I have already told you . . .'

'I know. It isn't. And it couldn't be if it was. But all I want you to do, Charles, is to pace out two hundred yards and have a look at the cellars of the Dog and Lobster.'

'The pubs aren't open yet,' said Kinsale weakly.

'For the scholar all doors are open, Charles. Even among Kurds and Yezidis. And Mr Bunn is a Christian innkeeper who at the moment will be staking his sweet-peas.'

Prior's Norton was full of Friday afternoon shoppers. Sir Matthew marched along the curb, counting aloud up to two hundred and raising his hat to the bicyclists and pram-pushers whom he incommoded. He arrived precisely in front of Miss Mallaby's tea-shop. Her neat window, decorated by home-made jams, pickles, cakes and scones, preserved a lady-like propriety between the coarser attractions of the Dog and Lobster on one side and James Ing, Butcher and Licensed Gamedealer, on the other.

Mr Bunn was not exactly staking his sweet-peas, but he was in the garden thinking about it. After ten minutes' talk on the weather and control of slugs, Sir Matthew asked if they might inspect the cellars.

'Nothing down there but empties,' replied Mr Bunn, looking suspiciously at Kinsale. 'What's he an inspector of?'

'Nothing! Am I the sort of man, Mr Bunn, to set inspectors on my neighbours?'

'Well, sir, you haven't been here long enough for us to make you out, like. Not that I've anything against inspectors,' he added hastily. 'A quieter, more well-be'aved lot of gentlemen you couldn't want when they ain't writing in their little books.'

'Mr Kinsale is the greatest living authority on the Later Roman Empire . . .'

'Matthew, I . . .'

'Shut up! If I knew a better one, I'd send for him. His University of Oxford'—Mr Bunn's brewers were in Oxford, and he made a sort of grunt of profound respect—'is interested in the history of our village. What Mr Kinsale wants to see is if there is any trace of Roman masonry in your cellar.'

The cellars ran under the whole length of the Dog and Lobster. In front they appeared to have been dug out of the gravel and lined with stone. At the back they had been cut from the hillside.

'Well?' asked Sir Matthew eagerly.

135

'My dear fellow, when the ceiling of a rock cave has been white-washed over and over for several hundred years, it's impossible to say off-hand who cut it. What's through the brick wall on the right?'

'That's Ing, that is, beyond the wall,' Mr Bunn replied. 'It all belonged to the Dog and Lobster once, when the Mallabys kept it. Four hundred years, father to son, they were here. And that's only what they knows of.'

'Miss Mallaby hasn't any cellars then?'

'What would she want with a cellar? Why, Ing and me, we don't use what we've got. No, she just owns the shop which 'er grandfather made for 'er when she wouldn't take over the pub. And that reminds me. There's a few bottles in the vault there from 'er grandfather's day. Would you gentlemen like to tell me what's in 'em? I'm told they drink a lot of old wine in them colleges at Oxford.'

'In moderation,' said Kinsale. 'In moderation. Don't wave it about, Mr Bunn! Here—let me!'

Borrowing Mr Bunn's corkscrew, he opened the first bottle with reverent care. It was dead and undrinkable. So were the next two. But the fourth was a brown sherry in the flower of great age.

'Prefer a drop of Scotch myself,' said Mr Bunn, tasting it with disapproval. 'But if you gentlemen are that 'appy with it, why, you can't do better than finish it up!' He refilled the tumblers.

'Any more bottles of it?' asked Kinsale.

'No. Nothing 'ere but what you can see.'

Mr Bunn whacked the back of the vault with a brewer's mallet. 'Solid!' he said regretfully. 'Solid rock!'

Half an hour later Fowlsey and Kinsale emerged into the daylight, thanking Mr Bunn profusely and a little noisily.

'Now we will call on Miss Mallaby,' said Sir Matthew, pacing the length of her shop window and balancing himself with too obvious concentration as he placed one foot in front of the other along the narrow curb. 'That niche was Roman, damn it!'

'Might just conceivably be, Matthew,' shouted Kinsale. 'Not, I beg you, *is*!'

Miss Mallaby withdrew a plate of cakes from the window. She was tall and dark with a faint and greying moustache. She had a maiden lady's penetrating stare in which alarm and authority were equally mixed.

'And I am not calling on her with this breath, Matthew.'

'Perhaps you are right. To Ing then!'

'He is the man who makes the sausages?'

'He is.'

'Then at least I have the excuse of telling him what I think of them.'

Mr James Ing was evidently accustomed to enthusiastic compliments. He received them with a nervous dignity. For a butcher he seemed a reserved little man. He had the blue-striped apron, round face and ruddy complexion of his trade, but all in miniature. He consented to accept a monthly order for sausages to be sent by post. The distinguished address of Kinsale's college appeared to take a weight off his mind.

'Always like to know whom I'm dealing with,' he said. 'Can't be too careful with strangers.'

He was quite willing to show what was under his shop, and led them down a semi-circular staircase with a dark recess beneath it. The cellars were obviously a continuation of those of the Dog and Lobster.

Sir Matthew paced out the length. 'I make it an eighteen-inch wall between Mr Bunn and Mr Ing,' he announced. So Grandpa Mallaby sold the lot.'

'Why shouldn't he?' asked the butcher with a blank stare.

'No reason at all. What's through there?'

'Cold store,' replied Mr Ing, throwing open a door which closed one of the vaults in the inner wall.

'Containing,' Kinsale added impatiently, 'no departed Caesars, but two pigs, a bullock and a lamb.'

'Four sausages on the floor, two and a half pigs, a bullock and a sheep,' Sir Matthew corrected him.

'To a butcher all sheep are lambs.'

'No, they are not, sir, begging your pardon,' said Mr Ing, 'not when a customer asks for mutton.'

After a long walk up the lane which once had been a Roman highway, Sir Matthew and Charles Kinsale regained a Roman dignity. When they returned home in the cool of the evening, the house smelled delectably of the famous sausages. They carried a martini for Muriel into the kitchen. She did not seem to be responding correctly to their compliments and attention.

'My dears,' she said, 'Miss Mallaby has been here.'

'Oh, ginger cake—good!' Sir Matthew exclaimed.

'I am afraid you have upset her rather badly. You have been staring at her shop and bothering Ing and Bunn.'

'What's the matter with the woman? There's nothing alarming in archaeology. Even Kurds and Yezidis . . .'

'But not an English village, dear. And you never know how loud your voice is.'

'I didn't say anything. I never went near Miss Mallaby. Charles looked at her through the window.'

'You were measuring it, Matthew,' said Charles promptly.

'Well, what about it?'

'Don't boom at me, dear. Are you sure you were both quite . . .'

'Muriel!' exclaimed Charles Kinsale, much shocked. 'The pubs

137

were not open, and the vicar didn't offer us anything.'

'Yes, of course. Perhaps I misunderstood Miss Mallaby. She was so very agitated. But if you *have* to excavate the only shops in the village who ever have anything fit to eat, Matthew, do let me handle it for you!'

'Excavation,' said Kinsale, using the full prestige of learning to divert the conversation to a higher level. 'I always feel it is a tragedy. A hundred years hence they will do it so much better.'

He continued to lecture, changing the subject when the bronze mound of sausages was on the table, from archaeology to analysis of flavour.

'Sage and pork of course,' he murmured after his fifth, 'and there is a suggestion that somewhere along the line of ancestry was a black pudding. But am I a medieval schoolman that I should discourse upon the ingredients of heaven? For the moment they are supplied by Muriel and James Ing—whose efforts you, my dear Matthew, like an amiable and attendant angel, have underlined by this admirable claret.'

When Muriel had left them alone with it, Sir Matthew refilled the glasses. 'Very nicely to the rescue, Charles! Damn Miss Mallaby! But have you seriously been thinking of excavation?'

'Not for a moment! You have made your usual find with your usual luck. But excavation wouldn't produce any more sherry.'

'Sherry? The sherry, my good man, is a clue not a discovery! Mr Bunn was distracting our attention from his cellar to its contents. That was obvious to me when Muriel mentioned Miss Mallaby's visit. Why should she be driven to hysterics by my balancing feats upon the curb-stone?'

'I suggest she was subconsciously devastated by your physical attractions.'

'Nonsense! Miss Mallaby is grim, but sane. No, they are all hiding something, and it's behind the back wall which Bunn was so anxious to prove solid. In a remote spot like this the worship of Mithras might still be carried on.'

'With James Ing sacrificing the bull?'

'Pah! That's all forgotten. What I mean is a mild little centre of vague superstition with Miss Mallaby as presiding witch—except that she's a pillar of the church and runs the Women's Institute.'

'They generally do, Matthew. But covens are very rare. An illicit distillery would be more likely.'

'Then you agree they are hiding something?'

'The evidence is more convincing than for Vagliodunum.'

'Five minutes in Ing's cellar without Ing is all we need. Look here! Muriel will make a fuss that she wants mutton not lamb. James Ing will go down to the cold store to fetch the carcase.'

'This comes under the head of upsetting the housekeeping.'

'Hm, yes. I suppose it might. We'll leave Muriel out of it. Then I myself will order a leg of mutton. When Ing goes down, you tip-toe after him.'

'Damn it, Matthew, I draw the line at burglary.'

'It's only trespassing. While he is inside the cold store you hide under the stairs. Ing comes up with the carcass. When he has served me, he'll hang it up in the store again. I follow him down and join you under the stairs.'

'How and when do we get out?'

'Easy as pie. Whenever Ing comes down for meat and is safely inside the cold store again. Then we tip-toe up the stairs and walk boldly past the customers, if any, with our parcels.'

Next morning after breakfast Kinsale flatly refused to play his part; but Sir Matthew, aware from long experience that men of books invariably felt inferior to men of action, shamed him into it, and explained to Muriel that they intended to spend an hour or two at the excavation in the main street.

The butcher's was empty, for Prior's Norton did not do its shopping before eleven. All went well. Kinsale, started by a merciless push, vanished downstairs behind James Ing and did not reappear. After cutting and wrapping the leg of mutton, Ing returned to the cold store with the carcass. Sir Matthew prepared to follow him, but was interrupted by the vicar who wanted sausages, and two housewives in need only of conversation. It was no good hanging around the shop. He went over the road to talk to the foreman at the excavation.

At last Mr Ing got rid of his customers and took the opportunity to deliver a loin of pork to the Dog and Lobster. Sir Matthew strolled back across the road, entered the butcher's, looked out through the window to ensure that he was not observed and an instant later was in the cellar.

'You've been the devil of a time!' whispered Kinsale.

'Couldn't help it. Found anything?'

'Yes. There's a sliding door at the back of the cold store.'

'Where does it go?'

'Really, Matthew, I don't know,' replied Kinsale testily. 'We are responsible persons, not little boys on a treasure hunt. And any way the door was locked.'

'Oh, my God!' Matthew Fowlsey suddenly exclaimed, creeping up to the curve of the stair and listening.

'But I saw him go in, Mr Ing,' insisted Muriel's voice, 'when I was down the road, and I am sure he has not come out.'

'Indeed, madam?' James Ing answered politely.

The probable explanation appeared to dawn on him. He repeated with indignation: 'Indeed, madam!'

Determined steps sounded overhead. Sir Matthew dragged Kinsale into the cold store and shut the door.

'You don't know what it is,' he whispered frantically. 'You're not married. I've been told not to monkey, and I've monkeyed. I tell you, this could mean she'd go on strike and make me live in a flat in London!'

The sliding door at the back, partly hidden by the two halves of the bullock, was not noticeable at a glance, but not particularly secret. Mr Ing could well have bought a double-doored refrigerating unit cheap.

'I don't believe it goes anywhere,' Sir Matthew hissed. 'He got it off a bankrupt butcher and installed it as it was. Hell! It doesn't open. Hell!'

The handle on their side had been removed. He thrust the small blade of his pocket-knife into the socket and turned. The blade snapped, but a second operation with the stump did the trick. The steps of Muriel and James Ing were already audible in the cellar. He pushed Kinsale through the door and slid it shut again, breathing heavily.

Sir Matthew switched on his torch. They were in a long, narrow cellar under the hillside. To their left was a stone stair evidently leading into the back of Miss Mallaby's shop. The flags of the floor were spotlessly clean.

At one end of the cellar were various tubs and buckets; at the other was an immense butcher's slab of solid oak, scored and hollowed by long use. Knives and choppers were neatly laid out on the scrubbed surface. The delectable, spicy smell alone was enough to tell them that this was where Ing's sausages were made.

They stared at each other, completely puzzled. There was the click of a switch above the staircase. The cellar was lit up. Miss Mallaby, a formidable figure in black, stood upon the third step looking down on them.

'Sir Matthew,' she pronounced with dignity, 'I am quite prepared to be reported to the police. But I must request you to leave my premises immediately.'

She stood a little to one side, pointing to the way past her. Fowlsey and Kinsale were hypnotized into a slow march before the power of speech returned.

'B-b-but why should I report you to the police, Miss Mallaby?' Sir Matthew asked.

'I presume that now you are in possession of the evidence you will consider it your duty.'

'I still don't see . . .'

'Inspectors! I do!' Kinsale exclaimed. 'Making sausages of unknown ingredients upon unlicensed premises! Hygiene! Modernity!

Stainless steel! If the beaks knew Miss Mallaby was making sausages down here, they'd slap a fifty-pound fine on her. Good Lord, we ought to be hanged! May I assure you, madam, that you are a public benefactor and that nothing would induce either of us ever to open our mouths?'

'Then what are you gentlemen doing here?'

'Miss Mallaby, that arch over your head is very probably Roman. Your cellar was—I mean, may have been—cut out of the hillside some seventeen hundred years ago. That accounts for our curiosity, our perhaps discourteous curiosity. I am an authority upon the period. Sir Matthew is—er—a more general authority.'

'When you come to my age, madam,' said Sir Matthew pathetically, 'you will realize that it is most difficult to pace distances while preserving balance.'

'Oh, sir!' Miss Mallaby exclaimed, joining them on the floor. 'But you will understand my agitation. Only Mr Bunn and Mr Ing are in the secret.'

'But why run the risk, dear Miss Mallaby? Why not go into partnership with Ing?'

'My grandfather wished the dispensary to remain in the family,' Miss Mallaby explained stubbornly. 'The Mallabys, Sir Matthew, always took a pride in the preparation of comestibles. Everything which they sold or served in the inn was home-made on the premises. You will no doubt be surprised to learn that there is a reference to Mallaby's Faggots in the kitchen account of Queen Elizabeth.'

'These sausages did seem to me somehow out of Ing's character,' said Kinsale. 'An excellent fellow—but not the type to have a magic touch. How *do* you make them, Miss Mallaby?'

'Like everything else, it's a matter of care and exact measurements, Mr Kinsale.'

'Scholarship. Precisely! You hear that, Matthew? Unsound methods can only lead to the sort of blundering which Miss Mallaby has been good enough to overlook.'

'Yes, Charles. What does the Dog and Lobster remind you of?'

'Are you thinking of Dr Johnson's cat which ate oysters?'

'No, I'm not! There's a good reason for the name of every pub in England—usually the arms of some great family. But no arms have as supporters a dog and a lobster. Then some actual occurrence? A lobster, for example, which delighted the peasantry by catching hold of a dog's tail? But Prior's Norton is too far from the sea. I suggest that if the villagers, centuries ago, were familiar with the reliefs upon an altar of Mithras, they would have noticed his hound and scorpion.'

'Of all the wild, preposterous . . .' Kinsale began.

'Nonsense! The names of pubs are historical documents. It's the soundest piece of evidence I have produced yet. Miss Mallaby's ancestors had no idea of the origin of the altar. They couldn't move it. They were tired of the pictures. So they covered it up and put it to use. That faint suggestion of black pudding in the sausages—isn't one of the ingredients a little bullock's blood, Miss Mallaby?'

'I don't see how you guessed it wasn't pig's, Sir Matthew. But you are quite right.'

'And that is all which remains of a great religion after sixty generations,' Fowlsey declared. 'That, and a little of the power of the god, would you say, Charles? It was you who mentioned magic in the sausages.'

'I'd say—to use an Americanism—that you've gone nuts.'

'No. You are looking at the altar of Mithras.'

'Where?'

'There!' Sir Matthew shouted, pointing to the butcher's slab. 'There, where the bull died and gave life to the people!'

'Assuming that is the altar, the niches are in the right place,' said Charles as if he disbelieved his own voice.

'Miss Mallaby, may we?' begged Sir Matthew. 'Without letting another soul into the secret I can lift the casing off the altar with a block and tackle and do no damage to either.'

'I am afraid you would, for the dowel pins have shrunk. I think perhaps the front of the slab would come away if you were to extract them. No, not with that knife, if you please, Sir Matthew! I will fetch you a gimlet.'

'Madam, you must be the only woman in the world to realize that a gimlet can be used like a corkscrew to extract a wooden peg!'

'I have been compelled by circumstance,' said Miss Mallaby primly, 'to do all repairs to the cellar myself.'

Sir Matthew removed the dowels without much difficulty.

'If you will now lift the top slightly, Charles, the whole front will be free.'

The noble slab of oak fell down. There, cut in the marble of the altar, was the god Mithras slaying the bull. The reliefs, except to eyes familiar with the composition, were not immediately obvious. In the upper half, the knife, the bull's head and the face of the god were worn faint. But at the bottom the scorpion and the waiting hound were clear and vivid as if they had been chiselled the week before.

'There is only one other to be compared with it in all Europe,' said Charles reverently. 'Miss Mallaby, Miss Mallaby, what are we to do? Your cellar will become a place of pilgrimage.'

'The sooner the better, Mr Kinsale. No doubt Mr Ing and I will be able to come to some mutually profitable arrangement. Whatever my ancestors may have thought, *I* should not wish to continue making sausages upon a heathen altar, and I am sure the dear vicar would agree.'

THE GREEKS HAD
NO WORD FOR IT

'May I say ten pounds?' the auctioneer asked. 'Five? Thank you, madam . . . Six . . . Six, ten . . . Seven . . . Seven, ten . . . At seven pounds, ten. Going at seven pounds, ten. An ancient Greek drinking bowl of the best period. Going at . . .'

Sergeant Torbin had at last wandered into the auction because there was nothing else to do. It was early closing day at Falkstead, and the shops were shut. There was nowhere to sit but the edge of the quay, and nothing to watch but the brown tide beginning to race down to the North Sea between grey mud-banks. The only sign of animation in the little town was around the open front door of a small box-like eighteenth-century house, the contents of which were being sold.

'Eight!' said the sergeant nervously, and immediately realized that nothing could give a man such a sense of inferiority as a foreign auction.

But the atmosphere was quiet and decorous. The auctioneer acknowledged Bill Torbin's bid with a smile which managed to express both surprise and appreciation at seeing the United States Air Force uniform in so rural a setting. He might have been welcoming him to the local Church Hall.

'May I say eight, ten?'

A military-looking man, overwhelming in size and manner, nodded sharply.

Bill could hardly hope that the bowl was genuine. He liked it for itself. Angular black figures chased one another round the red terra-cotta curve. He recognized Perseus, holding up that final and appalling weapon, the Gorgon's head. Very appropriate. A benevolent goddess, who reminded Bill of his tall, straight mother, looked on approvingly.

He ran the bowl up to ten pounds. When the auctioneer's hammer was already in the air, he heard someone say: 'Guinness!'

There was a snap of triumph in the word, a suggestion that the whole sale had now come to a full stop. It was the military man again. To Sergeant Torbin he was the most terrifying type of native—a bulky chunk of brown tweed suit, with a pattern of orange and grey as pronounced as the Union Jack, and a red face and ginger moustache on top of it.

143

'It's against you, sir,' the auctioneer told him hopefully.

Bill knew that much already. But the mysterious word 'Guinness' sounded as if it had raised the ante to the moon. He panicked. He decided that he had no business in auctions. After all, he had only been in England a week and had come to Falkstead on his first free afternoon because it looked such a quiet little heaven from the train.

'Going at ten guineas . . . At ten guineas . . . Sold at ten guineas!'

Hell, he ought to have guessed that! But who would think that guineas would pop up at auctions when they belonged in the time of George III? Bill Torbin walked out and sat on the low wall which separated the garden from the road, conducting a furious auction with himself while he waited for the 6.30 train back to his bleak East Anglian airfield.

He had just reached the magnificent and imaginary bid of One Hundred Goddam Guineas when the tweed suit rolled down the garden path with the drinking bowl under its arm.

'Nice work, colonel!' Bill said, for at last he had an excuse to talk to somebody.

'Oh, it's you, is it? I say, you didn't want it, did you?'

The sergeant thought that was the damn silliest question he had ever heard. He realized, however, that it was meant as a kind of apology.

'British Museum stiff with 'em!'

Again he got the sense. The Englishman was disclaiming any special value for his purchase. Bill asked if the bowl were genuine.

'Good Lord, yes! A fifth-century Athenian cylix! The old vicar had it vetted. His father picked it up in Istanbul during the Crimean War. That was the late vicar's late niece's stuff they were selling. Have a look for yourself!'

Sergeant Torbin took the bowl in his hands with reverent precautions. Round the bottom, which he had not seen before, two winged horses pulled a chariot. He wondered what on earth he would ever have dared to do with so exquisite a piece if he had bought it. He might have presented it to the squadron but, like himself, the squadron had no safe place to keep it.

'How the devil did you know I was a colonel?'

Bill did not like to say that he couldn't possibly be anything else unless it were a general, but he was saved by the bell. The church clock struck six.

'Ah, they'll be opening now,' said the colonel with satisfaction. 'How about a drink?'

Bill Torbin murmured doubtfully that his train left at 6.30. The colonel announced that Falkstead station was only two minutes from the pub, and that he himself had often done it in eighty seconds flat. Considering the noble expanse of checked waistcoat, Bill thought it

144

unlikely. But you never knew with these tough old Englishmen. Half of the weight might be muscle.

The colonel led the way to The Greyhound. It was a handsome little pub, built of white weather-boarding with green shutters, but Torbin had no eyes for it. He was watching the precious cylix, which was being swung by one of its handles as carelessly as if it had been a cheap ash-tray. The sergeant decided that the British had no reverence for any antiquities but their own.

In the bar were four cheerful citizens of Falkstead drinking whisky, two boat-builders drinking beer with the foreman of the yard, and, at a table near the window, the auctioneer and his clerk keeping up respectability with The Greyhound's best sherry. The colonel, disconcertingly changing his manner again, greeted the lot of them as if he had just arrived from crossing the North Sea single-handed, and enthroned the cylix on the bar.

'What have you got there, Colonel Wagstaff?' the innkeeper asked.

'That, Mr Watson, is a Greek drinking bowl.'

'Never saw 'em used,' Mr Watson answered, 'not when I was a corporal out there.'

Wagstaff explained that it was an old one, which possibly had not been used for two thousand years.

'Two thousand four hundred,' said the auctioneer, taking his pipe out of his mouth, 'at the very least.'

'Time it was!' Mr Watson exclaimed heartily.

'What are you going to put in it?' the colonel asked.

'Who? Me?' Watson said, not expecting to be taken literally.

'But you can't start drinking out of it!' Bill protested.

'It's what it is for, isn't it?'

'And an unforgettable experience for our American friend,' said the auctioneer patronizingly, 'to drink from the same cup as Socrates—or at any rate someone who knew the old boy.'

'Well, seeing as it's this once,' Mr Watson agreed, 'what would you say, colonel?'

'That Burgundy which you bought for the summer visitors is quite drinkable.'

The cylix was about two inches deep, and just held the bottle which Mr Watson emptied into it. The terracotta flushed under the wine. The figures blossomed.

'See?' said Colonel Wagstaff. 'Like rain in a dry garden!'

The company gathered round the bar. Wagstaff raised the bowl in both hands and took a hearty pull.

'Tastes a bit odd,' he remarked, passing it on to Torbin. 'Still, you can't have everything.'

The loving cup went round the eleven of them and Mr Watson.

'Fill her up again,' said the auctioneer.

The next round was the colonel's, and after that there was a queue for the fascinating honour.

'If you take the 7.45 bus to Chesterford,' Colonel Wagstaff suggested, 'there's sure to be a train from there.'

Bill was beginning to feel for the first time that England had human beings in it. But it was not the facile good-fellowship which persuaded him to wait for the bus. The bowl had become a local possession, and The Greyhound a club in which he was welcome to drink but might not pay. He was jealous. He could not bring himself to leave his goddess skittering along the bar in pools of Burgundy without his own hands ready to catch her.

The auctioneer said a fatherly good-bye to all, trod upon his bowler hat and left. Bill was astonished at the dignity with which he ignored his oversight and knocked out the dent. He looked at the clock. He felt bound to mention that it was 7.40.

'By Jove, so it is!' said the colonel, taking his moustache out of the bowl.

Till 7.45 he addressed them shortly on the value of punctuality in the military life, and then they all piled out into the street, led by Colonel Wagstaff, the bowl and Sergeant Torbin, and cantered through the village to the yard of the Drill Hall where the Chesterford bus was waiting.

It was a typical, dead, East Anglian bus stop on the edge of the North Sea marshes. The bus was not lit up, and there was no sign of the driver. The colonel swore it was a disgrace and that Sergeant Torbin would never catch his train at Chesterford.

'What time does it go?' Bill asked.

'I don't know. But you might very easily miss it. It's a damned shame! Here's a gallant ally trusting conscientiously to the Chesterford Corporation to get him to camp before midnight, and he lands in the guardroom because their bloody buses can't run to time! I've a good mind to teach them a lesson. Anyone want to go to Chesterford?'

About half a dozen of them agreed that it would be a reasonable act of protest to run the bus themselves, whether they wanted to go to Chesterford or not.

Wagstaff opened the driver's door and switched on all the lights. Bill was fresh from a lecture in which he had been told to behave in England with the formality of the English. He decided that he had better be American and hire a car. But the colonel had tossed the bowl on to the driving seat and was just about to sit on it. Bill rescued it with a quarter of an inch to spare, and found himself on the way to Chesterford.

The colonel was roaring along between the hedges when the auctioneer's clerk leaned forward and tapped Bill on the shoulder.

'Sergeant,' he said. 'It is 8.45 the bus starts, not 7.45. You had better go back and catch it.'

Wagstaff jumped on the brake, and Sergeant Torbin just managed to save the bowl from violent contact with the dashboard. Several of the passengers slid on to the floor, where they continued to sing 'Down Mexico Way' half a bar behind the rest.

'So it is,' the colonel exclaimed. 'Changed it last week! Well, I'll teach 'em to monkey with the timetable.' And he let in the clutch, cursed the gears, found top and put his foot down.

Bill was still wondering whether the auctioneer's clerk was sober or whether his liquor just made him more clerkly, when the man leaned forward again and tapped the colonel. 'Has it occurred to you, sir,' he suggested precisely, 'that it might be thought you had stolen a corporation bus?'

Sergeant Torbin cuddled the bowl, and this time only bumped his elbow.

'We'll get out here, chaps,' the colonel said, pulling up so close to the hedge that they couldn't and had to get out by the driver's door— all except the boat-builder's foreman who broke the glass over the emergency exit and managed to make it work. 'The Bull is just up the road.'

The Bull was a small riverside pub, empty except for two farm hands and a ferryman. It fulfilled, far better than The Greyhound, all Bill's expectations of the quiet English inn.

'Mr Baker and gentlemen,' Wagstaff announced from the head of the procession, 'we are celebrating the acquisition of a Greek drinking bowl. Could we allow it to go to America? Never!'

'Say, why not?' Bill asked.

'Because they don't drink wine in America. They drink gin.'

Bill was about to say that it was not true, and that works of art were appreciated a darn sight more than . . . but he was too late.

'What's wrong with filling her up with gin?' asked the boat-builder's foreman.

'Neat?' protested Mr Baker.

'It is indeed long,' said the colonel, 'since she was accustomed to those heights of felicity where you, Mr Baker, would be legally bound to refuse to serve us. So slowly, slowly. Gin and tonic. Half and half. Old Greek custom. Always put water with it. Not the men we are today.' And he began to sing 'Land of Our Fathers' at the top of his voice.

Mr Baker had just filled the bowl when Torbin's ear, trained by conversation in the presence of jet engines, heard the bus draw up outside. He shouted the news at Wagstaff.

The colonel sprang into action. 'Right, Bill! Our fault! Won't get you mixed up in it!'

147

He pushed the sergeant on to the window-seat, made him lie down and covered his uniform with a couple of overcoats. When the bus driver, accompanied by a full load of cops from a police car, crashed through the door, he was kneeling at Bill's side and bathing his forehead with gin and tonic out of the bowl.

'Now which of you gentlemen—' a policeman began.

The colonel kept his handkerchief firmly over Bill's mouth and explained in a voice which was the very perfection of quiet respectability that he had bought a priceless Athenian cylix at the late vicar's late niece's auction, and that an American art dealer had endeavoured to steal it from him outside The Greyhound.

Foiled by these gallant citizens and especially by this poor fellow— he tenderly mopped Bill's forehead with gin—the art dealer had made his escape in a corporation bus. They followed, some on foot, some clinging to the vehicle. The bus stopped suddenly just down the road, and the fellow bolted into the darkness before they could get hold of him.

'There was a tall, dark American sergeant in Falkstead this afternoon,' said another cop.

They all swore that it wasn't the sergeant. No, a civilian. A little, fairish chap.

'And six of you couldn't stop him?'

'He had a gun,' said the boat-builder's foreman, and choked into his handkerchief.

The bus driver, having no official duty to believe unanimous witnesses, went straight to the point which interested him.

'Which of you blokes broke the window above the emergency door?'

'I did,' answered the colonel magnificently. 'It was an emergency.'

Mr Baker polished glasses and said nothing. The ferryman and two farm hands waited patiently for free drinks. After telephoning a description of the art dealer to county headquarters, the police escorted the bus back to Falkstead.

'Now, Bill,' said the colonel, 'be reasonable! Whatever is the use of having allies if one can't put the blame on them?'

'Hell!' Bill replied, and accidentally kicked over the bowl which was on the floor at his feet. He picked it up and glared protectively at the lot of them.

'Bill, you have upset these gentlemen's liquor.'

Sergeant Torbin was in honour bound to have her filled up again. He discovered that he was delighted to do so, and reminded his conscience that the Athenian potter must have designed his wares to stand up to an evening's amusement.

What with one of them pointing out that the horses at the bottom seemed to trot whenever the tonic water fizzed on to the gin, and another swearing it was possible to hold a full bowl by one handle without spilling any—which it wasn't—the strength of the cylix was certainly astonishing. Mr Baker put the auctioneer's clerk to bed upstairs—explaining that he didn't want his house to get a bad name by turning him loose on the road—and that left Bill aware that he was the only member of the party with any worry at all in the back of his mind. Not that he hadn't been drinking his share. But in early days at The Greyhound, when the rest of them had been laying a foundation of Burgundy as if it were beer, he was too overcome by his respect for the bowl to commit more than a reverent sip whenever it came round to him.

At 9.30 he suggested that he ought to telephone for a taxi.

'Don't you bother!' the colonel said. 'We'll cross the ferry here, and then it's only half a mile to the junction. He'll get a train from there, won't he, Mr Baker?'

Mr Baker consulted a sheet behind the bar, and said pointedly that if he hurried, he would.

They all piled out on to the landing-stage, and Mr Baker locked up the bar though there was half an hour to go before closing-time. The ferryman unchained his punt, and twice took Bill and the colonel nearly over to the other side. The first time he turned round in midstream without noticing it, and the second time he had to put back because the boat-builder's foreman had fallen off the jetty while waving good-bye.

Bill and Colonel Wagstaff landed and set off along the creek-side path in single file—until, that is, Bill noticed that Wagstaff had left the bowl behind in the punt.

'Now, see here, colonel,' Bill recommended when they had recovered it, 'you let me carry that!'

'OK,' said the colonel. 'Catch!'

After a quarter of a mile, Wagstaff, who was leading, sat down on a tussock of grass and began to laugh. 'Bill—Guineas!'

Bill grunted. He had reached the sentimental stage of liquor, and his eyes were dramatically wet as soon as he was reminded that for a dollar and a half and a little courage he could have saved a priceless possession from the inevitable smash.

'Not fair! I knew guineas would fox you. Unsporting to take advantage of an ally. Funny at the time, yes! Bill, I present you with the bowl.'

'No, colonel, I won't take her.'

'Got to take her.'

'Say, we've had a lot to drink, and—'

'Boy, I was military attaché in Moscow.'

'Well, that sure makes a difference, colonel, but—'

It did. By the standards of his experience, Bill could not describe the colonel as drunk. He was merely incalculable.

'Also,' said Wagstaff repentantly, 'I have used it as a common utensil.'

'Not yet,' Bill answered. 'I guess you would if I wasn't carrying it.'

'But from now on it is yours.'

'Then you let me pay for it,' said Bill, handing the bowl to the colonel and feeling for his wallet.

'Not allowed to pay for it. That's an order from a superior officer. Even in retirement, sergeant, certain privileges attach themselves to—'

'Order, my foot!'

'If you won't take it, I'll pitch the bloody thing in the river.'

'Go on! You pitch it!'

The colonel did, with a neat back-handed action of the wrist. The cylix flew like a discus into the darkness and landed with a plop on the tidal mud.

Bill Torbin, after one horrified stare at the personified obstinacy of the English, drunk or sober, plunged after it. He squelched out towards the water, while the smell of primeval slime rose from the pits where his legs had been.

The sounds of progress became less violent. There was silence, except for the shunting of a distant train.

'Colonel, I'm stuck,' Bill said.

'Nothing to bother about, boy! We're used to it round these parts. Lie on your stomach!'

'I can't. I'm up to my chest.'

'Hard under foot?'

'I wouldn't be talking to you if it wasn't.'

'Then I'll come and pull you out.'

The colonel advanced over his knees and took off his coat. Keeping hold of one sleeve, he swung the other over to Bill. Between cuff and cuff were a good eight feet.

'I think I see her,' Bill said. 'You pull me clear and then I'll sort of swim.'

Wagstaff pulled. The sergeant emerged as far as the thighs, and flung himself forward down the slope. The object was an old white-enamelled basin with a hole in it.

Bill managed to turn, and floundered back like a stranded porpoise until the choice between sinking head first or feet first became urgent. The colonel took a step forward and flung the coat again. He, too, went in up to his chest.

'I guess this mud is covered at high water,' Bill said after a pause.

'Float a battleship!' Wagstaff agreed cheerfully. 'But there's an hour in the ebb still. Nothing to worry about. Round here everybody knows where everybody is.'

150

'Well, if you say so, colonel.'

'If I'm not home when the pubs shut,' Wagstaff explained, 'my housekeeper will telephone The Greyhound because she was expecting me home to dinner. Mr Watson will telephone Mr Baker. Mr Baker will telephone the junction. The stationmaster will say we never arrived, and somebody will come and look for us. You'll see. Cold, this mud isn't it?'

The comment struck Sergeant Torbin's mixed drinks as excessively funny. He began to hoot with laughter. The colonel, after two or three staccato explosions like an ancient truck protesting against the starting handle, warmed up and joined the racket an octave lower.

'But you shouldn't . . . you shouldn't . . .' yelled Torbin, trying to control himself, 'you shouldn't have drunk out of her.'

'Only pity for her, Bill. Only pity for her. How would you like to spend sev–seventy years on the vicar's mantelpiece remembering Alci–bibi–biades?'

Bill pulled himself together, mourning perfection farther out in the mud. 'She was safer there,' he said solemnly.

'At the mercy of any passing housemaid. Euphemia, she was called. I knew her well. But out of this nettle, safety, we pluck—'

'You've got it wrong.'

'Shakespeare, Bill.'

'Common heritage, Colonel.'

'What I mean to say is that when we pick it up it's yours.'

'Can't get at ten guineas. Under the mud.'

'Then that's settled. Do you know any songs to pass the time, Bill?'

'If I had my ukulele—'

'I'll do that bit,' said the colonel, 'if you don't mind it being a banjo.'

Bill's repertoire was good for an hour and a half.

'I could do with a drink,' Wagstaff said, giving a final plunk to his imaginary strings.

'That search party is sure taking a long time, colonel.'

'Must have slipped up somewhere. You'd have thought they would have heard us.'

'Your turn now.'

'I was considering that question in the intervals,' Wagstaff said. 'The trouble is, Bill, that the only songs I can ever remember were acquired during the sheltered life of school and university, and are of such monstrous indecency that even sergeants' sing-songs have been closed to me.'

After an hour of the colonel, Bill agreed that the sergeants might be right, and added that he thought the tide was rising.

'Eight hours down, and four hours up,' said Wagstaff.

'Not six?'

151

'Four.'

'Hadn't we better try to get out?'

'You can try, Bill.'

After ten minutes Bill said: 'I guess I'll learn some of those songs of yours, colonel, when I've got my breath back.'

'Repeat the words after me, Bill, facing the land.'

In competition with each other, they so concentrated upon the job in hand that neither heard the approaching craft until she was three hundred yards away. With the fast tide under her, she was abreast of them before their yells for help met with any response.

' 'Old on!' shouted the bridge. 'It ain't easy, yer know!'

The engine-room telegraph rang. The wash from the propeller slid up the mudbank, as the ship was held steady in the tide. A beam of light glared into their faces.

The captain certainly knew his channel well. Going gently astern, he edged into the bank until the bows towered above them. Prettily riding the crest of a wavelet, right under the forefoot of the ship, was the bowl.

'Look out,' Bill shouted. 'You'll run her down.'

'Never saw there was another of you!' bawled the captain.

The telegraph rang violently. White water swirled at the stern. Their rescuer withdrew, edging out a little into the current, and the tide promptly swung the ship in a quarter circle with the bows as centre. The captain went ahead in a desperate effort to regain steerage way, and there she was, aground fore and aft across the channel.

'Knew that would 'appen,' said the captain, addressing them conversationally from the forecastle. 'Now where's the lady?'

'No lady,' the colonel replied. 'She walked home.'

'What? And left you there?'

'Must have forgotten.'

'Cor! What I'd 'ave said if I'd known there was no lady! Well, catch 'old!'

The rope fell by Wagstaff. The captain, the mate and the one deckhand dragged him, wallowing, through the mud and up the side of the ship.

Sergeant Torbin followed, but left the rope in order to plunge sideways and recover the bowl. By the time the mate had recoiled the line and flung it back, very little sergeant was visible beyond his cap and an outstretched arm.

'What d'yer do that for?' asked the captain, when Bill too was safe on board. 'Balmy?'

'It's two thousand years old,' Bill explained.

'Like me frying pan,' said the mate. 'Went up to me waist for that one, I did. fifty-year-old it might be, and they don't make 'em like that no more.'

152

The captain led the way to a small saloon under the bridge. It reeked of fug and decayed vegetables but was gloriously warm.

'You take them things off, and Bert will 'ang 'em in the engine-room,' he said.

'Any old clothes will do,' the colonel invited, dropping coat and trousers in a solid lump on the floor.

'Ain't got none. Don't keep a change on board, not none of us.'

'Blanket will do.'

'Don't sleep on board neither.'

'What are you?' the colonel asked.

'Chesterford garbage scow. Takes it from the trucks and dumps it overboard at forty fathom, see? Never out at night, we aren't, unless we misses a tide like we done yesterday. Bert, give 'em a couple of towels and shovel up them clothes!'

Bill managed to make the towel meet round his waist. The colonel found his wholly inadequate.

'I'll try this,' said Wagstaff cheerfully, lifting the bowl from the cabin table and removing the tablecloth. 'Show you how they wear 'em in India!'

The cloth had once been red plush, but the pile was smooth with age and grease-stains. The colonel folded it diagonally, passed two corners through his legs, knotted the tassels and beamed on the captain.

'Well, I suppose,' said the captain grudgingly, 'that you'd both better 'ave a drop of rum, though it don't look to me as if it was so long since the last one.' He unlocked a first aid cabinet and produced a bottle.

'I admit with pride that we have been celebrating the acquisition of a priceless antique,' the colonel answered.

'This 'ere?'

'That there.'

'Sort of basin, like?'

'An old Greek drinking bowl, captain.'

'How's it used?'

'It was *not* used,' the sergeant shouted. 'They kept it to look at. On the mantelpiece.'

'Nonsense, Bill! They didn't have mantelpieces. I'll show you, captain. A slave took the jug, so!'—the colonel seized the bottle of rum—and emptied it into the bowl, so!'

'Hey!' the skipper protested.

'And then it went round like a loving cup.'

Wagstaff took a sip and with both hands passed the bowl courteously to the captain, who could only drink and pass it on to Bill. Bill despairingly lowered the level by a quarter of an inch, gasped and passed it to the mate—the mate to Bert.

153

'Good navy rum, that!' said the colonel, starting the bowl on its round again.

'Got to stay where we are for the time being,' the mate agreed. 'Bert, you take them clothes away like the skipper ordered, and then you can 'ave a lie-down.'

With the memory of the rising tide safely behind him, Bill felt that there was some excuse for the theory that an object should be used as its maker intended. Half an hour later, inspired by his towel, he was showing them a dance he had learned in the South Pacific when he began to think the saloon was going round.

It was. The stern of the garbage scow, gently lifted from the mud, swung across river with increasing speed and thudded into the opposite bank. Bill made a dive for the bowl as it slid across the table and landed in the captain's lap.

'Knew it would 'appen!' the skipper yelled. 'That's the last time I picks a Yank out of the mud!'

He jammed in the doorway with the mate. The bows came off the mud and described the same semi-circle as the stern. The engine-room telegraph rang like a fire engine. Wagstaff, flung off the settee on to the floor, sat there cross-legged shaking with laughter. Bill cradled the bowl grimly on his knees.

'Allies, Bill, allies! What did I tell you? It's all your fault, and your towel has come off!'

'Colonel,' said Bill, reknotting it round his waist, 'how come all the guys that tried to shoot you missed?' He dropped his head on the table, and instantly fell asleep.

They were awakened by Bert, flinging down two still soggy bundles of clothes. 'Skipper says 'e don't want no more to do with either of you,' he announced, 'and if you ain't off this scow as soon as we ties up 'e'll send for the police.'

It was light. Up the reach the town, the castle and the municipal rubbish dump of Chesterford were in sight. The clock on the church tower made the time eight-thirty.

'Bill,' said Wagstaff, breaking the silence, 'that piece of linen in which you have wrapped the bowl was once my shirt.'

'Say, colonel, I'm sorry. I wasn't thinking.'

'Not a word. It will dry there. And I can do up my coat collar. Thank heaven I am known in Chesterford!'

Bill took the remark on trust, though it seemed to him when he was escorted by the mate through the corrugated iron door of the garbage wharf, before breakfast and looking as if he had been dug out of the tip, that personally he would prefer a town where he was not known.

Striding up the main street of Chesterford, however, alongside the colonel, he understood. Wagstaff's air was guiltless, so full indeed of a casual manliness as he greeted an occasional acquaintance

154

that only one of them thought it proper to comment on his appearance.

'Showing our friend here some sport,' said the colonel. 'Mallard right. Teal left. Got 'em both. Lost me balance. And this gallant fellow hauled me out.'

As they resumed their squelching progress up the High Street, Bill remarked that he sounded exactly like a British colonel on the movies.

'A very useful accomplishment,' Wagstaff agreed, 'which has enabled me before now to rescue allies from well deserved court martial. Later in the day which is now upon us, Bill, or even tomorrow or whenever that damned bowl permits us both a reasonably sober countenance, I shall accompany you to your commanding officer and obtain for you a mention in your home town paper and probably a medal from the Royal Humane Society.'

'What's that?'

'It gives medals. Did you not leap into mud of unknown bottom to rescue me?'

'Don't mention it, colonel. It was the least I could do,' said Bill, and paused. 'Say, wasn't it the bowl?'

'The values are quite irrelevant, Bill. Me or the bowl? The bowl or me? We will now go into the Red Lion here for a bath and breakfast.'

'Will the bar be open yet, colonel?'

'Oh, that'll be all right. They know me there.'

'Then I'm not going in with this bowl,' Bill said firmly. 'Not to the Red Lion or any other of your animal friends.'

'Fresh herrings, Bill. I can smell 'em. And Bacon and eggs to follow.'

'We can have breakfast at a tea shop.'

'Too respectable. They wouldn't let us in.'

Sergeant Torbin, desperately searching the market square for safety, was inspired by the opening of the double doors of the Chesterford Museum. He ran, vaulted the turnstile in the vestibule where the doorkeeper was just changing into his uniform coat, and charged down an alley of Roman tombstones into a collection of stuffed foxes and weasels marked 'Natural History'. Hesitating wildly between 'Neolithic', 'Iron Age' and 'Gentlemen', he saw a door to his left with CURATOR on it. He leaped through it, and found himself facing a desk where a very tall wisp of a man in his seventies was quietly cataloguing.

'You take this,' he said. 'Lock it up in your safe, quick!'

Before the Curator could get over the shock of an American sergeant, covered with mud from head to foot and offering with outstretched arms an unknown object wrapped in dirty linen, Wagstaff also was upon him.

'Is it—is it a baby?' the curator asked.

'It is, sir, a fifth-century Attic cylix,' the colonel replied with dignity.

The curator tremblingly extracted the bowl, and at the sight of it instantly recovered an almost ecclesiastical self-possession.

'But this is an article of great value,' he intoned.

'I know it is. You've no idea of the trouble I've had preserving it from destruction.'

'This—um—er—has dispossessed you of it?'

'Lord, no! It's his.'

'Colonel, it is yours,' said Bill with what he hoped was finality.

The colonel took the bowl with both hands, pledged an imaginary draught to the gods and held it high above the stone floor of the curator's office.

'I've nowhere to keep it,' Bill screamed.

'Oh, that's all that is bothering you, is it?' the colonel exclaimed. 'Well, what's that damned owl doing?'

A stuffed barn owl in a Victorian show case stood on the curator's work-bench. Wagstaff lifted the glass dome from the ebony base, and removed the owl which immediately disintegrated into dust and feathers.

'Mouldy,' said the colonel. 'Disgrace to the museum. That reminds me, I believe I'm on the committee. Give you a new one and stuff it myself.'

'I was indeed considering—' the curator began.

'Of course you were. Quite right! Mind if I sit down at your desk a minute?'

The colonel printed a neat card:

LENT TO THE MUSEUM BY COURTESY OF

SERGEANT WILLIAM TORBIN, USAF

He laid the bowl upon the ebony stand and propped the card up against it.

'That will keep *you* quiet,' he said, replacing the glass dome, 'until Bill has a mantelpiece for you again. The sergeant has only to write to you to get it, I suppose?' he added fiercely to the curator.

'Yes, yes, but—'

'Any objection to the Red Lion now, Bill? It will be a pleasant change to drink out of glasses once more.'

EGGS AS AIN'T

Mrs Swallop had been working her twenty-acre holding single-handed ever since Tom Swallop was killed in the Boer War when she was seventeen years old and a six-months' bride. He left her his scrap of freehold land, no child, and apparently so pleasant a memory that she preferred to live with it rather than change her status.

Her farm—if you can call it a farm—was up at the end of a grass track: a patch of cultivation in a dry bottom surrounded by the thorn and bracken on the slopes, and well fenced except for short stretches of queer material such as old bed-springs and rusty sheets of corrugated iron. It had a name on the map, but no one for ten miles around ever called it anything but 'Noah's Ark.'

The birds and animals were not, however, in biblical couples. Mrs Swallop stocked her land with breeding females, for she had her own ways of encouraging them. There were two enormous turkey hens, a goose, a saddle-backed sow, a flock of undisciplined chickens, a black cow, a black nanny-goat and a big black cat who was fierce as a watch-dog when she had kittens. The only representative of the male sex was a buck rabbit who attended to the comfort of several prolific does.

She was a bright and cleanly old body—so far as one can be when farming alone—but her dress and her ways were odd. She might be wearing an old tweed skirt below an upper half swathed in sacking, or a new purple jersey with a horse blanket for a skirt. She had a black moustache, and she used to whisper under it to her animals.

Mrs Swallop would whisper for her neighbours, too, if she liked them; so they were always ready to lend her a male when she turned up driving one of her females in front of her, or pushing it, squawking, in the large dilapidated perambulator which was her only farm transport. If there were anything else in the bottom of the pram, such as eggs or cream, they would buy it from her by some careful method which would not draw the attention of Percy Crott.

Those were the days just after the war when farmers were making a lot more money than now. On the other hand, they had to put up with fellows like Crott. He had been a village schoolmaster till one of his fourteen-year-olds sent him to hospital; and when he came out he got a job in the Ministry of Food. How he rose to be an inspector, no one ever discovered—for all he knew about food were the regulations to prevent the public eating it. He had a blotchy pink face as smooth as a pig's, with a nasty little mouth in the middle of it and a round chin which he used to stick out when he was speaking—like one of those business men who are so proud of their faces that they put their pictures in the advertisements in spite of the sales they must lose.

Crott could never catch the big farmers who generally obeyed the law, and had a dozen inspector-proof ways of covering themselves up when they didn't. If he wanted to bring a neighbour before the courts and make an example of him, he went for the little man who was sure to be breaking regulations because he had no time to read them. And he made a dead set at Mrs Swallop because she built a breeding hutch for the rabbits out of all the pamphlets and government forms which the postman brought her. Those rabbits fairly flourished under the welfare state, but when Percy Crott saw the hutch he said it was a scandal, and carried on as if Mrs Swallop had built it out of a stack of Bibles.

All the same, it was difficult to find an offence by which he could put her out of business. She had no books or accounts—for she insisted that she could not write—and old Trancard was always ready to tell any lie for her. Crott's only hope was to catch her red-handed selling eggs to the public.

Trancard took a very friendly interest in the old lady, for his sheep-run surrounded her land on the north and east, and the luck he had with the lambing was marvellous. He guessed what Percy Crott was up to when he saw him hiding behind a hedge and counting Mrs Swallop's birds. So he persuaded her to turn over a new leaf, and register herself as a poultry producer.

'It won't give 'ee no trouble at all, missus,' he told her. 'I'm a licensed packer, and you hand over your eggs to me for grading and packing, and get paid by the government at fifty shillings for ten dozen. But what you must not do, missus, is to sell 'em to anyone who ain't licensed. And if that young Crott catches you at it, you'll fetch up before the beaks.'

'I don't want no more of 'is papers,' Mrs Swallop answered.

'Ain't no papers, not to speak of, me dear! You delivers your eggs to me whenever you happens to be passing, and along comes the money and your National Poultry Food regular. If you mixes it up with a bit of barley, which maybe I can find for 'ee, the hens won't hardly know what they're eatin'. Oh, it's all as easy as kiss your 'and, missus, begging your pardon,' he said.

Trancard was obviously making money out of his fine flock of Rhode Island Reds, so Mrs Swallop decided to take his advice. While there was plenty she wouldn't understand, there was nothing she couldn't once she got her lips moving silently round the problem. She collected another score of hens, one by one wherever a bird caught her eye, and a shocking lot of mixed breeds they were; but she soon had them in the pink of condition and laying up and down the hedgerows as fast as if they had been their orderly sisters in Trancard's deep litter house.

When Mrs Swallop came up with her third load of eggs, six inches deep in the bottom of the pram, Trancard graded them and gave two dozen back to her. They were too small or too crooked.

'And what must I do wi'' 'em, mister?' she asked.

'Do what you likes with 'em. The government don't want 'em.'

'They be all egg inside,' she said.

'But the public won't buy 'em in the shops, missus.'

'Can I sell 'em,' she asked, 'without that young Crott comin' up after me wi' the constable?'

'No, you can't. Not to say sellin' 'em as *is* sellin' 'em. But you can give 'em away, and I'll tell 'ee where. And that's Mr Buckfast up at The Bull, with all his guests wanting two fried eggs to their breakfasts when he can't hardly give 'em one. He'll take all you can give 'im, and it wouldn't surprise me if 'e was to pay you at seventy bob instead of the fifty we gets from the government. But 'e won't be paying you for eggs, mind, but for carrots or such-like.'

Mrs Swallop leaned against the gate-post, calculating in so fast a whisper that she couldn't keep listening to herself; so she fell into a sort of trance, and old Trancard had to take her up to the house and bring her round with a glass of port.

'And there's no point in you bringing eggs as ain't legal eggs up to me for grading,' he said, when he had given her an arm back to the pram. 'You know an egg as ain't when you see it as well as I do. But don't you go giving away an egg that's an egg within the meaning of the Order, because it's not worth the risk.'

Next week it was all over the district that Mrs Swallop had another male to keep the buck rabbit company. He was a black leghorn cock of a fine laying strain, with a certificate to prove it; but his breast-bone was twisted over to one side like a plough-share, so that when he stretched out his neck to crow he had to spread his tail the other way to balance himself. Mrs Swallop, naturally enough, did not have to pay a penny for him, though she may have done some little favour to the bees in passing.

In spite of his looks the hens took to this young cripple, as females will. And Mrs Swallop groomed his tail feathers and whispered to him and stuffed him with National Poultry Food till the old buck was so jealous that he set about him and got a spur down his ear-hole before they could be separated.

When spring came, Mrs Swallop was not delivering anything like

159

the proper number of eggs, in spite of the fact that she and the black leghorn between them had raised her flock to nearly a hundred birds, most of them laying pullets of her own breeding. Trancard went down to her holding to see if he could help at all, and a repulsive sight the yard was for a careful farmer. He stared at those miscoloured, lopsided, sinister-looking freak pullets, and went purple in the face with the pressure of all he did not like to say.

'Why, what's wrong wi' 'em?' she asked him.

'Missus,' he said, 'there's everything wrong with 'em. But if they're yourn, they're laying—and that young Crott has been up, lookin' at me books.'

Mrs Swallop gave him a sly smile under her moustache, with a twitch of the lips that must have enchanted Tom Swallop fifty years before.

'Don't 'ee worry over me, me dear,' she said.

But Trancard did worry. He knew Mrs Swallop was making a mysterious profit. So did Percy Crott. She had had her fences repaired, and a pipe laid to the spring where she got her water instead of old lengths of rusty gutter stopped with clay. And there was nothing to account for all the eggs in town, especially at The Bull, except the visits of Mrs Swallop's pram.

Crott timed it nicely. He watched Mrs Swallop deliver a parcel of eggs—which should have been all she produced—to Trancard, and he let her go down to the town with her pram. Then he took his government car and the local cop from behind the haystack where he had parked the pair of them, and drove into Trancard's yard and asked to see the books.

Old Trancard tried to muddle him by passing off some of his own eggs as Mrs Swallop's. The cop did his best to help. But the ink was hardly dry in the book, and there was no getting away from the figures. Mrs Swallop had delivered only two dozen eggs that morning, and nothing else for a week.

'She'll be on her way to The Bull now, constable,' said Percy Crott, pushing him into the car.

He started to drive slowly down the hill so as to reach the hotel about the same time as Mrs Swallop. All Trancard could do was to rumble behind in a tractor wondering how Mrs Swallop could ever pay the fifty pounds or so which the beaks would have to fine her, and whether they would give her six months if she didn't.

When they stopped in front of The Bull, Percy Crott and the constable nipped round into the backyard, with Trancard a second or two behind them trying to look as if he had just called to return the empties. There was Mrs Swallop talking to Buckfast, the proprietor.

'Madam,' asked the inspector, 'what have you got in that perambulator?'

'Nothing but eggs, sir. Nothing at all,' she answered, pretending she was frightened of the cop.

'And were you thinking of selling them?'

'No, she weren't,' Buckfast told him pretty sharply. 'She was giving them to me. And it's legal.'

'Uncommonly kind of her!' said Percy Crott in a sarcastic way, and he whipped the cover off the pram.

It was stuffed with eggs. And not one of them was fairly oval. There were eggs which might have been fat white sausages, and round eggs and oblongs and lozenges, and pear-shaped eggs and eggs with a twist like a gibbous moon with round points.

Inspector Crott pushed them aside with the tips of his fingers as if they were something the dog had been rolling in. They were all the same quality right down to the bottom of the pram.

'Don't your hens lay anything fit for human consumption?' he asked.

'No, sir,' she told him, 'they don't. A poor old woman can't afford good 'ens like you gentlemen.'

Then Buckfast was taken with a fit of the sniggers, and old Trancard slapped his breeches and grinned at Mrs Swallop as if she were the knowingest farmer in all the county.

'Damme if she ain't been breeding for rejects!' he roared. 'Damme, and I tried to tell 'er how to run fowls! I tell you, Mr Percy Crott, that if only she 'ad a cock with a face like yourn, them 'ens would lay eggs and bacon, and burst out laughin' when they turned their 'eads round to look at what they 'ad done,' he said.

ABNER OF THE PORCH

When my voice broke, even Abner and MacGillivray understood my grief. I did not expect sympathy from MacGillivray, for he had no reason to like me. But he knew what it was to be excluded from cathedral ceremonies. He was the bishop's dog.

Abner was masterless. I would not claim that he appreciated the alto's solo in the 'Magnificat' when the organ was hushed and there was no other sound in the million and a half cubic feet of the cathedral but the slender purity of a boy's voice; yet he would patronize me after such occasions with the air of the master alto which he might have been. Though not a full Tom, he knew the ancestral songs which resemble our own. To our ears the scale of cats is distasteful, but one cannot deny them sustained notes of singular loveliness and clarity.

Abner's career had followed a common human pattern. My father was the gardener, responsible for the shaven lawns and discreet flower beds of the cathedral close. Some three years earlier he had suffered from an invasion of moles—creatures of ecclesiastical subtlety who avoided all the crude traps set for them by a mere layman. The cat, appearing from nowhere, took an interest. After a week he had caught the lot, laying out his game-bag each morning upon the tarpaulin which covered the mower.

Fed and praised by my father, he began to pay some attention to public relations and attracted the attention of visitors. Officially recognized as an ornament of the cathedral when his photograph appeared in the local paper, he ventured to advance from the lawns and tombstones to the porch. There he captivated the dean, always politely rising from the stone bench and thrusting his noble flanks against the gaitered leg. He was most gracious to the bishop and the higher clergy, but he would only stroke the dean. He knew very well from bearing and tone of voice, gentle though they were, that the cathedral belonged to him. It was the dean who christened him Abner.

To such a personage the dog of our new bishop was a disaster. MacGillivray was of respectable middle age, and had on occasion a sense of dignity; but when dignity was not called for he behaved like any other Aberdeen terrier and would race joyously round the cathedral or across the close, defying whatever human being was in charge of him to catch the lead which bounced and flew behind.

His first meeting with his rival set the future tone of their relations. He ventured with appalling temerity to make sport of the cathedral cat. Abner stretched himself, yawned, allowed MacGillivray's charge to approach within a yard, leaped to the narrow and rounded top of a tombstone and, draping himself over it, went ostentatiously to sleep. MacGillivray jumped and yapped at the tail tip which graciously waved for him, and then realized that he was being treated as a puppy. After that, the two passed each other politely but without remark. In our closed world of the cathedral such coolness between servants of dean and servants of bishop was familiar.

MacGillivray considered that he should be on permanent duty with his master. Since he was black, small and ingenious, it was difficult to prevent him. So devoted a friend could not be cruelly chained—and in summer the french windows of the Bishop's Palace were always open.

He first endeared himself to choir and clergy at the ceremony of the bishop's installation. Magnificent in mitre and full robes, the bishop of the head of his procession knocked with his crozier upon the cathedral door to demand admission. MacGillivray, observing that his master was shut out and in need of help, hurtled across the close, bounced at the door and added his excited barks to the formal solemnity of the bishop's order.

Led away in disapproving silence, he took the enormity of his crime more seriously than we did. On his next appearance he behaved with decent humility, following the unconscious bishop down the chancel and into the pulpit with bowed head and tail well below horizontal.

Such anxious piety was even more embarrassing than bounce. It became my duty, laid upon me by the bishop in person, to ensure on all formal occasions that MacGillivray had not evaded the butler and was safely confined. I was even empowered to tie him up to the railings on the north side of the close in cases of emergency.

I do not think the bishop ever realized what was troubling his friend and erring brother, MacGillivray—normally a dog of sense who could mind his own business however great his affection for his master. When he accompanied the bishop around the diocese he never committed the solecism of entering a parish church and never used the vicar's cat as an objective for assault practice.

His indiscipline at home was, we were all sure, due to jealousy of Abner. He resented with Scottish obstinacy the fact that he was ejected in disgrace from the cathedral whereas Abner was not. He could not be expected to understand that Abner's discreet movements were beyond human control.

The dean could and did quite honestly declare that he had never seen that cat in the cathedral. Younger eyes, however, which knew where to look, had often distinguished Abner curled up on the ornate stone canopy over the tomb of a seventeenth-century admiral. In winter, he would sometimes sleep upon the left arm of a stone cru-sader in the cavity between shield and mailed shirt—a dank spot, I thought, until I discovered that it captured a current of warm air from the grating beside the effigy. In both his resting-places he was, if he chose to be, invisible. He was half Persian, tiger-striped with brown-ish grey on lighter grey, and he matched the stone of the cathedral.

As the summer went by, the feud between Abner and MacGillivray became more subtle. Both scored points. MacGillivray, if he woke up feeling youthful, used to chase the tame pigeons in the close. One morning, to the surprise of both dog and bird, a pigeon failed to get out of the way in time and broke a wing. MacGillivray was embar-rassed. He sniffed the pigeon, wagged his tail to show that there was no ill-feeling and sat down to think.

Abner strolled from the porch and held down the pigeon with a firm, gentle paw. He picked it up in his mouth and presented it with liquid and appealing eyes to an elegant American tourist who was musing sentimentally in the close. She swore that the cat had asked her to heal the bird—which, by remaining a whole week in our town in and out of the vet's consulting room, she did. Personally, I think that Abner was attracted by the feline grace of her walk and was suggesting that, as the pigeon could be of no more use to the cathedral, she might as well eat it. But whatever his motives, he had again made MacGil-livray look a clumsy and impulsive fool.

MacGillivray's revenge was a little primitive. He deposited bones and offal in dark corners of the porch and pretended that Abner had put them there. That was the second worst crime he knew—to leave on a human floor the inedible portion of his meals.

The verger was deceived and submitted a grave complaint in writ-ing to the dean. The dean, however, knew very well that Abner had no interest in mutton bones, old or new. He was familiar with the cat's tastes. Indeed, it was rumoured from the deanery that he secreted a little box in his pocket at meals, into which he would drop such delica-cies as the head of a small trout or the liver of a roast duck.

I cannot remember all the incidents of the cold war. And, anyway, I could not swear to their truth. My father and the dean read into the animals' behaviour motives which were highly unlikely and then shamelessly embroidered them, creating a whole miscellany of pri-vate legend for the canons and the choir. So I will only repeat the triumph of MacGillivray and its sequel, both of which I saw myself.

That fulfilment of every dog's dream appeared at first final and overwhelming victory. It was 1 September, the feast of St Giles, our patron saint. Evensong was a full choral and instrumental service, tra-ditional, exquisite, and attracting a congregation whose interest was in music rather than religion. The bishop was to preach. Perhaps the effort of composition, of appealing to well-read intellectuals without offending the simpler clergy, had created an atmosphere of hard work and anxiety in the bishop's study. At any rate, MacGillivray was nervous and mischievous.

While I was ensuring his comfort before shutting him up, he twitched the lead out of my hand and was off on his quarter-mile course round the cathedral looking for a private entrance. When at last I caught him, the changes of the bells had stopped. I had only five minutes before the processional entry of the choir. There wasn't even time to race across the close and tie him up to the railings.

I rushed into the north transept with MacGillivray under my arm, pushed him down the stairs into the crypt and shut the door behind him. I knew that he could not get out. Our Norman crypt was closed to visitors during the service, and no one on a summer evening would have reason to go down to the masons' and carpenters' stores, the strong-room or the boilers. All I feared was that MacGillivray's yaps might be heard through the gratings in the cathedral floor.

I dived into my ruffled surplice and took my place in the procession, earning the blackest possible looks from the choir-master. I just had time to explain to him that it was the fault of MacGillivray. I was not forgiven, but the grin exchanged between choir-master and precentor suggested that I probably would be—if I wasn't still panting by the time that the alto had to praise all famous men and our fathers that begat us.

St Giles, if he still had any taste for earthly music, must have approved his servants that evening. The bishop, always an effective preacher, surpassed himself. His sinewy arguments were of course beyond me, but I had my eye—vain little beast that I was—on the music critics from the London papers, and I could see that several of them were so interested that they were bursting to take over the pulpit and reply.

Only once did he falter, when the barking of MacGillivray, hardly perceptible to anyone but his master and me, caught the episcopal ear. Even then his momentary hesitation was put down to a search for the right word.

I felt that my desperate disposal of MacGillivray might not be appreciated. He must have been audible to any of the congregation sitting near the gratings of the northern aisle. So I shot down to release him immediately after the recessional. The noise was startling as soon as I opened the door. MacGillivray was holding the stairs against a stranger in the crypt.

The man was good-dogging him and trying to make him shut up. He had a small suitcase by his side. When two sturdy vergers, attracted by the noise, appeared hot on my heels, the intruder tried to bolt—dragging behind him MacGillivray with teeth closed on the turn-ups of his trousers. We detained him and opened the suitcase. It contained twenty pounds' weight of the cathedral silver. During the long service our massive but primitive strong-room door had been expertly opened.

The congregation was dispersing, but bishop, dean, archdeacon and innumerable canons were still in the cathedral. They attended the excitement just as any other crowd. Under the circumstances, MacGillivray was the centre of the most complimentary fuss. The canons would have genially petted any dog. But this was the bishop's dog. The wings of gowns and surplices flowed over him like those of exclamatory seagulls descending upon a stranded fish.

Dignity was represented only by our local superintendent of police and the terrier himself. When the thief had been led away, MacGillivray reverently followed his master out of the cathedral; his whole attitude reproached us for ever dreaming that he might take advantage of his popularity.

At the porch, however, he turned round and loosed one short, triumphant bark into the empty nave. The bishop's chaplain unctuously suggested that it was a little voice of thanksgiving. So it was— but far from pious. I noticed where MacGillivray's muzzle was pointing. That bark was for a softness of outline, a shadow, a striping of small stone pinnacles upon the canopy of the Admiral's Tomb.

For several days—all of ten I should say—Abner deserted both the cathedral and its porch. He then returned to his first friend, helping my father to make the last autumn cut of the grass and offering his catch of small game for approval. The dean suggested that he was in need of sunshine. My father shook his head and said nothing. It was obvious to both of us that for Abner the cathedral had been momentarily defiled. He reminded me of an old verger who gave in his resignation—it was long overdue anyway—after discovering a family party eating lunch from paper bags in the Lady Chapel.

He went back to the porch a little before the harvest festival, for he always enjoyed that. During a whole week while the decorations were in place he could find a number of discreet lairs where it was impossible to detect his presence. There may also have been a little hunting in the night. We did not attempt to fill the vastness of the cathedral with all the garden produce dear to a parish church, but the dean was fond of fat sheaves of wheat, oats and barley, bound round the middle like sheaves on a heraldic shield.

It was his own festival in his own cathedral, so that he, not the bishop, conducted it. He had made the ritual as enjoyable as that of Christmas, reviving ancient customs for which he was always ready to quote authority. I suspect that medieval deans would have denied his interpretation of their scanty records, but they would have recognized a master of stage management.

His most effective revival was a procession of cathedral tenants and

166

benefactors, each bearing some offering in kind which the dean received on the altar steps. Fruit, honey and cakes were common, always with some touch of magnificence in the quality, quantity or container. On one occasion, the landlord of the Pilgrim's Inn presented a roasted peacock set in jelly with tail feathers erect. There was some argument about this on the grounds that it ran close to advertisement. But the dean would not be dissuaded. He insisted that any craftsman had the right to present a unique specimen of his skill.

That year the gifts were more humble. My father, as always, led the procession with a basket tray upon which was a two-foot bunch of black grapes from the vinery in the canons' garden. A most original participant was a dear old nursery gardener who presented a plant of his new dwarf camellia which had been the botanical sensation of the year and could not yet be bought for money. There was also a noble milk-pan of Alpine strawberries and cream—which, we hoped, the cathedral school would share next day with the alms houses.

While the file of some twenty persons advanced into the chancel, the choir full-bloodedly sang the 65th Psalm to the joyous score of our own organist. The dean's sense of theatre was as faultless as ever. Lavish in ritual and his own vestments, he then played his part with the utmost simplicity. He thanked and blessed each giver almost conversationally.

Last in the procession were four boys of the cathedral school bearing a great silver bowl of nuts gathered in the hedgerows. The gift and their movements were traditional. As they separated, two to the right and two to the left, leaving the dean alone upon the altar steps, a shadow appeared at his feet and vanished so swiftly that by the time our eyes had registered its true, soft shape it was no longer there.

The dean bent down and picked up a dead field-mouse. He was not put out of countenance for a moment. He laid it reverently with the other gifts. No one was present to be thanked; but when the dean left the cathedral after service and stopped in the porch to talk to Abner he was—to the surprise of the general public—still wearing his full vestments, stiff, gorgeous and suggesting the power of the Church to protect and armour with its blessing the most humble of its servants.

FRANCE

THE SWORD AND THE RAKE

Young Georges Dumont, garage proprietor and agricultural engineer, crashed his motor cycle into first gear, roared the engine and dismounted at the door of Papa Arneguy's cottage. On the valley slopes
the silent, orderly beds of the market garden were intensely green and
black in the last of the setting sun.

'Attention!' he yelled. 'Radishes into column of troop, right wheel!'

Père Arneguy looked up from the seedsman's catalogue upon
which he was making notes—without glasses, though he was well over
sixty. He found the youth of France a little comic; it did not believe in
doing anything with hand or foot which could possibly be done by
electricity or a two-stroke engine. But, if motor cycles had to exist,
that was the way to stop them—with a flourish.

'It never existed, your order,' he replied peaceably. 'Will you take a
glass?'

'Willingly.'

Père Arneguy always had excellent wine, though heaven only knew
how he had the ready cash to buy it after feeding his large self and his
larger horse.

'But I have little time,' Georges Dumont added. 'An urgent
duty . . .'

'It is always the same with the young,' said Arneguy, wiping out
excuses from the air around him with a wave of his massive hand.
'You spend so much time mending your machines that you have none
for anything else.'

'And you, you old cave artist, how many hours a day do you spend
grooming the Shah?'

It exasperated the younger generation of the village of Achard that
Papa Arneguy should continue to work his three hectares of land with
hand tools and a horse when a cultivator—as Georges Dumont had
proved to him a dozen times—could be bought on hire purchase and
would pay for itself in two years. Fathers and grandfathers were just
as obstinate, but from sheer inability to understand the economics of
machinery. The infuriating thing about Papa Arneguy was that his
arithmetic remained sound and his intelligence quick. He was not
out-of-date because he couldn't help it. He chose to be out-of-date.

He was a typical Basque, individualist all through. In 1914 he had gone to war as a cuirassier, helmeted, breast-plated and making as much noise at the trot as a cart-load of cymbals. When provoked—which was often, since his thundering good humour in argument could entertain a whole café—he maintained that such gay and useless ironmongery had been far more satisfying to the human spirit than sitting at the bottom of a trench with a lot of machines which might or might not work when they were needed.

He still looked the part. Those great shoulders and long grey moustache belonged to the cuirassier. Georges Dumont admitted that a squadron of Arneguys might indeed have had the moral effect of a tank. Yet, while working his land, the same shoulders and moustache gave an impression of the utmost peace and benignity. So did the Shah, a barrel-shaped half-bred Percheron whose keep alone used up one of Arneguy's three hectares.

'It's always when I can't stop that someone offers me Burgundy as good as this,' said Dumont, regretfully finishing his glass.

'What's your hurry? There is plenty more.'

'Flood warning. I am on my way down river.'

'There has been no flood here since Noah. Look at the river—decently in her bed like a good bourgeoise!'

'All the same, she may not be alone between the sheets tonight.'

'So they have made a mistake up there, have they?'

Père Arneguy had no respect whatever for the contractors and engineers who were damming and tunnelling the foothills of the Pyrenees above his village.

'At that level one does not make mistakes,' Dumont answered, rushing to the defence of fellow technicians. 'And you have nothing against their electricity, I suppose?'

Arneguy mischievously shrugged his shoulders. In fact, he had a high opinion of electricity.

'It's true one hasn't got to take a spanner to it,' he said.

'And what in God's name is wrong with a spanner? This from him, who farms with a sword and rake like an ancient Roman!'

Père Arneguy grinned at the retort. He enjoyed a ferocious mock battle with Georges Dumont. He did, in fact, keep a vast cuirassier's sabre hanging on the wall of his cottage, and it was not wholly for decoration. In one point he obeyed the laws of economics; he kept nothing he did not use. The sword, which had as fine an edge on it as his scythe, was occasionally drawn from its scabbard for odd jobs too delicate for the bill-hook and too heavy for the pruning knife.

As for the rake, it was the proud jest of the village. Arneguy liked beds of noble width—parade grounds of crumbly loam where lettuces, radishes and spring onions were massed in column. Once the crop had been thinned, no weed was allowed to grow so large that a hoe would be required to remove it. The rake was sufficient. It was a formidable weapon of his own invention with four-inch tines and a nine-foot handle. His immense forearm handled the tool as delicately as a toothpick, stirring the soil between a dozen lettuces simultaneously.

'All the same, when I make a dam it lasts.'

'The dam is immovable for ever, Père Arneguy. But one cannot foresee freaks of geology. There must be a cave in the limestone below the centre of the lake. They say there was a swirl on the surface as if a plug had been pulled out.'

'The water has reappeared?'

'It is beginning. In the gorge east of the dam. If they cannot control it, the flood will come tonight and last four or five hours. Achard is in no danger, but all livestock and farm machinery must be moved from the bank of the river. Incredible, the activity! Dynamite, echo soundings, bulldozers lowered into the gorge!'

'And the island?'

'There will be a team and trucks in half an hour to evacuate the island. Will you let the widow Ibarra know, and see that she is sensible?'

'At once,' said Père Arneguy, driving right home the cork of the bottle with his grey-haired fist.

As the roar of the motor cycle faded away between the hills he tramped down to the river at the bottom of his land. For most of its course it was a mountain torrent, but at the lower end of the little Achard valley it was blocked by the boulders of an old moraine through which the water tumbled down to the Gave d'Oleron. Above these rapids it gave the impression of some peaceful tributary of the Loire with a fertile island floating in the middle of it upon which was an ancient, white-washed farmhouse standing well above the level of the spring floods.

Now, in autumn, it was hardly an island at all. On the eastern side the water divided into several little branches running between pebble shoals. To the west it was separated from Arneguy's land by a channel some eighty feet wide, knee-deep and flickering with small trout shaped like miniatures of the island itself.

Père Arneguy hailed the farm. Marie-Claire came to fetch him with the punt, pulling herself across the channel by a slack and dripping cable which stretched between two little, stone landing-stages—one beneath the farm-house windows, the other on the river bank.

It was a very wet and primitive method of ferrying. Père Arneguy had several times offered to install a running mooring instead of a single cable fastened to ring-bolts. Marie-Claire who was twelve years old and prided herself on being up-to-date, was all in favour. Her mother, Madame Ibarra, was not. She insisted that they would never feel safe in their beds if anyone could pull the punt back from the island.

Marie-Claire was excited by the news. Her island was to be the centre of fascinating efficiency merely for the sake of a foot of water on the ground floor. Madame Ibarra, however, was incredulous, then tearful, then appalled. She imagined the dam emptying in a wall of water as high as itself. Arneguy considered they were both wrong, but long life as a fatherly bachelor had taught him that women found comfort in exaggeration.

Georges Dumont, at any rate, had been exact. Five large trucks appeared on the river bank with a team of thirty men under the supervision of one of the contracting engineers. His first duty appeared to be public relations. He assured Madame that the entire organization was at her service. She and her charming daughter would be spared all possible inconvenience and indemnified against any financial loss.

Even while he was talking, the farm as a human home began to disappear. The punt was unshackled and pulled on shore ready for loading. A timber ramp and rolls of wire netting went into the channel. The trucks began to cross and pull out again loaded with furniture, implements and animals. All breakables were carried up to the top floor, for there might be no time to pack them. Urgency was in the flood lights and the silent figure who sat on the bank with his walkie-talkie, continually in communication with the dam site.

Père Arneguy felt old. There was nothing for him to do, not even a haul for the powerful quarters of the Shah. It was no longer a neighbour's business to deal with emergencies. Trained men did it better. By ten o'clock the farm had been stripped, and Madame and Marie-Claire were housed with relations in Achard. There was even a champagne supper laid out with the compliments of the dam contractors.

He went to bed with his clothes on—aware that it was no more than an old cuirassier's gesture—and slept soundly. Before breakfast he examined the river and its lifeless island. The water was discoloured and had posibly risen an inch or two; but there was no sign of flood.

At half past eight he was cleaning out the stable when he heard the whoosh of powerful rockets. One would have said it was the fourteenth of July. He approved of the technicians. That was the good old way to give warning—better than the telephone and their little wireless sets.

He strolled round the corner of the stable in time to see a wall of water higher than a man sweep down the bed of the river and break on the bows of the island, throwing up a curtain of spray which hid the trees. There were no rockets. The noise had been the rush of the wave.

When the spray fell, the island was not there, only the farm and its buildings standing in a lake. Beyond them, over the pebbles and fields to the east, the river had risen to its fullest spring width. The current

174

steadied. For second after second the water climbed the stubble on the lower slope of Père Arneguy's land. It would do no harm there. The Shah's rations for the year were already in the barn.

The shutters of a top-floor window flew open, and Marie-Claire came through on to the iron balcony. The lake which surrounded her again became a torrent as the water surged clear over the boulders and narrows at the lower end of the valley. The old cow-shed upstream from the farmhouse crumbled and vanished.

Both banks were filling with the inhabitants of Achard accompanied by firemen, police, the mayor and a newsreel cameraman. As he ran to meet them, Père Arneguy looked, from force of habit, for the town band. The dam contractors had sent a powerful rescue squad in case of unforseen emergency: men, ropes, an amphibious vehicle and a rubber dinghy. He waved to them, pointing to Marie-Claire. The thunder of the water made shouting useless.

They were fast, the engineers. No denying that. In two minutes they had launched their amphibian well upstream. Two minutes later she was hurled back into the shallows, riding at the end of her cable over Arneguy's stubble.

They tried again, attaching light lines to the crew of two and providing the boat with an anchor weighted by a block of concrete. This time her engines took her far enough out. The anchor went overboard and the crew paid out the cable, bringing her nearly into position under the balcony. But anchor and weight were rolling together down the bed of the river. The amphibian vanished. The crew were pulled ashore.

It was clear that in such a race boats were as useless as Madame Ibarra's outstretched arms and the incoherent advice which she screamed across the water. Marie-Claire herself, now that rescue was on the way, seemed astonishingly self-disciplined. The poise of the fair head and brown school uniform impressed Père Arneguy. She belonged to the youth which knew so much. Perhaps she was right to be confident.

'But what happened, Madame?' he asked. 'I cannot conceive . . .'

'She forgot her homework.'

'You mean—for a damned exercise book?'

'But who would have thought it?' wept Mme Ibarra. 'I wondered why she left so early for school. Who would have guessed what she intended? When one's home is destroyed, does one think of bits of paper carried up to the attic? She must have crossed from the other bank. She often does so at this time of year when she is too impatient to pull herself over in the boat. *Mon Dieu! Mon Dieu!* She jumped from shoal to shoal like a little deer! It used to delight me to watch her.'

'But the warning, Madame?' protested the smooth young engineer who had supervised the removal the night before. 'Achard had ten minutes' warning.'

'She was already on her way here. And I who thought she was at school!'

'Tell Madame there is no need to worry, Père Arneguy,' whispered Georges Dumont. 'To you she will listen. They have ordered up a helicopter.'

'How long will it be, your helicopter?'

'Half an hour at the most.'

The outbuildings upstream, which had been acting as bastion to the house, disappeared. There was not even a splash. The old grey mortar had quietly reached a limit of resistance as the water sucked at the dry holes where generations of lizards had hidden and bred.

Someone in the crowd hoisted a placard for Marie-Claire to read: HELICOPTER ON THE WAY

The child waved, and then turned in alarm as she felt the house shudder. The ground floor was divided by a wide archway where in old days the farm carts had been kept. Arneguy saw the great wooden doors which closed it give way. Immediately afterwards there was a swirl at the downstream end of the house. The wall of the coach-house had gone. The top floor was nothing but a doubtful bridge over the current.

'We will try to catch her at the narrows,' said the engineer.

He spoke into the machine on his back, asking his headquarters for a heavy steel net.

'Keep your men here!' Père Arneguy recommended. 'They can help me.'

'Your farm, I assure you, is quite safe.'

The former cuirassier towered above him, pulling his moustache. Then he turned away and lumbered up to his cottage.

'They are amazing, these old peasants!' said the engineer, and then shouted: 'Ah, but here at last is Jean-Paul!'

Jean-Paul rolled through the shallows, a monstrous squat crane on six sets of caterpillar tracks. Jean-Paul turned, lowered the sixty-foot jib of his crane and roared straight for the island. He would be recovered when the flood went down. Meanwhile, if he could get far enough before the engine stopped . . .

Jean-Paul stopped and rolled slowly over on his side. His driver jumped for it and was dragged ashore. The monster continued to wallow in the river until the crane jib jammed on the bottom.

To the onlookers it was a relief, after that colossal fall, to see Papa Arneguy trotting down the slope of his land bareback upon the Shah, with his sword in his right hand and his great rake over his left shoulder. There was a ripple of nervous laughter.

'He has forgotten his helmet.'

'What's he going to do with his one horsepower?'

'One would say, a Basque Quixote!'

He rode up to the engineer and delivered his orders. 'You!' he roared, using the disrespectful second person singular of the old army. 'Occupy yourself with a cigarette! For five minutes I command here. After that, do what you like!' His eyes crossed those of a grey-haired foreman who had volunteered for the amphibian and was still coughing the water out of his lungs.

'You—second-in-command! On your feet, and take another glass! Lying down like that, you don't give the brandy a chance to mix with the water. Pick me the best of your men! A light line round the Shah here—pull him ashore if he's in trouble! The rope I take with me round my waist. Get your men to pay it out as soon as you see what is happening! Don't let them drag me back—understand? When I have the rope across, rig a loop to run on it and take your rubber boat over. It offers no resistance, that boat. One could do a Christopher Columbus with it. To work!'

'It's not possible, Père Arneguy,' Dumont begged. 'Don't get yourself killed for nothing! The helicopter will be here in a moment.'

Arneguy leaned over the Shah's withers and tapped him affectionately on the shoulder. 'And then another moment while he comes down to borrow a spanner. You know where you can put your helicopter, Georges?'

He wrapped the end of the rope round his body and rode the Shah over the familiar field until the water was up to his thighs. As he approached the old bank of the river he turned the horse's head to the current and edged him sideways. The water swirled against the Shah's great chest. The foreman, quick to see what was needed, led his men into the shallows as far as they could safely go, and kept a strain on the line.

Père Arneguy reached down and began to rake the bottom far out to his left. Even Madame Ibarra did not see what he was up to. The racing surface of the water looked so permanent. It needed an effort of imagination to recover a memory of what the channel had been a quarter of an hour earlier.

At last he raked up the ferry cable. It was still far from obvious what use that was. Neither man nor rubber dinghy could cross by it. The sheer weight of slack, waterlogged rope would drag them under.

He clung to the cable and let his rake go. There was no holding it without a third hand. He shouted: 'Tell the neighbours down stream! It is useful, my rake!'

Then he drew the full length of his sword twice across the cable, and twisted a severed strand round his left wrist. He slipped off the Shah's back and sliced at the cable a third time. It parted, and the current had him.

At last on land they understood. 'Pay out! Let him go!'

Père Arneguy, clinging to the long end of the severed cable, was hurled down and across the stream in a quarter circle with the ring-bolt on the island landing-stage as its centre. In twenty seconds the cable was taut, stretched parallel to the wall of the house and some six feet out from it. He pulled himself up river, yard by yard and hand over hand, until he was below the balcony.

The problem now was to pass up to Marie-Claire the end of the second rope which was round his waist. If she could haul it through the window and make it fast, the dinghy could, with luck, travel along the rope like the old punt.

But Marie-Claire was now, he saw, incapable with fear. These little ones! It took some time to make them understand the difference between what was real and the excitement of pictures they made for themselves. Useless to give her orders yet. If only she had been a man, a little army language would be just the thing to bring her to her senses.

'Listen, Marie-Claire,' he said gently. 'Have you a pair of sheets or table-cloths or even strong cord?'

'No, no, no! Nothing!'

'Go and look, *ma mignonne*! Go and look in the attic! There is plenty of time and no danger.'

While he waited he lay on his back. Like that he seemed to plane easily over the rush of water which no longer piled up against mouth and nostrils.

She came back with an old carriage rein. He expected to find it rotten, but never mind! Once started on activity, she could go off and find something else.

'Good girl!' he said. 'Take a turn round the balcony corner-post! At the bottom—that's right! Now throw me the end!'

The leather seemed solid enough. Madame Ibarra, years before, must have stored it away well greased.

'There! I shall now tie this rope which is round my middle to the reins,' he announced in the tone of a village conjuror. 'No deception! You see that I have only one hand free. Therefore the knot will be poor. Pull it in quickly and gently, and then tie the rope to a beam! Tie it well, for the lives of men depend on you.'

Marie-Claire at last smiled. She hauled in the rope and vanished through the window with the end of it. Père Arneguy could see the excitement on the bank. The grey-haired foreman was up to his waist in the shallows paying out the other end of the rope. Behind him were his men, rigging a block and pulley on the rubber dinghy.

But Marie-Claire returned, still with the rope's end.

'I cannot reach the beam, M Arneguy.'

'Stand on a chair, *ma mignonne*.'

178

'There is no chair. All the furniture and the chests have gone. There is nothing.'

'What is in the room with you?'

'Only our crockery and our wine.'

Père Arneguy let go the streaming ferry cable, and tried to pull himself up to the balcony by the reins. He had not the strength. He looped the reins under his arms and rested. That, then, was the end of his plan.

'Could we not wait for the helicopter?' she asked.

He could feel through the leather the shuddering of the house. While they talked, a stone quoin had fallen from the corner.

Ah well, the town band would have something to do after all. At sixty-three one couldn't feel cheated. And to rest when one was so tired—at the moment it was perfectly acceptable even if one had to rest for ever. All the same, Marie-Claire wouldn't agree at all. At twelve one hadn't nearly enough of one's own absurdities.

'If the wine is there, you might as well pass me a bottle, Marie-Claire.'

'Willingly, M Arneguy. But I have no corkscrew.'

'Never forget, my child, that there are very few tools necessary to the life of men. A corkscrew and a good blade are among them. I have both together in my pocket.'

Marie-Claire showed no more sign of panic now that she had companionship. She lowered the bottle by means of a stick, her belt and a hair ribbon. Père Arneguy drew the cork and swallowed a quarter of the contents. He felt better. It seemed a pity not to let his last taste of wine rest on the palate. He drank a second quarter more slowly. His imagination revived.

'They are perfectly right,' he informed Marie-Claire, 'when they say that old men cannot change their plans in a hurry. I will return you to your mother in one-third of a minute.'

'I will do what you tell me, M Arneguy.'

'Have you the courage to slip down the reins into my arms?'

'It doesn't need much to do that, M Arneguy.'

'And then you must not struggle. Even if we are under water the whole way, we shall recover. They'll soon empty us out on the other side.'

'I promise.'

'Very well. Then since there is nothing in the house to which you can tie the rope and the posts of the balcony cannot be trusted, it shall go round my stomach again. How curious that neither of us has a waist! You are too young, and I am too old. So pass me the rope's end, if you please, Marie-Claire.'

Père Arneguy knotted the slack under his arms. He was now attached to the balcony by the reins and to the far bank by the rope. As soon as he cut the reins he would cross the channel exactly as he had done before, sweeping down and across in a quarter circle with—this time—the foreman as its centre.

'Down then, my little one!'

She hesitated. Only in a nightmare could mass move at the pace of those smooth tons of water. Even that kindly head and dripping moustache, like those of some zoo seal waiting for fish, could not take away the menace.

The balcony and its wall began a slow, hardly perceptible swaying. The moment had come to use the voice of the cuirassier. 'Quick!' he roared. 'Quick, will you, *Nom de Dieu*!'

Marie-Claire climbed over the balcony railings. Her hands slid down the leather held taut by Père Arneguy's weight. His knife notched the edge of the reins, and they ripped apart.

It was a worse journey than the first. For two there was no chance of keeping upon the surface of such a battering of water. His last conscious thought was that all the trout must have been carried away and pulped in the rapids. They were the last two. But caught. Held fast on the line by his second-in-command. A good type, that. He locked his fingers into Marie-Claire's hair.

It seemed to him that Mme Ibarra was trying to pry them loose. He held on tight. It was only when he felt without doubt Marie-Claire's smaller fingers among his own that he loosened his grip.

'Incredible!' he heard someone say. 'And to think he had the coolness to down a bottle while he waited! We are not the men our fathers were.'

'I am ashamed of myself,' Georges Dumont confessed.

'What's that? What's that rubbish?' murmured Père Arneguy in the ghost of a roar. 'No reason to be! It's not that you lack courage, Georges. It's that you have too much faith in machines.'

CHAMPION ANTIOCHUS

Dear Desmond:

No, I will not sell Antiochus. Even if your man improves on his offer, as you think he might, I won't take it. It is not that I don't want him to go to Ireland, and it's not altogether that he is accustomed to being a personal friend, though of course that counts.

Because I brought him back from Syria and had something to do with sending him there in the first place, people like to say it was not the same bull. It was, and his papers prove it. But in a way they are right. We went through an odd experience together, which is the real reason why I will not part with him. After all your kindness, I can't in decency leave it mysterious. As a superstitious Celt you will have no difficulty in believing the facts, though, when it comes to my reasonable interpretation of them, you may say that I am—well, too down-to-earth.

In the autumn of 1954, I was in the Middle East—a last trip abroad for the firm. Because I spoke clumsy but intelligible Arabic, our exports of seeds, fertilizers and machinery were helping to make the Fertile Crescent a bit more fertile. While I was staying at Aleppo, a friend of mine in the Ministry of Agriculture advised me to go up and see Pierre de Valence. He had given his heart to Pierre in that frank, unarguable way of the Arabs, and considered him an adopted citizen of enormous value. I was assured that the Bukeia estate was more meticulous and scientific—on a small scale of course—than any of the Ministry's agricultural stations, and a place I ought to inspect. It was remote and almost without communications; but he would get in touch with the nearest police post and order up a gendarme with a message.

The car and driver which de Valence promptly sent down to fetch me were both efficient without being smart—the sort of pair which might have belonged to some cheerful and irregular military unit. We crossed the Orontes and started climbing into the Alaouite Mountains by a narrow metalled track built by the French between the wars to serve a small holiday resort which never came to anything. We bounced off that on to a solid dirt road, which was just as narrow but more purposeful. Where the top dressing had been swept away by spring rains I saw flagstones, still showing the ruts of chariot wheels between the skid marks of de Valence's trucks.

This Roman road led us over a pass into Bukeia. It was more of a bowl than a valley, surrounded by low crags on the south and west and rising on the east to the even round breast of a hill. I was at once impressed. The arable, now brown and lifeless, was here and there divided by white stakes, indicating experimental seeding. Water was plentiful. A small blue reservoir lay under the shade of the southern cliffs. The driver told me that there was also a powerful artesian well. Paddocks between irrigation channels held some fine cattle and still finer horses. The house was flanked on one side by an Arab hamlet, all straightened up and re-roofed, and on the other by orchards with the pomegranates showing red.

I expected to find Pierre de Valence the sharp-featured, emphatic type of go-ahead Frenchman. Something of that he was, but with an unusual dreaminess about him. His lined face was rather still, his eyes far-sighted. I don't mean that he looked over the person or animal he happened to be talking to. Far from it. But he often gave me the impression that his tall figure was brooding over all the valley, not just the object which occupied his attention. The place was an organic unity to him, and he was always conscious of the whole to which the individual cells were contributing.

He received me with a touch of the effusive formality of the Syrian which fell away as soon as he began to feel that we were fellow Europeans with a common interest. He could be equally genial in either part. I rode all over the estate with him, stayed the night and let him talk.

Pierre's was an eccentric life, which must have been lonely in spite of the fact that he was obviously loved and trusted by his employees. Two irresistible young Alaouite girls served at meals. They were very discreet, and their duties were no business of mine. There was also a library from which I could guess that my host had had a university education of such French thoroughness that he still read Latin and Greek for pleasure. Agriculture, genetics and history were well represented, too. I was surprised to see nothing on field sports. One would have expected this expatriate of eighteenth-century flavour to shoot his game or run a pack of hounds as decorative as his other beasts.

He gave me this side of his character over dinner, telling me that there was a leopard in the district which had a preference for the crags above the reservoir. It was twenty years since the last had been reported. He wouldn't have it interfered with, and paid compensation when it killed the odd sheep or goat. It never raided Bukeia, he said, just as if it had accepted a gentleman's agreement. He became indignant and romantic as he described how the poor devil must have trekked five hundred miles from the headwaters of the Tigris with every man's hand against it.

He talked just as familiarly of all his beasts. His hobby—I wouldn't call it a business though he probably broke even—was racing his Arabs and half-bloods in Damascus and Beirut. He was so unreasonably successful that the public never got anything like the fair odds from the tote.

Over the brandy—distilled from his own grapes and very drinkable—he asked me if there were any white cattle in England. I mentioned the famous Chillingham herd, but explained that they were a curiosity for zoos and parks, possibly unobtainable. Then, of course there was the Old English Dairy Shorthorn sometimes pure white, but bred primarily for milk yield.

'So nobody would keep a bull just for its colour?' he asked.

I replied that it was unlikely. The only reason for raising a bull was the gallons-per-year record of his female ancestors for two or three generations. If they were not outstanding for milk yield, the bull calf would go for veal or perhaps be fattened as a beef steer.

'When you are at home, would you try to get me a white bull with no markings at all?'

His request seemed to me to be in character. After all, our figures for yield could not be approached on his sun-baked grass, marvellous though it was for Syria. So there was nothing out of the ordinary in buying a bull of good breeding just for its looks. It would do quite as well as some wildly expensive beast and produce a very handsome herd.

We had taken to each other unreservedly, so when I got home I went to some trouble for him, though I didn't suppose I should ever see him again. His bull was hard to find, for a calf was seldom raised unless it had the makings of a champion. Then I came across a go-ahead fellow in Northamptonshire who was experimenting with the new craze for bull beef. Among other breeds he had Old English Dairy, and there I found Antiochus. He was nine months old, entire, and fortunately had no ring in his nose. De Valence had insisted that he should not be mutilated in any way.

He hadn't even a name then. He was just Buttercup's No 5 or Daisy's 3, or something undistinguished of that sort. His mother was only in the 700 gallon class. But pure white he was, with a forelock which curled like a ram's. A really lovely little beast! Thirty years ago no small breeder would ever have cut him or sold him. In these days, however, when a dairy farmer sends round to the Ministry's station for a phial of whatever qualities he wants, he was worthless as a sire. He was not at all fond of human beings then. Bouncy rather than vicious. I remember you protesting that I go in and out of the bull pen as if I were sharing an armchair with a favourite cat. So I do. But at our first meeting I would have betted that he would grow up to be a treacherous old devil.

I sent a wire to de Valence who replied at once that he wanted him and would I have him flown out by freighter? He had some pull with the government air line. At any rate it was not nearly so expensive as you would think, and ensured his arrival in the pink of condition.

That winter I found a good man to replace me in the firm, and was free at last to enjoy every acre of the six hundred my father had left me. When I gave up the pace of doing two jobs at once, I fell ill. It's a very common occurrence—as if a man were fated to it, but could hold off fate so long as he was busy enough. And the damned thing had not been brewing in me all the time. It was the devastating result of a long thorn broken off in the upper arm. Infection spread to the lung, and I was three weeks in bed being drained and hacked about and stuffed with injections. The doctors told me to get out of England for the rest of the winter if I could afford it.

The obvious choice was Syria where I was well known and would not be confined to some sleek hotel with a lot of rich old women playing bridge. Unlike the bull I went all the way by sea, and by the time I reached Beirut I was feeling so well and impatient that I wished I had never left England at all. I spent a week between Damascus and Aleppo and then drove up to Bukeia to see how Pierre de Valence was getting on.

He would not let me go. The perfect hospitality. A self-contained flat at my disposal, absolute freedom and horses to ride. He hoped I would be kind enough to give him the pleasure of my company every day at dinner and any other time I chose. He insisted that he needed my help. I took that a mere courtesy; but, as you will see, from his point of view I had dropped on him from heaven—or the moon, let us say.

At that time of year when the spring rains were just ending, the beasts were in magnificent condition. The white bull was running free in a well fenced meadow below the eastern hill, sheltered from the rest of the estate by a belt of eucalyptus. It was Pierre who named him Antiochus. He visited him daily to clean out his private spring and give him something pleasant to crunch. I recommended that, if he wouldn't hear of a ring in Antiochus' nose, at least the bull ought to have a headstall. But Pierre saw no need. His animals were all a part of that organic whole, and he expected them to know it and to behave as reasonably as playful children. Mukhtar, his Arab stallion, used to follow him around licking the back of his neck. I have never seen so consciously proud a horse. He was generous with his strength, whether he was obliging his master or his mares.

That was the prevailing mood of Pierre de Valence. And animals in close contact always reflect the character of the human friend. He was an immensely appreciative man—of his life, his estate and his abiding luck. He didn't like to talk about it. Who does? But one morning when

184

we were gazing down on Bukeia from the upland stream which fed the reservoir he did go so far as to say: 'Looking after Bukeia—there must be something.'

I was encouraged by sun and scented distances and wind from the sea—all far away from the gropings in darkness which worry and get us nowhere—to ask him what sort of something he believed in.

'I do not know,' he answered frankly. 'But in this country the unseen is always present.'

That was true enough. There are seventeen separate religions between the Taurus and Jerusalem. The One, the Merciful, with whom a Mohammedan is content to be alone in the desert, is not enough for the fullness of the Syrian shore.

He dismounted from Mukhtar, and I from Lys. She was a big, eight-year-old brood mare from Turkestan with a will of her own. Mukhtar stayed close to his master, listening for whatever important event had caused him to take to the ground.

'Sometimes I want to worship,' he told me. 'Just to say "thank you". That's all. Not asking for this, that and the other! Not bothering powers which, if they exist, don't want to be bothered!'

We had been to visit the Greek Orthodox monastery in the next valley. Pierre had bought part of his land from them and frequently sent the monks casual gifts of the season. They struck me as a lot of dirty, greedy old men; but they were warm and grateful, and their chanting was marvellous. I suggested that Pierre could say his 'thank you' very well within the conventional limits of Christianity.

'I can't accept those monks as intermediaries between me and the divine,' he said. 'They are just creatures of habit. They have been at it so long that all the goodness has gone out. And I—I am a revivalist, if I'm anything.'

It was a queer word to use, yet it pointed his meaning. A revivalist brings the fresh, emotional content back to any religion, often with spectacular results—which you, as a good Catholic, very rightly distrust.

'I always felt you would understand,' he went on. 'That's why I wanted to talk to you about it. Let's go!'

I thought he was about to ride down to the house. Instead, he led me round the edge of the bowl towards the bare hill which closed his valley on the east. It was higher than I thought. From the top the view was limitless, all the dust of the air washed out by rain. I could see the golden flash of the Orontes at a bend, and if the earth had been flat I could have seen the Euphrates too. To the north-west, through a gap, was a broad arrow of Mediterranean around Antioch.

Just over the brow of the hill was the marble pavement of a small temple, the stones of its precinct and the drums of slender columns scattered over the turf. I asked Pierre if anything was known of it—a stupid question in our Europe which treasures its remains of the classical period, but a reasonable one in the Syrian hills where there are so many exquisite little sacred sites never mentioned in the literature of the time and still awaiting the spade to identify them. What was exceptional about this ruin was that the altar still stood: a block of stone indestructible, though cracked, weathered and tilting.

'Yes, a little,' he replied. 'It's a shrine of Artemis. They used to ride up here after sacrificing to Zeus Casios on the Jebel Aqra above Seleucia. You can see the heaps of ash and bones on it to this day—' he pointed out the peak to me, forming part of the slope which framed the wedge of sea '—I feel I know why they came. For a sort of spiritual picnic. No holocaust of victims. Just a single sacrifice for the more fastidious. There may have been another reason, too. Artemis was much more like a living woman than other goddesses—jealous, very easily offended, very fussy about her sacrifices. And there all day long was the smoke rising from the Jebel Aqra, and nobody paying any particular attention to her!'

I saw the direction in which his thought was running, and that he had jumped at the conversational opening I had given. I said awkwardly that Artemis, the goddess of hunting, wouldn't be much good to him.

'Of the beasts as well as hunting,' he answered. 'I like to think that she had her sacred park at Bukeia.'

Behind the altar, the substructure of the temple had all vanished under lumpy turf infested by big, black ants of one of the scavenging species. Pierre suggested that they had been there, generation after generation, ever since the first colony fed on the dried blood from the sacrifices. Like so many of his imaginings, that could very well have been true. One reads of the intolerable cloud of flies over the pagan altars, so why not ants? And, if experience on my own land is anything to go by, once ants, always ants. Even modern insecticides only reduce the number.

This lot was decidedly carnivorous. While I was looking for reliefs on the eastern face—which the winds had long since scoured away— four of the little devils were crawling up my socks. They all bit in very quick succession, I suppose because they reached bare skin at nearly the same time. That was not the only shock which had to be relieved. I remember being ashamed of my language in such a thyme-scented silence and hoping that the virgin goddess was broadminded.

'After three thousand years of angry Syrians,' Pierre said, 'I expect she finds you unimaginative.'

The dry, ironic voice was uneasy. He had been following my eyes as I closely examined the carved sump of the blood channel.

'It was you?' I asked.

'Yes. A lamb.'

'But you don't believe?'

'It isn't a question of belief exactly. I told you. I must show my gratitude. As well here as elsewhere.'

That was true enough. It was a place made for worship, where prayer alone would have its greatest possible effect. When I said so, he replied that prayer received but could not give: that life could only communicate with Life through life.

An obscure theory. I did not know enough of pagan mysticism to argue. I could only say that I thought he hated killing.

'I do. But sacrifice—well, you *must* feel pity. You *must* admire the victim. Oh, I don't suppose the priests did. Like the monks, it became a habit and there was no response.'

'Was there any for you?' I asked.

'No. I felt revolted. Partly by the blood. Much more because I knew I had not done the thing properly. Such a sense of inadequacy implies a standard of comparison. Whose standard? I haven't any myself. What was disappointed and telling me that I had made a mess of it?'

I exclaimed that of course he had, that it wasn't surprising he felt a fool.

'I did not,' he replied. 'I felt incompetent. I was much too afraid to feel a fool.'

He told me how he had studied and rehearsed the rites, his own purification, everything proper to the worship of Artemis and the moon goddess Astarte, which was her Syrian avatar. In a thin voice he chanted to me a bit of the Greek hymn, then translated it into French.

I saw him for the first time—in spite of his Syrian friends and the Ministry of Agriculture—as a hermit, cut off from his kind and finding the lost Europe in its roots: roots which had meant a lot to him in some sun-lit library of sweet France, fired his imagination and left it receptive to the city walls and temples which still stood serene among agitated Arabs. And I was sure that he, like most hermits, was escaping from himself and something in his past which made him unworthy of his beloved Bukeia. Rumour had it—but rumour would—that awkward questions might be asked if he went home. Nobody knew how he had acquired his capital.

'Will you help me?' he asked. 'It's difficult alone, and my people would be horrified if they knew.'

I couldn't refuse outright. I was already very fond of him, and he depended on me. You, Desmond, will feel pagan sacrifice to be actively wrong. I did not. Both he and his hill-top made it seem pure and even beautiful. And his motive was unexceptional. I have stretched out my own arms in gratitude when some combination of life on a spring morning has made me thankful to be part of it, though I have never imagined that killing could help me to express what I thought.

I explained that I had not the sort of tingling temperament which

187

would welcome Artemis into the twentieth century, and that he would not get me anywhere near the altar. As an act of disapproving friendship I was prepared to come along and hold the horses, but that was all. He thanked me warmly, promising that, if I liked, I could go away at once after I had helped him to lead Antiochus as far as the temple.

The name exploded inside me. It was utterly unexpected, yet plain and obvious once mentioned. I protested. I said it was indecent to waste the life of such an attractive young creature. And then I began to splutter away into nothing as I realized the hollowness of my argument. If Pierre decided that the beast ought to go for beef—which was all he was worth—a Mohammedan butcher would give him the same quick, clean end as he was going to get. And if he preferred to feed himself spiritually instead of on steak, he had a perfect right to do so. In any case, Antiochus had had an idyllic year of life to which, economically, he was not entitled.

Pierre had it all worked out before he made me buy the bull. That was why Antiochus was in a field by himself, near to the hill and far from the herdsmen; that was why only Pierre himself attended to his wants. He proposed to make it look as if he had carelessly left the gate open, and the bull had wandered off into the mountains. He doubted if the ritual roasting of the meat was necessary; the offering and the sincerity of the spirit behind it were the essentials. Jackals would do the rest, as they always had, with the leopard helping if he happened to be in residence. He knew where to hide the carcass, and intended to drive his breakdown truck, tracked and with a winch on it, up the hill the day before.

There was a new moon two nights later: an acceptable occasion, I gathered, for this dubious act of worship. I was glad of that. A delay of a week or more might have tended to exaggerate my reluctance. For twenty-four hours Pierre was not to be seen. Somewhere in the silence of the house he was fasting and submitting his body to the formalities of purification. I could not help being impressed. A certain reverence was unavoidable. The man had nothing in common with the lunatic fringe, playing about inefficiently with witchcraft and black magic. What he was doing was holy and had, after all, been holy to men and women of first-class intellect with spiritual yearnings just as eager as our own.

At dusk we rode down to the bull's pasture—myself keeping well behind Pierre on the narrow path, for he had asked me not to touch him even by accident. He was dressed like an Arab in a white kaftan, bare-legged and bare-headed. Antiochus, a big, grey ghost in the last of the twilight, came plunging up. He tried to eat the garland of wild iris and narcissus as Pierre lifted it over his head, but after that was docile and affectionate. Pierre walked alongside him, caressing the curls between the horns. Mukhtar followed to heel. I led Lys up the steep grass track, curiously moved and even wishing that I had not excluded myself from all participation.

Near the top we passed the dark bulk of the truck and its winch. It was a mistake to have that cold, modern reminder on the spot. It should have been further away and forgotten. I find it hard to explain what I mean. Put it this way: one does not want a bed in the aisle at a wedding service. We know that the ceremony leads to it; but for the moment proceedings are on a higher plane.

As our heads rose above the last slope, the brilliant new moon came into sight as if it had been climbing up from the Orontes to meet us. I stopped fifty yards from the ruins with Lys and Mukhtar. Pierre and Antiochus walked together to the altar, his hooves clattering on the marble. He was interested and submissive. Vanity? It might have been. Animals of high intelligence can all feel something of the sort. But I retained in the rag-bag of memory that it was always considered a favourable omen if the sacrifice walked willingly to the altar. So it must once have been a common occurrence, whatever the reason.

They were all silver—the mass of Antiochus, the crescent moon, the curved blade lying on the altar. Pierre murmured some prayer which I could not hear and picked up the knife. He buried his left hand in the curls and pulled back the head, throwing his full weight into the movement. The steel flashed in the moonlight, and that was all. He let the head drop, and turned for a moment to the altar with out-stretched hands. Then, with a sudden attack in which I thought I could discern desperation, he tried again. I saw the meekly elongated throat very clearly against the sky. It seemed to remain erect even after the knife had tinkled on the pavement.

Pierre came straight over the turf to me, shaking with emotion. 'I cannot do it to him,' he said. 'I cannot do it.'

'Of course you can't!' I answered with a heartiness which offended me. 'It amazes me that you ever thought you could.'

'Take him back, will you?' he asked.

I left him with the horses and walked up to Antiochus. He waited, perfectly motionless, his eyes shut. His neck under my hand felt slightly unnatural: a stiffness either of hair or muscle. He was in a kind of trance. The double flash of the steel under his eyes may have caused it.

While I wondered whether to give him an irreverent slap, there was a commotion among the horses. Pierre came running, twisting like a snipe, followed as usual by Mukhtar. But not in the usual way. He just managed to get in among the fallen stones as Mukhtar struck at him with his forelegs. The stallion chased him round to the back of the altar, and then seemed to come to his senses. Myself, I took cover behind the still motionless Antiochus, yelling out to know what was wrong.

'I cannot imagine,' Pierre answered. 'The scent of fear, perhaps. Or of shame.'

He realized that the fit of hysteria which had possessed the stallion was over, and leaned across the altar to stroke his nose. Mukhtar whinnied with pleasure; he seemed quite unaware of what he had done. Pierre gentled and petted him for a good minute, then led him out through the tumbled masonry. He was so confident that when they reached the open he sat down to pick off the ants. I was never so impressed by his self-control in the presence of animals, and told him so. He replied that he had been forced to be patient, that any exclamation or excitement might have upset Mukhtar all over again.

Meanwhile, Antiochus returned to normal, more than normal. He began to behave like a healthy young bull waking up from a pleasant dream and impressed by his own excellence. He butted me in the wind and cavorted around inviting me to butt him back. Pierre and Mukhtar headed him off and let him work his energy out of his system on the way down the hill. We returned him to his paddock and went home ourselves.

Next day we hardly discussed what had happened, for it was only too evident, when considered in the light of the sun upon a scientifically managed estate, that the four living beings concerned—I leave out Lys who, as befitted an experienced mother, had remained a mere spectator—could not look back on themselves with approval. I left Pierre to his business, and in the evening drove the truck down from the hill for him and put it away in the barn.

On the third day I noticed that he was walking with a limp. When I asked him if he had sprained an ankle, he replied that he might have wrenched something running away from Mukhtar, but that he had not noticed it at the time. The leg, he said, was a bit painful in the thigh and groin.

That seemed a likely result of dodging among the drums of fallen columns, and I thought no more of it till the following morning when one of his little Alaouites visited my flat. She said that she had been giving her lord hot fomentations, that he had fever and that she did not like the look of his leg. He had insisted that it was nothing, that he had probably caught a chill and that his leg hadn't anything to do with it.

I was up in his bedroom at once. The girl was right. He had such a temperature that he was incapable of clearly examining his leg or any other object. The flesh was noticeably dark, with streaks of red. The doctor who attended him and the Bukeia families was down at the coast in Latakia—many hours away if one had to open up communications by messenger and police post. So I took command. I got some of his men to smash down the door-posts of his bedroom so that we could lift the whole bed out without disturbing him. We lashed it down to a two-ton truck and made a bolt to Latakia hospital.

God, the speed of the thing! It was too late to amputate, and he seemed resistant to penicillin and every other injection in their dispensary. When they had given him up and the fever dropped in the hour before death he had a short interview with his lawyer—he wouldn't hear of a priest—in which he left Bukeia to a co-operative of his workers. He whispered to me: 'I have left you Antiochus. Do not tell them why!'

I couldn't have done, because then I did not really know why.

Forget, my dear Desmond, all about the supernatural! There had been nothing inexplicable, except for the momentary possession of Mukhtar when he chased Pierre to the wrong side of the altar. And I think your vet could give you a dozen reasons for that. As for the fact that the ants were more effective avengers, it's nothing but tragic co-incidence. The hospital said that the resistant staphylococci which my body was still tolerating could be transferred by an insect bite, though the odds against any of the same four individual ants biting Pierre seemed enormous.

There was no other connection between our moonlight expedition and his death. Those primitive old monks in the next valley might have insisted there was; but my own conscience sees nothing reprehensible in a sincere act of worship directed at Artemis, Astarte, whatever her name and address. As a jealous virgin goddess, kindly only to animals, she seems a fair choice for farmers. As the Moon, we all worship her in our way.

No, there's nothing supernatural. Even the motive, assuming there was one, is simple and very human. It was no way to treat a woman: to offer, to excite and then to say 'I cannot'. One sees a parallel to what Pierre had done. With a bull I thee worship. That was in the hymn. For better or for worse, and so on. And then he deserts her on the altar steps. Literally the altar steps.

I don't think I believe in disembodied spirits: but I confess I wondered uneasily whether I, as best man, could be involved, and comforted myself with the thought that anyway her character was bold and decisive. Pique, yes. Fury, certainly. But not against me and not against Antiochus. He was already and for always sacred to her—if that was what Pierre meant. I felt that there might even be some contemptuous hand-out. 'It's not your fault, you poor bastards' she might say to us over her silver shoulder, and throw us the bridal bouquet, as it were, to remember her by.

I took Antiochus home with me by ship. There was no one else worth talking to, or else I did not feel like talking. So we got to know each other. Four years later, his cow calves began to go straight into the 2,000 gallon class. His bulls don't carry the hand-out until it has been passed through the female line. Then the second generation is most promising. All I can do in return is to keep the ministry boys and their test tubes off the premises. Antiochus and I both prefer the personal touch.

It would be good business to sell him. I do not need so valuable a beast. I detest all the correspondence he costs me, and I could do with the capital he represents. But it's unthinkable. For example, it would obviously pay you to dredge out that attractive, hidden spring of yours and stop the seepage which bogs the lower meadow. Why don't you brick it in? And why is there sometimes a little crock of milk among the ferns?